Jail Fever

by

Lexie

Conyngham

First published in 2017 by The Kellas Cat Press, Aberdeen.

Copyright Alexandra Conyngham, 2017

ISBN: 978-1-910926-34-5

Lexie Conyngham

DEDICATION

With thanks to Gabi, Kath and Nanisa, for all their help

JAIL FEVER

Jail Fever was written in the year 2000. When I came to consider publishing it, I thought about bringing it up to date, but when I reread it I realised it made more sense to publish it as it was. For one thing it would have meant a huge amount of fiddly work on the details: both the Archaeology Department and Edinburgh Royal Infirmary have moved since then, and mobile phones, while around, were not as ubiquitous as they are today (ah, halcyon days!). 2000 was a year of millennial twitchiness, too: GM foods, mad cow disease, superbugs, computer chaos, all contributed to a particular paranoia that has, if not abated, at least changed in the intervening years. So I present this now, not a historical novel, but one grounded in the time in which it was written, for those of us who remember it.

1 - PLAGUE

I

'Oh, no, oh no, oh no.'

The woman in the plastic chair whispered her prayer as she rocked, backwards and forwards, wrapped around her folded arms. The rhythmic movement was reflected dully in the antiseptic walls. Her eyes were closed, scrunched up hard, and she muttered her denial continuously, through in-breaths and out-breaths, perpetual and desperate as if even a moment's lapse could let in the demons that would destroy her world.

This part of the hospital was quiet at this time of the night, though she would not have noticed if a pipe band had marched past. In her mind she was back in the Benefits Agency, where it had all started, where her universe had begun to crumble.

The office there was always full of brats, running screaming between the rows of hard chairs, fighting, pulling at the posters, slamming the doors of the toilets, using language she did not even want Vicky hearing, never mind using. The mothers let them run wild. She always kept Victoria back, held her firmly between her own knees as she sat waiting for service, sometimes reading to her, sometimes just the pair of them staring away through the multiple glass layers of offices into the distance, dazed by the warmth and the noise and the smell of other humans, not even alert enough to wish themselves anywhere else. But today, Vicky had been grumbly, wriggling free, being deliberately aggravating. She had slapped her leg at one point, and then sat, shamefaced, believing that everyone in the office was staring at her in disapproval. Then she was called up to the counter, finally, and when Vicky had broken free of her hand again, while the clerk was explaining about some new form, she had let her go without looking. It was only when the room fell silent that the clerk tried to see past her, and she looked around.

Vicky was lying on the floor, writhing She was beside her daughter in a second ready to smack her again for this appalling display. But it was not a tantrum. Vicky's eyes were screwed shut and when her mother touched her clammy forehead she did not even twitch. The sweat sparked on her pallid skin, her teeth ground. The other children stood around open-mouthed, staring and pointing.

The security guard had his St. Andrew's Ambulance: he hurried forward importantly, waving his arms to push them back, to give the child and her mother room to breathe. But even he stopped when he saw the blotches.

No one breathed. No one moved, except for Vicky, rigid and shaking on her side. She could not believe her eyes, could not take in what the all-too-distinctive greenish blotches meant as they began to appear, rising slightly from the surface of Vicky's bare arms and legs. She looked up. Hands clapped over their mouths, the crowd in the Benefits Office swayed slightly, still staring down at Vicky, and seemed to slide backwards, away from her. Anyone near the door had vanished. Behind the glass screen, in the preternatural silence, she could hear the clerk, dialling frantically for an ambulance.

She prayed all the way in the ambulance, sometimes out loud, though she did not notice. She had prayed a lot in the last two years. She had always been a sort of Sunday morning Christian, appropriately dressed in a pew near the back, Vicky in the Junior Sunday School, nodding pleasantly to the right people. That had all changed two years ago. When the police had come for Andy, she had stopped going to church, unable to hold up her head, but prayers had begun to bubble up, in all kinds of places she would previously have thought ridiculous: the supermarket, the Benefits Office, even the visitors' waiting room at the prison where she went weekly with Vicky to see Andy.

She had thought at first she could pretend to everyone that Andy had been posted overseas for three years, but it was harder than she expected. For one thing it was the money. Andy had never spoken much about his job, but they had been comfortable: a new house on the outskirts of the city, tasteful furniture, new clothes when she wanted them, no pressure on her to work. But the 'wee touch of white-collar fraud' that the C.I.D. man had referred to so casually when they arrested Andy – that had paid for a good deal of it, and the job Andy had lost the day he was convicted had paid for the rest of it. Suddenly she had had to find her way through the paper maze of income support and housing benefit – the new house had had to go – with hardly any time for shame. And Vicky had taken it all with the calm acceptance of a three year old who could not remember it being any different.

The ambulance men, anonymous behind their masks and gloves, worked around Vicky to make her comfortable. They had her on oxygen, but nothing more. If she had had eyes for anything but Vicky, she might have seen her own fears reflected in their eyes, too.

When the ambulance doors opened, they were not at the Sick Kids in the Meadows, as she had expected. They seemed to be round the back of the Infirmary somewhere, an unmarked double doorway with the mottle fluorescent light from inside making no impression on the bright daylight. They were in before she had the chance to wonder. Not running, not like you saw on the American T.V. shows, but walking briskly along a glossy grey corridor towards heavy security doors.

Once they were through, a nurse in a mask divided her neatly away from Vicky's trolley.

'The doctor'll take a look at her straight away,' the nurse said before she could open her mouth. 'If you could just step through here and we'll do the formalities, eh?' He ushered her, without touching her, into a Spartan office: desk, computer, two hard chairs, clock on the wall. Only a few minutes since she had gone up to the counter at the Benefits Office. It seemed like hours.

'Now, what's the wee lassie's name?' asked the nurse, taking the chair behind the desk. His eyes above the mask were professional, reassuring.

'Vicky. Victoria Emma Larssen.' She spelled the surname automatically.

'Date of birth?'

'Twentieth of the fourth of ninety-seven.'

'Three in April? A spring birthday – that's lovely for a wee girl.' He spoke with absent care as he tapped at the computer keyboard. 'And are you her mother?'

'Aye, that's right. Her mother.' She glanced back at the office door as if the words strengthened the link between her and Vicky, tweaking the chain of love and blood between them.

'Your name?'

'Shona Larssen.'

'Address?'

She gave it, the sad little council flat in Silverknowes that she had tried to brighten with sheets of cheap wrapping paper and old birthday cards.

He took a little time typing it in, and she had a moment to formulate her question.

'Why did they not take us to the Sick Kids?'

He glanced up at her, his eyes taking in not the worn clothes and home-cut hair but the blank anxious expression. Poor girl, he thought, it hasn't even hit her yet.

'It's for infection control,' he said gently. 'This is a special unit.'

'A special unit for what?' she asked, still unable to get past the wall in her mind.

'For SAIDS.' He saw no response. 'For swift-acting immuno-difficiency syndrome.' He paused again. 'For jail fever.'

Jail fever. That was what the tabloids called it, though the broadsheets stuck to SAIDS. Either way there was the stigma.

It was amazing how quickly stigma could appear. This thing, this disease or syndrome or whatever it was, had first arrived in January, just six months ago. The first few cases had been in a prison in the Midlands. The authorities tested the water, the food, the air, and even the paintwork, and eventually declared that this was a form of Legionnaire's Disease. The water tank and the air-conditioning were replaced, the victims were buried, and everyone settled down. Then the following week two men died in a prison in Dorset, and three in one near Cardiff. The authorities wriggled. Enquiries were demanded by the opposition. The press wanted a name. Scientists provided one, just as the next victims died in Yorkshire, Lancashire and Norfolk. They called it SAIDS, swift-acting immuno-deficiency syndrome, and sat back for a while to see how it went. Of course, various eminent epidemiologists had to explain that it looked like AIDS in name only: it did not reflect at all, no, not in the least, on the behaviour of prisoners within Britain's jails. It was hard to say what it looked like, in fact. And the bravest, or most foolhardy, of the scientific community confessed quietly that they had no idea at all where it came from, what caused it, or how it spread.

By February the tabloids had come up with 'jail fever' – not typhus, the old jail fever. That was no longer a bogeyman in the popular imagination. Not one case had occurred without an intimate connexion with prison. In March the first prison warder died, and in April, when the first cases were appearing in Scottish jails, a prison doctor died at the wheel of his car on the M6, causing a multiple pile-up. By the summer, forty-three people had died, and the Westminster parliament and its satellites were in uproar, and epidemiologists all over the country were running themselves ragged, but no cause or cure was to be found.

There had been cases at Saughton, but Shona had told herself not to worry about Andy. He was not in Saughton: he was in the new privately run prison, Sinclair House, out along the Old Dalkeith Road, one of the ordinary prisoners put there to show it was not a two-tier system. There had not been a single case in the private jails. And besides, he was a decent, clean-living man. How could he catch it?

The nurse fetched her a cup of tea, a proper one from the kettle in the staff room, he said, and put her to sit in the corridor. He said there weren't great facilities yet, and apologised. She sat where he told her, and let the tea grow cold between her fingers, and prayed.

'Don't let it happen, let it be all right, let it be all right, oh, please God, let it be all right, please, God, please, God, please, God, please ….'

When the doctor came out he looked exhausted, and he sat down next to her as though his back hurt, his hands taking his weight first on the plastic chair. He, too, was wearing a mask.

He was a kind man, even though he was tired. He broke the news to her with his eyes before he ever said the words out loud. Vicky had SAIDS. He explained a little of the very little they knew about it, and how quick it was.

'Vicky is the first child we know of to contract it,' he was saying, though his voice made odd echoes in her head and she could not follow his meaning. 'It is possible, with a young child's immune systems, that she could pull through this, but I must tell you that there is very little hope, and very little time. Is there anyone we should call? Her father? Grandparents? Brothers and sisters?'

She shook her head quickly.

'No, no one.' She could not have them call Andy, not to see his daughter like this and think, somehow, that it was his fault. And what would he say, this nice doctor, if she told him her husband was in Sinclair House? But of course, he would know there had to be a link somewhere. Jail fever. Vicky had jail fever. How could it have happened?

'Do you want to see her now?' the doctor was asking. 'She's unconscious, but she wakes every now and again. It would be good for her if you were there,' he added, standing up stiffly. 'We don't think she's in any pain.'

'Give me a wee minute, eh?' she said, not recognising her own voice.

'Sure,' said the doctor. 'Call the nurse to show you in when you're ready. And later, when – there's an opportunity – we'll have to do some tests on you, as well.'

He nodded and disappeared through the swing doors, walking as if he were trying not to move his back. Shona slumped in her plastic chair, her arms wrapped tightly around her body.

'Oh, no,' she murmured to herself, closing her eyes as the world crashed around her. 'Oh, no, oh no, oh no …'

II

Catriona Lindsay was blonde, blue-eyed, slim and intelligent. She was more likeable than she thought she was, and truth to tell, not particularly happy.

When the radio alarm clock switched on the *Today* programme in mid-sentence, she rolled, already wide awake, from her otherwise unoccupied bed, and disappeared into the shower. From there, plaiting her long, silvery blonde hair while it was still wet, she went to the kitchen in a sensible towelling robe and pressed the switch on the kettle she had filled the previous night, and popped down the toaster, before returning to the bedroom and pulling the curtains.

From the third floor, the view of the serried Victorian tenements of Leith was moderately interesting. Across the street, neighbours whose names she did not know followed their nevertheless familiar morning rituals, while down on the cobbled street binmen shifted and stacked heaps of splitting binbags. Above the roofs, the distinctive outline of Calton Hill, the Nelson Monument and the Disgrace stood out from the morning haar, misty round their ankles. For Edinburgh, it was going to be a hot day.

The wardrobe was splendidly ancient and smelled faintly of cigar smoke. She pulled a clean teeshirt out of a drawer labelled 'Collars' and a pair of chino shorts from a drawer labelled 'Dress shirts', and put them on, flicking her heavy plait out from the teeshirt collar. She cast a quick, shy glance at her reflection – nothing noticeably wrong this morning, apart from the dark circles under her eyes and the ingrained dirt under her fingernails. She poked uselessly at one grubby nail, then gave up and tiptoed barefoot into the kitchen to have her breakfast.

Over the years and with many judicious hunts in junk shops, she had the place pretty much the way she wanted it: one bedroom, a windowless boxroom she used as a study, bathroom, kitchen and living room with one of the small, angular bay windows common in Leith flats. The furniture was neatly and plainly upholstered, the kitchen was clean and uncluttered, and the radios were permanently tuned to BBC Radio 4. There was a stereo, but she rarely used it unless she had guests. And yes, sometimes she did have guests, and she would look forward to their arrival and cook for them and often they would come to stay, sleeping on the futon in the living room, but when they left she would always breathe a sigh of relief, rearrange the furniture, retune the radios, put the CDs away, and relax again.

She wiped the table clean of toast crumbs and put the kettle on to boil again to wash the few dishes, and stood waiting at the sink, staring out of the window. This one faced the back, not the street, a small stretch of wasteland behind the shared greens and then the backs of other houses, probably a Second World War bomb site left undeveloped. She wondered if there was anything worth digging there, if there was anything underneath but the old nurseries that used to stretch between Edinburgh and the port of Leith.

A small movement attracted her attention: a cat, black and white as a magpie, was choosing a good position on a garden wall from which to survey its territory. She grinned and pretended to wave at it, four floors down. She called that one Adrian, to herself, after the head of her department, who surveyed and expanded his territory in much the same way as the magpie cat. She would have liked a cat of her own. Neil had liked them, and they would have had them if he had been here, she was sure. Aye, well, Neil.

She found that she had unwittingly opened the fridge and pulled out today's allocated chocolate bar. The smooth brown brick splintered between her teeth, warm and cold at once. She would only eat half of it now, she told herself, and put the rest away for later.

The kettle boiled with a ferocious gurgle and a click, and she emptied it into the washing up bowl, added hot water, finished the chocolate bar and began to wash up, contemplating the day ahead.

This dig was, to all of them, a miracle of convenience, though for the students it lacked some of the adventure and excitement they had been promised. Usually the summer excavation was somewhere far from Edinburgh, Orkney, or some peel tower on the Borders, or a mediaeval kirkyard in Kirkcudbrightshire. But this year there was no heap of rucksacks and tents to transport, no all-pervading stench of wet socks, corned beef and last night's beer in the minibus – well, not to the same extent, anyway. They were digging near Rosslyn, just outside Edinburgh, on land now owned by one of the big research companies eager to be in on Dolly the Sheep and the Edinburgh Science Belt. The land had belonged to the Sinclairs at Rosslyn Castle, but what they were hoping for was something older, a Roman encampment of some description, and as far as the students were concerned, the bigger the better.

She drove round through Queen's Park, the morning rush hour traffic incongruous beside the rocky bulk of Arthur's Seat, and made easy progress out of the city going against the flow of cars heading towards the great battle for parking spaces. It was not long before she was in the countryside, bright green as the haar lifted, the sun flinging off its veils high on her left like an abandoned belly dancer.

The gateway to the site was only the outer entrance to the research company's land, but it boasted a security guard and a fresh coat of white paint. She slowed to a halt and produced her temporary pass, and was waved through as the guard worked the gate from his hut. Just beyond the gate a discreet white sign read, in elegant green italics, 'Elysian Fields', and underneath, in take-me-seriously print, 'Food Science Research'.

Another car turned through the gate behind her, and while it continued along the tarmac lane to the Elysian Fields buildings, she turned off on to a rocky track, trying not to scrape her sump, following a handwritten sign on A4 file paper saying, in black marker pen, 'U of E Dig' with a rough arrow.

The centre of the dig was a mound, not noticeably regular or in any casual way interesting, probably mostly a natural formation. Tucked against the side of it, sheltered by some gorse bushes, was the dilapidated shell of what had once been a shepherd's hut or perhaps some kind of animal pen, it was difficult to tell, even though they had set some of the students to stripping out the nettles with a slasher. They had had nettle soup that night, thanks to one enterprising students who had watched too many wholefood cookery programmes: it had been disgusting, but the staff had been too polite to say so.

She stopped the car beside the departmental minibus, opened the door to wave a greeting to the students already on the mound pacing out theodolites or filling basins at the stream, and turned in her seat to flip off her espadrilles and change them for hiking socks and boots. From the boot of the car she collected a leather belt holding a paintbrush, two different trowels and a pair of gardening gloves, and a cotton hat, cricket umpire-style. Thus fortified, she locked the car and briskly climbed the hill to join in the work.

Robbie Dean was holding a site meeting at the top of the hill. He grinned at her as she attached herself to the back of the small group, and went on with what he had been saying.

'The stone of that building below the hill, well, you saw yesterday the ones we picked out that were Roman workings. So from maps we know that building was here from about the fourteenth century, so the Roman remains must have been above ground level at that time. When was the main Roman incursion this far north?'

'First century A.D.,' said one or two students.

'Right. Then they retreated to what became Hadrian's Wall.' Robbie was from Carlisle and had grown up with the Wall, ranking it in world importance somewhere above that minor structure in China. His teeth glinted amidst the hair of his black beard. 'You've seen the geophysics results on this hill: we're probably looking at a small fort, stone-built, so they were here a fair while. Look back at the area: a grand little hill in the middle of flat land, with pani – water to you sad non-Cumbrians – just down there.' He waved at the stream below.

Catriona cleared her throat.

'Robbie, do you not think we should extend the geophys down around this hill?'

'Why's that?' he asked. His eyes, soft and brown, seemed to say they both knew the answer but were helping the students.

'I was thinking,' she said, 'that if they were here long enough to build a stone fort, there might be a bit of a vicus.'

'Vicus?' repeated Robbie, looking about for a response.

'Suburbs,' said one student. 'Service industries.'

'Camp followers,' said another lubriciously, and the rest laughed.

'Aye, well, a supply town, of sorts,' agreed Robbie. 'Tradesmen, wives, and other hangers-on. Not a bad idea, either,' he smiled at Catriona, and she nodded back. She did not smile much now. 'I think the project design will allow for that,' he went on. 'I'll check with Elysian Fields this morning, but there's no reason why the geophysics chaps can't get on with it while I do.'

The meeting only lasted a few minutes longer, and then, with everyone assigned to their various trenches, the site fell into quiet, unexciting activity. Robbie signalled to Catriona to meet him over at the old quartermaster's tent that they used as a site headquarters, and she went willingly.

'Are the troops happy?' asked Rob when they were inside.

'The ones that think they're on Time Team are running out of stamina and want some V.I.P. visitors: the ones that want to be Indiana Jones when they grow up could do with a few priceless treasures and rifles,' Catriona replied, straight-faced. 'But the good weather is keeping them together.'

Rob laughed.

'Amazing, eh? Rained all last year in Greece, and this year sunburn in East Lothian!'

His own nose was already red and peeling: he never had the sense to wear a hat. Catriona felt a small surge of motherliness come over her, and quickly looked down at the site map, spread out on the trestle table and tacked into place. She had wondered quite a lot about Robbie in the last few years, whether he might finally be the man to make her – not forget Neil, but slide him more comfortably into the past where he belonged. Her life was in the present, she told herself briskly, sometimes several times a week. But of course it was not true: she was an archaeologist, and whether it was a Roman camp-follower or a man four years ago, they were all alive to her.

'I picked up the report on the finds we've made so far. It was in my departmental pigeonhole when I popped in this morning.' Rob handed her a thick transit envelope, much used, and she drew out the contents.

'Second century Samian shards, yes,' she read aloud, picking out key words. 'Second rate tesserae ... that's much what we thought, isn't it? No surprises there.'

'What about the coin Emma picked up the other day? She'll be thrilled to hear about it.' He answered her frown. 'I only picked the envelope up and threw it in the car. I haven't had a chance to look at it yet.'

Catriona nodded, and ran her gaze down the report.

'Ah, there we are – 'Find EM/2000/9, early Scottish farthing coin, post 1280, probably circa 1290.'

'Oh, damn it. Not Roman, then.'

'I don't think she'll be much distressed,' Catriona said, closer to the students than Rob. 'She's never thought much of the mighty Roman Empire – prefers Scotland the Brave.'

Rob the Roman enthusiast made a disparaging noise which he would no doubt have followed with a matching remark, but there came a sound at the tent flap and an uncertain-looking undergraduate made a token knocking motion at the tent pole.

'Excuse me, Dr. Lindsay, Dr. Dean ...' She was a little wide-eyed, and against the sunlight she seemed to be shivering slightly.

'What's the problem, Alison?' asked Rob. 'Found Mons Graupius? Or lost a trowel?'

'I think,' said the girl, definitely shaking now, 'I think I've found human bones!'

III

'Aw, no!'

The alarm clock fell on its back on the bedside table, and an arm flailed the covers back and the radio on in one panicked sweep. Tom swung to a sitting position and peered at the clock again. He must have switched off the alarm without waking up.

He stumbled to the bathroom, swearing comprehensively, and threw cold water at his face, as hard as he could. Honest grey eyes in an over-old grey face stared at him, emptying handfuls of water over his curly black hair, from the droplet-spattered mirror, trying to stay open. He sighed, and stepped into the shower.

There seemed to be no clean clothes in the bedroom, which came as a shock until he remembered he had hardly been at home and awake for more than about twenty minutes all week. His only consolation was that everyone else in the lab must be in much the same state, or the ones that lived alone, anyway. The last girlfriend had moved out of his life months ago, and would not have touched his laundry anyway, preferring to segregate her designer wear from his objects of clothing. He flopped on to his knees beside what seemed to have identified itself as his laundry pile, and began to hunt through it.

'… a spokesperson at Holyrood has denied the rumours,' the radio was saying. 'And now to our main story again. Health chiefs at Edinburgh Royal Infirmary NHS Trust have confirmed that a child suffering from SAIDS has been admitted to the hospital, the first child known to have contracted the disease since its appearance in January this year. The child, who is not being named, is believed to have a close relative serving a sentence in a Scottish prison. Doctors said the child's condition was critical but stable. No further details were given.'

A child. This would make their work twice as urgent. A child.

He found he had stopped searching for cleanish clothes and started again, his arms heavy and tired. A child … how could a child have contracted it? And which prison? One they'd looked at before? What was the setup for visitors? Pity for the unknown victim made way – had to make way – for analysis. This was the first child, the first visitor, to have caught the disease. What was special about this child? How had it happened? Could – you always had to hope – could this be the key they needed?

He dressed with renewed vigour, his ears alert for any further news, but the newsreader had moved smartly on to the continued anxious coverage of the debate over GM crops, accidental plantings and unforeseen contaminations. He left the radio on, muttering more mysteriously to itself the further he left it behind, and it was only when he had taken the long stone tenement stair two at a time and reached the street door below that he remembered that he had omitted to have breakfast. But at the end of the road he could see the great maroon double-decker waiting at the traffic lights, and he broke into a sprint for the bus stop, willing the lights not to change until he reached it. If he missed this one, there would be no direct one for hours …

'One to Roslin, please.' He hurled himself up the steps and felt in his pockets, finding a heap of loose change. The bus driver watched him morosely as Tom counted it out in his hands.

'Ye bin busking in Princes Street again?'

'Not so well, either, to look at this,' Tom agreed, joining the joke.

The bus angled its way through the late rush hour traffic, stopping awkwardly every few hundred yards as if scraping an acquaintance with an unfriendly pavement. As they neared the centre of town the traffic, like the threads on a spider's web, grew denser, and Tom stared out at the Catholic cathedral and the long, straight, throng of Princes Street while the bus lurched ever upwards, crossing the end of Princes Street and climbing North Bridge over Waverley Station in a sudden surge of empty road. By the time the bus became completely bogged down in the chaos of South Bridge, Tom, sticking to the plastic seat, was already in the laboratory in his mind, deep in the possible results of the experiments he had set going the previous night. He hoped they would work this time.

The bottleneck of South Bridge and Nicolson Street opened up into South Clerk Street and Newington Road, then broadly swelled to Minto Street – still the same road but now spaciously residential and peppered with hotels. The bus turned off and on to Dalkeith Road, and began the task of leaving the city behind.

'Tom, you look absolutely dreadful, my boy.' George Mackay's anglified accent greeted Tom as he blundered through the doors of the Establishment. As Tom's eyes adjusted to the change in light levels, George came into focus, tall, square-jawed like a film star, black eyebrows and silver hair. He wore a perfectly pressed white lab coat that glowed almost radioactively in the fluorescent glare. 'Did you have breakfast?' he asked, avuncular as ever. Tom shook his head. 'Or much sleep? I see from the computer you were here till two again this morning. You're as bad as young Price, and I'll say the same to you as I did to him ten minutes ago: straight to the dining room with you and have something to eat. You're no good to my laboratory unless your brain is functioning, and it won't do that without fuel. Go on, now!'

Tom staggered past him, feeling underdressed and inadequately groomed. No one else caused quite that reaction in him, but George Mackay could manage it in seconds.

The canteen – only George ever called it the dining room – was pleasant, with large sunny windows, a choice of high tables with hard chairs or low tables and comfortable armchairs in cool, relaxing blues, echoing the huge photographs of lighthouses in high winds that adorned the white walls. It could be chilly in winter, but on a hot summer's day like today the effect was almost calming. It was empty, except for the one discordant feature at a table in the middle: Gavin Price was indeed already there, drinking coffee out of the side of his mouth so as not to obscure his reading of the journal article in front of him. He was around Tom's age, skinny and with the look of youth that red hair and freckles often give. Today, however, he was crumpled, shabby and weary, with great dark circles under his eyes.

He glanced up as Tom approached. Tom grunted a greeting, glanced longingly at the counters of hot food and counted out more of his small change to buy a coffee and a chocolate bar from the vending machines against the wall. He went back to sit by Gavin.

'Sleep in?' Gavin asked economically.

'Aye.'

'Me, too.'

'Uncle George caught me at the door,' Tom added. One whiff of the chocolate bar was enough to remind him just how hungry he was, and he laid his change out on the table to see if he had enough for another one. 'Said he'd seen from the computer how late we left this morning.'

'Aye, well,' responded Gavin, with a humourless grin, 'it's the only way he'd know. When was the last time he was here past six?'

'There was that night his car broke down and he had to wait for his wife to collect him,' Tom pointed out reasonably. 'He was here till maybe a quarter to seven, that night.'

'True, true,' Gavin allowed, though he did not look amused. He rubbed his crinkly hair vigorously and took a mouthful of coffee, draining the plastic cup. The coffee was good, because George Mackay said it had to be. 'I suppose he has his uses,' he added, waving a hand around the canteen.

'Well, he's the great one for getting us the funding grants, isn't he? And even business sponsors.'

'Oh, aye. Ever seen him at a posh party? He just cruises like the QE2 amongst the rich and famous, and his tastefully-attired handmaidens scuttle behind him with the baskets for the cash.'

'He didn't have to try too hard for this one, anyway,' Tom pointed out, slightly uneasy at Gavin's new levels of bitterness. 'Government and drugs companies falling over themselves to find a cure for jail fever.' He returned to the chocolate machine with his coins.

'And how long will that last, eh?' Gavin raised his voice to continue the conversation. 'If we don't see some success soon, someone, somewhere will start to think about pulling plugs. And I don't know about you, but I'm on a short-term contract here.'

'Damned if we find a cure, damned if we don't,' agreed Tom through his chocolate bar. 'And all we really know so far is that it isn't airborne.'

'Doesn't *seem* to be airborne,' Gavin corrected him with disgust. 'Swift-acting from first symptom to death, not airborne, and goes for the immune system.'

'It's not much for five months' work, is it?' said Tom. 'Come on, we'd better go and see if we can add anything to that vast body of knowledge.'

'Tom – did you hear about the girl?'

Tom stopped. Gavin was standing and rolling up his journal, but his eyes were on Tom.

'What girl?' he asked.

'The wee girl in the Infirmary – the one with jail fever.'

'I didn't know it was a girl,' Tom said, 'but yes, I heard it on the

21

news this morning.'

'That's the first child to get it.'

Gavin had two young children of his own, Tom knew. If Gavin had not wanted to get home to his children, and had not offered Tom his only chance of a lift back to town at that hour of the morning, Tom probably would not have gone home at all.

'I'm wondering if it might be the very thing we need,' said Tom encouragingly. 'Let's go and see if there are any reports in yet.'

He ushered Gavin out through the canteen door, letting it swing shut behind them. The nearest lighthouse picture lifted slightly like a sail, causing the sea within it to surge and swell.

IV

Nicholas Eliot had no regard for the sea.

That did not mean he had no respect for it. No, he had been in bad enough storms in his life, and seen enough strange wonders, to respect the sea and its strengths, its peculiarities, its deviousness. But he did not care for it, and he did not loathe it. It was simply a means to an end.

That silly old fool up in the prow, with his rich furs and velvets and with the lad he said was his nephew – that was the kind of thing Eliot thought ridiculous. Striding about the wooden deck and pointing and staring, and enthusing about the whole voyage, learning the names of every rope and sail and bit of plank as if they were going to be examined on it in Paris, making friends with the sailors, trying their food and drink, prattling about the romance of the sea – oh, it was nonsense. It was enough for Eliot that the broken-down old barrel would survive the journey, for there was a cold, yellow light in the sky that even he knew was cause enough to worry, and he could not quite convince himself that the black strips of land in the distant west was really the coast of Scotland, or Ultima Thule, or even land at all.

Nicholas Eliot was going home. He did not go particularly willingly or with much sentiment, and it was not to see family or friends that he was undertaking this inauspicious voyage. Nor did he go much laden down with merchandise. When he wanted to impress people, usually guards at gates and women in the better class of inn, he said he was a merchant, but he was closer to being a trader. He had a few packs below decks, nothing of great value or moment. He had sold most of his stock on the long journey from Amsterdam to Stockholm, lightening his load, selling, one by one, his mules as there was nothing with which to load them, leaving some of the money with old and trusted friends along the way but converting most of it to gold. A little gold had gone to pay for this voyage – he had paid in silver so as not to attract too much attention. His looks were unmemorable: a longish, thinnish face, wrinkled now and sagging, with mud-coloured hair and eyes. His clothes never marked him out, either, though just at present they were his most valuable possession as the rest of the gold was well-hidden into the various seams and linings, the unremarkable material thick with unsuspected richness. If the ship foundered now he would go straight to the bottom, he thought, and bared his yellow teeth in a mocking grin. That would solve all his problems, anyway.

He leaned against the rail and regarded the oily sea with misgiving. The ship, such as it was, slid up and down on the swell, sails comfortably full. He had heard one of the sailors tell the young man they were tacking, some method, he gathered, of going across the wind.

The yellowish light went flat, and suddenly everything was wrong.

The wind, springing on them out of the sky, whipped and cracked the sails till it sounded like spars breaking above them. The old man and his nephew, silly grins shock-frozen on their faces, leapt back from the rail as the salt spray lashed their finery. It stung the eyes, smarted on the skin. Eliot left the rail as though it had turned white-hot: he grabbed at some part of the cabin wall behind him, and as he tried to steady himself the first sizeable wave hit them. It flailed over the rail at the old man and his nephew. They crashed to the deck, sprawling, clutching for a handhold. Open-mouthed, they tried to cry out, but the wind whipped their voices away. Sailors sprang nimbly over them, their first concern the ship. Serve them right, thought Eliot, turning away, let them drown, stupid fools.

But some spark of folly in himself – probably the same spark that had him on this graceless ship in the first place – made him turn back, even as he cursed himself for doing so. Ears singing in the howl of wind and water, he seized a loose rope with one hand, and using it as his link to the cabin he inched forward, as far as he could, slithering on the flooded deck. He grabbed feet, hands or head, whichever came nearest, thick with soaked furs, and dragged first the old man, then the nephew, back to the lea of the cabin wall. He left them there, sodden and spluttering, and staggered back to the comparative safety of the cabin.

He was something above the middle height, and had to lurch about the cabin with his head hunched far down between his shoulders. The cabin itself was Spartan, and his belongings had not made it less so. He looked about, peering through the gloom. The daylight through the one small window was now dull and sick-yellow, no use for anything but warning of worse to come. His bed roll was done up neatly on one of the flat wooden benches, a practice borne of frequent necessity to leave places fast. He did not value it: if the ship went down, as seemed all too probable, he would not be seizing that. The packs in the hold mattered little, too. But the leather satchel on the little three-legged stool – that was something he had not wish to have far from him. He quickly took off his coat, slung the satchel over his shoulder and shrugged the coat back on again, feeling its unnatural weight. He was a strong man, but had he the strength to swim with all this? But arriving without it, he reflected with a shudder, might well be worse than not arriving at all.

Outside, the cries of the sailors, ripped by the wind, were as incomprehensible as the cries of the gulls. Occasional footsteps pelted past the cabin door. He sat on the bench, feet apart, swaying with the roll of the ship, trying to sense whether it was growing worse or easier. He could not tell.

After some time the old man and his nephew appeared, soaked and subdued, making their way gingerly to their side of the cabin, where they had hung a few choice pieces of tapestry in the confined space and arranged their cups, spoons and plates on a board. The pewterware was all now on the floor, the cups rolling pointlessly, but the nephew's attention was taken up with getting the old man on to his bench bed. The old man was bone-grey. The nephew found their supply of wine – Eliot could smell its fruity richness – and poured it into a recovered cup, holding it with the old man's hands up to his uncle's face.

The old man sipped at it and began to shake, though that in itself seemed to be an improvement in his condition. A little colour returned to his shivering cheeks. The nephew helped him to finish the cup and then laid him back tenderly on the bench, tucking a fur blanket around him. All the time he murmured softly to his uncle, a susurration of sound beneath the racket of the waves and the wind and the creaking ship. Eliot did not recognise the language, which was unusual: he had travelled so long and so widely in the cold countries of the North that he recognised all the tongues, and could understand most of them. And these two were fair, like the Northern races. The old man spoke a few words in the Frankish tongue, which Eliot knew and which made sharing the cabin possible, if not comfortable: Eliot supposed he could have asked him where they were from, but it had not crossed his mind until now. He eyed them sideways as he sat with the weight of his coat pulling his shoulders down. Like his, all their belongings came from a variety of places: Russian furs, Flemish tapestries, boots in a leather he did not know, well-tooled and exotically cut.

The storm neither diminished, nor increased. The noise of the sailors' efforts lessened, just sitting tight, somewhere, Eliot supposed, only emerging if something else came loose. And they sat tight, too, in the dark little cabin. The old man slept, on and off. Eliot pulled a tallow candle from his bedpack and lit it, using its own melt to stick it firmly to the end of his bed-bench. The nephew poured himself some of the wine, and then had second thoughts and with the wide-eyed, over-emphasised expression of one who does not share a language, he held the cup out to Eliot, spreading his other hand, palm up, making the offer generous. Eliot paused, then leaned forward, reaching for the wine with a not-unfriendly nod, missing it at the ship slid suddenly down a wave. The wine slopped. The nephew made an apologetic face, Eliot made an 'it doesn't matter' sign with one hand. The nephew topped up the cup and the handover was more successful this time. Eliot grinned his thanks. The nephew smiled in return, his face showing dull in the candlelight, pulled another rolling cup towards himself with one foot, and poured himself a helping, too. Eliot and the nephew raised their cups in a toast and tasted the wine. It was warming, rich, strong. Eliot regretted even the little that had been slopped on the floor.

They sat for a long while. The boy, accustoming himself to the heavy sea, swayed with a look of blank betrayal on his face: the journey was not as wonderful as he had thought. He'll dine well on this for months, though, thought Eliot – if we live. But he himself had grown – if not more optimistic, at least more resigned. The wind must have caught them at the wrong angle, that was all. The ship had proved itself unexpectedly sturdy, and the sailors seemed to have it under control again. Perhaps he was not going to drown tonight. The darkness deepened, and lulled by the unaccustomed strength of the wine, he fell asleep.

The crack that woke him sounded like the heavens breaking in two. As he leapt to his feet, confused, the wind turned its hollow roar to a scream. He ran for the cabin door. A path of ragged moonlight led to it. Beyond it the sea, steel grey, lurched and broke into dirty foam.

He ran out on to the deck, looking up. Something was wrong with the sails. He watched, falling against the rail but still staring up as a sailor tried to catch an end of broken rope. Then he saw that the great solid mast had cracked in two.

A hand clutched his arm. Beside him crouched the nephew, staring wildly ahead. The boy pointed, crying out something Eliot could not understand. He turned to look.

Ahead loomed a rough, black mass. In the moonlight, shadows cast across it, catching white specks and the torn foam at its base. The whole thing was so close it towered above them.

'The May Isle,' breathed Eliot.

With a crash that echoed off the rocks, the mast above them finally gave way. The sailor, tangled in the ropes that were finally in his reach, fell shrieking into the waves. Then, as if stuffed with gunpowder, the bows exploded. Wood showered around them. Moonlit rocks flashed on either side. In the howling wind, driving motion and cold, black and white light spun in Eliot's eyes, then inside his head, and then he knew nothing but darkness.

V

Tom's mind was blank. He looked around him at the open refrigerators, the broken stands, the shredded paperwork. Underfoot, as Gavin stepped slowly forwards, the shattered glittering remains of slides and test tubes crunched like new-fallen snow. To complete the image, Tom found he was shivering.

'What the hell is this?' Gavin managed first. 'Is it - is it some kind of an accident?'

Tom found himself nodding, trying to believe it was possible, though to a certain extent it was obvious what had happened. Vandals had wrecked their laboratory.

'How did they get in?' asked Tom, though he was still looking more at the destruction than at the method. His voice sounded hollow in his head. Someone had put something heavy through his computer screen – his desk chair, by the look of it. He hoped it was only the monitor that was damaged.

'Look,' said Gavin, still inching into the L-shaped room. 'The fire door is open. It looks as if someone forced it.'

'Well, it would have to be that or this door,' said Tom. His brain was slowly returning to normal. 'It's not as if there are any windows.' He ran a hand through his hair and rubbed the back of his neck. Even the poster of Shania Twain, the object of their affection and of George Mackay's perpetual despair, had been ripped from the wall. 'I'll go and call the police. Eh, you'd better not touch anything, right?'

'Oh, aye,' said Gavin absently. 'Here, I'll come back to the door, stop anyone else getting in, eh?'

'Good idea.' Tom stepped back to the door and made off to reception, with the sound of Gavin's crunching, uneasy footsteps following him down the corridor.

He felt foolish calling the police. It had a great deal to do, he felt, with the woman on the other end of the line being so calm, taking down the details slowly and carefully. He had not dialled 999 – there was no one dying, he would have felt like an imposter – but he was still made to feel that what he had to report was so commonplace that he was on the verge of being charged with wasting police time. He put the receiver down and sat on one of the low leather seats provided in reception, and some part of his analytical mind said that the police attitude was probably geared towards people panicking, to calm them down. It was just a bit too calming for him, because of course he was reacting perfectly rationally and placidly, wasn't he? It was only a break-in, no one hurt, nothing on fire …

He leapt an inch from the seat as a long, pale hand landed on his shoulder.

'Tom! Are you listening?'

It was George Mackay, expression paternally anxious. The crease on his trousers was at its sharpest just about level with Tom's bare knee at the scuffed edge of his shorts. It was all Tom needed to put the cap on his morning.

'What?' he asked, not bothering to tone down his voice to the polite moderation George preferred. George drew a little breath into his kindly smile, patient, understanding.

'I saw Gavin – I saw what had happened to your laboratory. He says everything you left out to work through last night has been destroyed. Is that right?'

'Gavin looked more closely than I did. If he says so,' said Tom, terrified that Gavin might indeed be right. These experiments took long enough to set up, and to work through, and every day they lost meant more deaths. What about that child?

'He also said,' George went on more carefully, 'that you were going to call the police. Have you done so already?'

'I have,' Tom confirmed.

A look of mild disappointment passed over George's face.

'That's a shame. I'm sure we could have dealt with all this, ah, internally.'

'But the fire door was smashed in!' said Tom, confused more than shocked.

'Oh, indeed. But consider: there are three laboratories concentrating on the cure for SAIDS nationwide.' George never called it jail fever. It was not in his nature. 'If we are the first to find and develop it – and I hope and trust we shall be – then we want nothing to taint that glory. No breaches of security, no possibilities of mistakes or, ah, contamination. And really,' he added, moving smoothly into his argument-winning smile, 'the police cannot really help us, can they? We are *scientists*.' As ever, he invested the word with a meaning somewhere between physician, mystic and God.

'Well, it's too late now,' Tom said flatly.

'Oh, never mind.' George's long hand patted his shoulder kindly. 'Come along, let's wait somewhere a little more comfortable.'

And less conspicuous, Tom thought, as he peeled himself off the seat and nodded to the receptionist at the switchboard. George led him back to the canteen and, extraordinarily, bought him a coffee. Gavin was already there, still pale with shock.

'I locked the lab door,' he explained, 'and Eck the Door said he'd go round to the fire door and make sure no one got in that way.'

Tom nodded. George seemed satisfied, too.

They were still sitting there, pretty much in silence, when the receptionist tripped in ten minutes later to announce the arrival of a police inspector.

'An inspector, eh? I'm glad they're taking this seriously. I shall deal with them,' said George, magisterially, but it was not to be. Hard on the heels of the receptionist arrived a lop-sided gentleman in a tweed suit, with a tie beneath in an obscene shade of orange.

'Hello,' said the man amiably, smiling roundly at the room in general. 'My name is Detective Chief Inspector McAlester – well, obviously it isn't all my name, you know,' he finished apologetically. 'I'm not really here. My constable's the one in charge, but I've always loved laboratories.' He said the word with a kind of rubbly relish. The constable, taller but somehow self-effacing, kept a straight face. 'Who is it that works in the laboratory that was broken into?'

'Ah, me,' said Gavin, standing awkwardly with the shadow of a grin on his face. George was frozen in his attitude of affable scientist, completely bypassed by the little policeman.

'Ah!' The policeman shook Gavin's hand delightedly.

'Gavin Price,' Gavin added in response to McAlester's questioning look.

'But you didn't call us, did you?' asked McAlester.

'No, that was me,' said Tom quickly. He could see hysteria bubble up in Gavin. 'Tom Buchan. I work in the lab, too.'

'Excellent, excellent!' said McAlester. 'Will you show me?'

The four of them headed for the laboratory. Tom had the impression that George had been left in the canteen still standing in the same position, unaccustomed to such abandonment.

'Who discovered the damage?' asked McAlester as they led him along the corridor.

'We both did,' said Gavin. 'We came through from the canteen together –'

'Just like this?' asked McAlester in mild excitement

'That's right.'

'And when had you last been in?'

'Around two o'clock this morning.'

McAlester made a sympathetic tutting noise through loose lips. They reached the door of the laboratory, and Gavin unlocked it, first with a mortice key, then with a swipe card. A low beep told him the door was released, and he opened it.

'Oh, dearie me.' McAlester surveyed the mess within, standing half on tiptoe to peer down the long room. 'And what do you do in here?'

Tom felt faintly surprised that he had to ask. His own life was so consumed by his work at the moment that he half-expected that everyone else's must be, too.

'We're epidemiologists,' he explained, used to the blank expression that followed. 'We're trying to analyse and find a cure for jail fever.'

'Jail fever?' said McAlester vaguely, almost as if he had never heard of it. He tutted again, shaking his head and staring into the laboratory. 'Then who would want to do this?'

'Absolutely no idea,' said Gavin. Bitterness was taking over from shock in his tone. It was impossible to calculate yet how much work had been lost, where they would have to go to start again.

'Can you see – I know it must be difficult, just from here – can you see if anything is missing?'

'It's hard to tell,' said Tom. 'I think all the equipment is there, but how many trays or slides or tubes are in that mess on the floor – you would never know.'

McAlester swung a beatific expression from him to the self-effacing constable behind him.

'I think, John, that you should perhaps ask the Scenes of Crime ladies and gentlemen to come and take a look at this.'

The constable nodded, and turned away, pulling a mobile phone out of his pocket.

'How long is all this going to take?' asked Gavin. 'Our work is kind of urgent, you know?'

McAlester favoured him with an apologetic smile.

'We'll try *very* hard to let you back in this evening, if that would help. There is a lot of very complicated-looking things in there, you know, and it might take us a little while.'

Try as he might, Tom could find no trace of sarcasm in the chief inspector's tone. He frowned. McAlester turned to him.

'Would you both like to walk round with me to the fire door? I understand that, ah,' he glanced at a piece of paper he seemed to have been clutching in his hand for some time, 'that Eck the Door is guarding it for us.'

He led the way back to the front door and they went outside into the hot sunshine, leaving the gravel path for the parched grass. George had had some very particular landscapers in to do the grounds. Noisy gravel, combined with attractive planting of thorny and inhospitable shrubs, made the place distinctly discouraging to the average intruder. However, there was a clear path to the fire exit, a substantial double door opening outwards. The chief inspector scuttled forward, followed more sedately by the young constable, and they began a minute examination of the forced door. Gavin drew Tom away a little, out of immediate earshot.

'I was thinking,' he said, 'that we should tell him about the other things, too.'

'What other things?' asked Tom, looking back cautiously.

'Oh, come on, Tom, you know! All the wee accidents we've been having with the work – the refrigerator breaking down, then the generator going, and the bug in the computer system. Think about it. All in all we're probably weeks behind where we should be. What if they weren't accidents? What if someone is behind it all?'

'But who could it possibly be?' asked Tom. He wondered if he was being stupid. Could these really all have been caused by one malevolent individual? Certainly there were times he had thought the whole project was jinxed, but then they were rushing, and tired, and that was when mistakes happened. He had always privately wondered to himself if the refrigerator thing had been his own fault, anyway. And maybe because they were rushing, and tired, he had failed to see this genuine pattern in the whole thing, the pattern of sabotage.

'Who could it be?' he repeated. 'Who *could* do it, and who *would* do it?'

'There's that bunch that writes to the newspapers,' said Gavin. Clearly he had been thinking it through. 'The ones that say that jail fever is God's revenge for the abolition of capital punishment. Or there are our rivals, I suppose …'

'Oh, they're as dedicated as we are!' Tom objected. 'But maybe the newspaper lot, now … That's a possibility. Oh,' he drew a deep breath, 'you're shocking me here, Gav. I never looked at it this way before.'

Gavin gave a grin little nod.

'Shall we tell him, then?'

They went home after that: there was nothing else they could do until the lab was clear again. George, recovering from being passed over, came into give his account of the various mishaps affecting his project, to admit he had not been near the laboratory that morning, and to point out, a little acidly, that the fire door was connected to the alarm system. Detective Chief Inspector McAlester took careful notes in longhand, his eyebrows almost up in his spiky white hairline with the effort of concentration.

Gavin gave Tom a lift, for which he was grateful, and at his request left him at the big Tesco at Fountainbridge. He filled a trolley with pizzas and frozen pastas, bread, milk and beer, and took a taxi home to spend the rest of his unexpected liberty, feeding the washing machine and the tumble dryer, planning a distant cycling holiday with a motoring atlas, and watching Carry On Caesar on video while he ate and drank properly for the first time in weeks.

VI

'Down by the river?' Rob was asking in some agitation as they left the quartermaster's tent. 'We aren't digging there yet. We haven't even surveyed it.'

Catriona saw Alison the student blush as she led them over to the site of her discovery.

'I didn't do any digging,' she said, a plaintive note in her voice. 'I'm not on digging today.'

'No, you're on washing, eh?' said Catriona, trying to make up for Rob's abruptness.

'That's right. I was filling a bowl of water – just here,' she added, reaching the stream. Where she stood was a small, pebbly shore by a sharp wriggle in the river's course. Next to the shore, the mud bank rose sharply, overhanging the curve slightly. A foot-wide bite of this had fallen out and presumably been swept away by the stream, and in the gap was what could easily have been mistaken for a large, rounded, greyish-yellow stone.

'Oh, well spotted!' cried Rob, instantly cheered. He leaped towards the spot, and Alison beamed with pleasure.

The skull was within a few inches of the surface at the point at which it had appeared: the ground then sloped upwards slightly, away from the river, and Rob crouched slightly away from a direct line above the skull, keeping his shadow and his weight off the site.

'Face up, I think,' he remarked. 'Got a brush?' Catriona handed him a two-inch paint brush from her tool belt. He dusted a little earth off the exposed arc of the skull, whistling softly through his teeth, then rolled back to sit on his heels.

'Right,' he said, his face solemn, 'We're going to take this slowly. Alison, call the others over, tell them to leave what they're doing and come down here.'

Alison scurried off. Rob eyed Catriona, and she had suddenly the warm feeling of being part of a team.

'We weren't expecting bodies, were we?' he asked, his voice hovering between casual and ominous. She could see he was not yet sure whether to milk the drama or to pretend he dealt with this kind of thing every day.

'Not exactly,' Catriona agreed. She peered over the edge, careful not to tread where she might damage anything under the thin top layer of soil. Never assume more than you're offered, she thought. 'It might be nothing more than the skull.'

'Aw, come on, Catriona! You know the archaeologist's saying: one stone's a stone, two stones are a wall and three stones are a house. At least where there's a skull let there be a reasonable chance of a skeleton!'

The students arrived in a rush, trying to look cool in the face of their first freshly dug corpse.

'Right,' said Rob, raising his voice a little. 'Were we expecting bodies?'

'No,' chorused most of the students, who had read the project plan.

'Why not?' asked Rob.

'Romans at this period favoured cremation,' said Alison, quietly. She was a hard-working girl. Rob beamed approval, and Alison stared at the ground, quite pink.

'Right,' said Rob. 'It's possible that there were inhumations here, but they were more likely either in urns or just layers of ash, possibly with some bone tissue. Good. So, everybody take a look at what we've got here, then.'

This involved most of the students leaping joyously into the river to see the protruding skull at close quarters. At last they were huddled round it – it came to around their hip height. Rob gave them a moment or two to look their fill, and then asked generally,

'So, what do we do next, eh?'

'Excavate from this end?' said someone tentatively, and was shouted down.

'Take photographs!' called several others, looking smug. Rob was known for being very insistent on careful record-keeping on a site – archaeology was a destructive science. Now he nodded approval for the idea, but was still looking for something more.

'Geophysics?' asked Emma warily. 'To make sure we're not disturbing anything else?'

'Not a bad idea,' Rob conceded with a grin. 'Suitably cautious for an archaeologist. However, there is something else we should at least consider first. Think about what we've just been saying. We weren't expecting to find bodies out here. This one is near the surface … anyone make the connexion?'

'Call the pollis,' said one student morosely, and everyone laughed. But Rob waved down the noise.

'He's right, you know. How do we know someone didn't nip out ten years ago and stash their old granny out here?'

A little anxious laughter followed this remark: for some you could see a sudden realisation in their eyes that a skull two thousand years old was not at all the same as one two decades old. For the rest there was the shameful, irresistible frisson of someone else's car accident or murder.

'So back to your work and not a word to anyone outside the dig just yet, eh?' He turned to Catriona. 'Keep an eye on things here, Catriona, and I'll nip up to Elysian Fields and ring the Sheriff's office from there, okay?'

He made off with long, outdoor strides, and Catriona waved the students back to their allotted jobs, chivvying them with sarcastic remarks. Alison made for the basins and tables near the stream where she and several others had been preparing to wash the day's finds. Others drifted reluctantly back up the hill to their spits and sondages, surrounded by neat hedges of cut turves.

It was lunch time, and they were seated near the stream munching their various sandwiches when an official-looking car drew up, and out of it stepped a smart young man and a dilapidated older one, who wore a tweed suit and a violent orange tie, and walked with a rolling gait. They approached the group a little circumspectly.

'Dr. Robert Dean?' asked the older man generally when they were within a reasonable distance. Rob pulled himself up from the ground, eyebrows high in surprise.

'Detective Chief Inspector McAlester,' said the man, his eyes half-shut as though he were trying to remember it all. 'I hear you have a body for me to look at,' he added happily.

In a pair of wellingtons intended for larger feet, McAlester waded into the little stream and peered, as the students had done earlier, at the promising dome of bone sticking sideways out of the mud bank.

'Oh,' he said, on a note of surprise.

'It's just,' added the constable apologetically, 'we normally get them with a bit more flesh on, if you see what I mean.'

'Oh,' said Rob, exchanging a glance with Catriona. 'This tends to be the way we always find them. Would you like us to excavate further, then?'

'Ah –' said the constable, but McAlester beamed.

'Oh, yes please,' he said. 'May I watch?'

'We rather hoped you would,' said Rob, 'in case it's a bit too recent for us. What we'll do,' he went on, 'is to take the turves off back this way, away from the river, for a couple of metres, and about a metre wide. That should show us any shading in the earth that'll tell us what's grave backfill and what's the surrounding earth. Catriona, do you want to get started on that? Alison could give you a hand, since she found it. There's only so many people can excavate a grave, Chief Inspector, if you think on it.'

Catriona finished a chocolate bar and went to fetch her tool belt, a shovel, and Alison.

All afternoon, in the baking heat, Catriona and Alison dug, scraped, fingered and brushed, tickling and smoothing the bones as they cleared them, leaving them neatly in situ. Every discarded grain of soil, every pebble, was removed by the washers, sieved and rinsed in the clean stream water and examined closely, but there were no finds apart from the bones themselves. The washers came and went, Rob left and arrived again with a man in smart shirtsleeves and office trousers from Elysian Fields, the other diggers stretched their digging breaks to watch the progress of this much more exciting trench, and the police officers settled themselves down to watch someone else digging up bodies for a change. Through it all, sweating in a way ladies were not supposed to, Catriona and Alison crouched in the shallow ditch or on its banks until at last all was clear, and they stood and stretched their muddy legs and snatched off their hats to fan their faces. The world, which a moment ago had been focussed on a dim trench and tiny specks of earth, suddenly seemed brilliant and enormous, the scrubby trees meandering at odd angles about the river, the little hill looming.

Rob brought them cans of fizzy drink from a net in the stream, and they gulped them thankfully while two other students took photographs and made drawings of the bones for the dig records. Catriona stared up at the glittering sky for a moment, stretching her back and her neck, before once again looking down at the remains in the trench.

'They must have been dug up and buried again,' Rob remarked, and Inspector McAlester, sporting a sunhat made from yesterday's *Scotsman*, scrabbled over to see.

'Why do you say that?' he asked eagerly.

'Easy,' said Rob with a grin. 'They're not laid out like a skeleton: they're all thrown down one end. And there was no dark staining in the earth that would have shown where flesh had decayed, was there,

Catriona?'

She shook her head, still gazing down at the little heap of bones, the tiny mortal remains of someone forgotten. For she was sure, now that she had touched them, that these were old bones, long-buried.

'What if –' the Chief Inspector began with a frown, ''What if they had been boiled, or scraped?'

'Bleagh,' remarked the student with the camera, pretending to vomit.

'Well,' said Rob, 'how would you know?'

The student stopped and stared down at the bones.

'There would be knife-marks if they had been scraped,' he said slowly. 'though that might only show up under a microscope. Same if they'd been chewed by wild animals. But boiled – I don't think we've covered that one yet, Dr. Dean!' He left, striding cockily back to the quartermaster's tent, but Rob stepped down delicately into the trench and picked up a thigh bone.

'If it had been boiled,' he explained, determined to educate, 'chances are the ends would be shiny. But they're not.' He showed the white ball of the hip joint to McAlester and then to the constable. 'Now, we'll take these back to the tent and lay them out to see we've got everything. Pass me that box, Alison, eh?'

'I wonder ...' said Catriona.

'What?' asked Rob, plucking bones from the pile as though he were playing jackstraws. He, too, had clearly decided they were old bones. She hoped the police would not decide otherwise.

'Why go to all the trouble of digging a full length grave if you are going to throw all the bones in at one end?

Rob stopped to look back at her. She sat on the grass, gazing at the trench, thinking.

'Maybe someone dug up a grave, took the grave goods and flung the bones back in,' he suggested.

'How did they know where to dig?' asked Catriona. 'This place was never a graveyard: we have copies of every old map we could find of this place. I know the stream moved about a bit over the centuries, but there was never a suggestion of a burial ground of any date here.'

Rob sat down. The policemen waited, alert.

'You have an idea, haven't you?' asked Rob, with one of those companionable smiles that she liked so much. She looked away.

'Mm. It just reminds me – reminds me of the pattern in some old kirkyards. You know, where they've been burying people for generations, and headstones are missing or records are gone. You know what they do when they're digging a new grave and they find old

35

bones?'

'Well?'

'They take them out and put them in the church till after the funeral. Then before the backfill is dug back into the grave, they put the old bones back into the hole.'

'Do you mean,' said the constable tentatively, 'that you think there could be another burial under there?'

Catriona nodded, biting her lip. Rob, his feet still in the trench, lifted one of them to give a little tap on the floor of the grave. Everyone held their breath, trying to decide if the sound had been hollow or not. No one was sure.

'Well,' said Rob, standing up and stepping out of the trench, 'let's go for it.'

Another couple of minutes was enough to remove the rest of the excavated bones and let Alison take her discovery back to the tent in a box. Then Rob and Catriona settled down to take a spit of earth out of the trench.

They knew, as they neared it, that there was something below them, something not simply subsoil. The trench smelled damp, and a little water seemed to be seeping in at the end nearest the river, which was worryingly close. They dug circumspectly, back to back in the narrow trench, feeling their way along the earth floor with expert fingers. The sun, now at six in the evening, was still Scottish-summer high and they worked in their own shadows, and in the shadows of those who stood to watch, trying to keep their feet to either side of the cut. And then in an instant Catriona brushed away a thin layer of soil to reveal a grey, flat surface. She gasped.

Rob spun, still crouching, and leaned to look over her shoulder. She could feel his chest touch her back as he suddenly breathed in.

'A lead coffin ...' he said on the outbreath, and she could feel it warm on her cheek. For a long moment they crouched there, not moving, then Rob reach round her to brush off a little more of the earth. The rudiments of a pattern were revealed, the crossover point of two decorative lines. He stopped, and slowly stood up, and she followed, and they stepped up carefully out of the trench.

'Bloody hell,' said Rob reverently. And then, after a long silence, he added, 'Well, that's it, I've peaked. I'm ganging yame!'

VII

The site security guard employed by Elysian Fields was large and tough. He was good with savage dogs and wore DMs as others wear slippers. He had tattoos on his arms and rings through parts of his anatomy that made many squirm to think about, but as long as they were not visible through his uniform Elysian Fields did not mind. And as a goodwill gesture they lent this useful gentleman to Edinburgh University for the night, at some cost to themselves, to guard an unspecified (to the security guard) treasure and a slightly mouldy tent full of plastic basins.

VIII

Rob and Catriona stood dinner for the excited students at a vegetarian curry place near the department, praised with enthusiasm by Rob for its insistence on organic, vegetarian, un-genetically-modified wholesome grub. Catriona privately wondered how they could tell. The atmosphere was fizzing after their discovery: a Roman lead coffin, miles from anything but a small military outpost, manned by what they thought might have been a Dacian unit or some other small body of men from the outskirts of the civilised empire. It would have to be someone important – and then the lead coffin itself added a new dimension. How well would the body be preserved? Sometimes bodies well sealed in lead coffins kept most of their flesh, even for two thousand years. Sometimes water crept in, making a kind of soup around the bones. And what would have been buried with the corpse? Grave goods, clothing, even weapons … the possibilities seemed endless, and the students screamed them across the table, causing the smiles of the waiters to become rather brittle.

'There is another possibility,' said Rob, with a warning smile. 'The bones we found today could be our body. They could have been taken out of the coffin by grave robbers and tossed back in after they had looted the grave. And we have no notion yet how well preserved the coffin is – or if we just have the fragment of a lid …' But his eyes belied his words – he was just as excited as the rest of them. Catriona watched him from the other end of the long table. The students all thought he was wonderful, a bit mad, a livewire, good crack in the pub after a departmental seminar. She thought she knew him a little better than they did, but did she? Was he a friend? Was he just someone good at recruiting team members? Was he likely ever to be something more – or was he simply about the only eligible man she ever met these days? She half-smiled at herself. Living in a dream world … She should be concentrating on the lead coffin, if that's what it was. When was the last time anything interesting had even come close to happening anywhere in her vicinity? And what would Neil have thought – of Rob, of her, of the coffin? Neil, always, in the end, came between the motion and the act, falling like a shadow.

They finished their curries, most of them still hyper. Someone suggested going on to a pub and then a club, and Rob and she were enthusiastically encouraged to join them – a great honour, she knew. But as Rob left in the midst of the crowd of students, she found herself drifting slightly aside, not quite confident enough of her own popularity, and soon she was back at her car in the departmental car park, and soon after that she was at home, raiding the fridge for semillon chardonnay and chocolate, and settling down with a book in the empty silence.

IX

In a grim, shiny room on the other side of the city, there was no such thing as silence. It was filled with the hum and whine of machines and the laboured heavy breathing of Vicky, flat in the bed. Shona had no idea what the machines did. She had no idea when she had last eaten, or what. All that mattered was that Vicky, amidst all these wires and tubes, was still alive – for now.

2 – AWAKENING

I

The howling darkness swept and receded about him like waves in the night. He thought he might be on a ship, though he was not sure where he might be going.

Eliot was a cautious man. Before he opened his eyes, he tried to feel with his other senses just what was around him, where he might be. Which way up was he? For a moment he could not even tell that, and a panic-stricken question raced across his mind – how long had he been asleep? And in the next instant, puzzlement: what was the hurry?

A slight movement of his fingers told him he was lying on his back. His fingers moved unwillingly, though, reluctant to straighten, hard to direct. It was a long moment before they could be brought to identify the rough blanket on which he lay, and the other two? Or three? that covered him. They felt heavy, but unfamiliar. He had no recollection of owning them.

He moved his hands again, stretching with infinitesimal speed to feel what might be beyond the blankets. All the time he listened hard, trying to hear anything that would tell him that his movements were being watched, but beyond the howling wind there was nothing near at hand. He carried on with his efforts, and in an inch or two his left hand brushed something, a wall, perhaps? It felt like some kind of mud structure, not very common on a ship. But then, now that he thought about it, there was no sense of waves beneath him, so it was unlikely, in this wind, that he was on a ship. He was indoors, though, for he felt only slight draughts on his face as from an ill-fitting door.

His thoughts were sluggish, but he whipped them on. Behind his closed eyes, he could see no hint of a light source. He sniffed, warily. There was an earthy smell and, he thought, the scent of bracken. A little more prodding with his fingers confirmed that the bracken formed his bed, beneath the blankets. He moved slightly, stiffly. It felt comfortable. Someone had been taking care of him – not a situation he was used to. Finally, tentatively, he opened his eyes.

Dim light, coming from cracks around some kind of door hanging, showed him the inside of what seemed to be a small, single-roomed hut. The walls were part stone, part mud, and the roof disappeared in the darkness, with a few pale shapes dangling from the rafters. A few other low beds, looking much as his felt, surrounded the remains of a fire in the centre of the floor. They were empty, blankets folded neat and flat.

It was nowhere he had ever been before, he was sure of that. He turned his head to look around further, but his neck felt even more stiff than his arms, his movement constricted. He put a hand up to feel it, and it seemed as if the skin had grown thicker on one side of his throat, short-cropped hairs prickling his fingers as he touched it gently.

That was strange.

He felt further, to the back of his neck, then up across his skull to the top of his head, and around the sides.

Someone had shaved his head.

Not yesterday nor today, for the stubble was growing back already. How long had he been here? And where was here?

He had hardly registered, in his confusion, the sound of footsteps soft outside the door, but suddenly the door cover was whipped back and a tall figure stood against the light for a moment before stepping into the room. It flashed across Eliot's mind that he had no notion at all of what language the man might speak. For a moment the man hesitated as if he, too, had the same doubts. Then he approached Eliot's bed, and as he came away from the light Eliot could see him more clearly. He wore a long, hessian robe with a rope belt and wide sleeves, into which he tucked his hands as if nervous. His face was weather-worn and his sandy hair was tonsured. Oh, no, Eliot thought. Not a monastery, please.

'Pax tecum,' said the monk, with a slight, uncertain inclination of the head. Latin was a universal language, after all: he was hedging his bets. Eliot opened his mouth to speak, but found it was dry. He nodded his response. The monk, seeing his problem, knelt by the bed and reached somewhere behind Eliot's head, producing an earthenware cup and jug. He poured water from the jug and held the cup to Eliot's lips, helping him to sit up and reach it. Nothing had tasted so good for a long time, it seemed to Eliot. He drained it, and signalled for more, but the monk hesitated again.

'Ah, just a wee bit at a time, eh?' he tried, watching Eliot for his response. He met the monk's blue eyes in surprise. The words had been in Scots, Eliot's own mother tongue. Eliot was relieved, but at the same time puzzled. Was he in Scotland? What in Heaven's name would have made him go back there?

'Where am I?' he asked, his voice strange and uncontrolled, like a young lad.

'Oh, you are Scots!' said the monk. 'We have had a fine time speculating on your origins, my friend!' He gave a reassuring grin. 'You're on the Isle of May, do you know it? Off the coast of Fife.'

'Oh, aye, I have heard tell of it,' said Eliot, still with difficulty. 'So – I came here by boat, did I?'

'There is no other way,' laughed the monk, 'unless you swim like a fish, or fly like a bird! Your ship foundered on the rocks by the east of the island: you were flung ashore, and we found you the next day. It is rare for us to have visitors, I can tell you!' He gave Eliot a quizzical look, and poured him another half-cup of water. Eliot swallowed it gratefully.

'There are just the three of us here, you see,' the monk went on to explain eagerly. 'Brother Fillan is in charge, then there is Brother Peter, and I am Brother Mungo. You will meet the others later when it is time for our evening meal.'

But the thought of having to face three monks all at once was suddenly too much for Eliot. He felt an enormous weariness overtake him, and though his mind buzzed with questions, he could not find the strength to ask them. Darkness was closing about him again, and the last thing he remembered was Brother Mungo's friendly, calming voice.

'You're tired, now, you need your rest. Call out if you need anything, we are not far away.'

II

Anyone wanting a quiet moment alone with the magical lead coffin would have had their work cut out for them, as Rob remarked. He and Alison and Catriona laboured on it in pairs while Rob and Catriona also took it in turns to supervise the digging which continued at the top of the hill. Nevertheless there was never a moment when some of the students could not find an excuse to go to the ever-widening trench by the stream, or when cars were not manoeuvring in the narrow gateway, bringing other lecturers from the department, proprietorial officials from Elysian Fields pleased to leave their hot offices for a stroll in the sunshine, one or two local journalists sniffing out a story, and even, on occasions, the two C.I.D. officers who had been there at its discovery, even though their own pathologist had confirmed on the day that the bones were old enough to be out on their own.

Rob was always the one to greet the visitors and play the genial host and tour guide. Alison, too, was popular: a young and pretty face always sold over-intellectual stories well, and the girl's confidence was growing daily. Catriona, however, preferred to get on with the work at hand, scraping earth away from the ever more beautiful coffin. They had had to divert the stream, a hot and happy day's work for several wet students with shovels, and then, recording the grave cut as they destroyed it, they had widened the trench so that they could dig down by the sides of the coffin, leaving it standing at last on a shallow platform of damp soil in the middle of a clean-cut hole in the ground.

It still seemed to be in perfect condition. The sides were almost plain, with only a simple border pressed into the lead using some kind of twisted fibre or rope. The same pattern had been used on the lid, but there, as well as the border, there was a line of the string marks down the centre of the coffin, branching into a Y shape to meet the corners at the head and foot. Between the lines, a large, flat seashell had been used to make additional decoration in the soft, silver-grey metal.

'It's not as elaborate as the one at Spitalfields last year,' Rob conceded to Inspector McAlester, implying, too, that *his* lead coffin was rather more tasteful. 'It's more like the one they found at York about 1875. It might be a more northerly design, but the string and shell elements appear on all three.'

'And what happens now?' asked the inspector, crouching eagerly by the graveside.

'Mm. Well, we have a lorry and a crane ordered. We want to open it in controlled conditions, you see, so we'll make a kind of cradle to slide under it to lift it.' Rob was breathless with excitement half the time now: he kept smoothing his beard down with one hand, as though calming it would calm the rest of him.

'Isn't that a bit of a risk, sir?' asked the younger police officer diffidently.

'Oh, aye,' agreed Rob, eyes glittering. 'An awful risk. But it's our only reasonable choice. If we opened it here, where we can't really shelter it properly, we could lose everything in it. If there is anything, of course,' he reminded himself sternly, and smoothed down his beard again.

They burrowed with girders under the coffin, using padding to stop it from being scratched, inserting boards at all kinds of angles until it began to look like a long grey egg in an untidy nest. Rob hurried about with ropes and chains, calling authoritative directions to students only too eager to obey, and for another day they laboured in the hot sun, praying that now the weather would not break until they had their lovely treasure safe indoors. This time, summoned by the publicity department of Elysian Fields, the press came in force, and Adrian the professor turned up with his boot full of new hard hats with the university logo plastered across the back, and made Alison scurry round distributing them. The whole site by the stream seethed with feverish activity, the trenches on the hill abandoned, and as the security guard from the gate helped to guide the great flatbed lorry and crane backwards down the lane, Catriona quietly took away the soil dug to make room for the girders and wheeled it over to the basins for washing and sifting.

From here, she could watch but not be much noticed, head down and cricket hat pulled low over her forehead. The water gathered from the diverted stream was cold on her hot hands and the soil trickled between her fingers. She used touch as much as sight, feeling differences in weight and density, and even temperature, all telling her that this was old soil, not backfill: the coffin had been placed in a newly dug grave, never used before, virgin earth brought to the light of day only two thousand years ago and now.

She wondered who he was – or perhaps even she – this high-class Roman, buried with such glorious ceremony at a military outpost on the muddy hemline of the sweeping skirts of Empire. He was probably not a native Briton, but miles from home, a Dacian, maybe, or Iberian. What sights had he seen, travelling so far in his lifetime, and had he expected to end up here? Had he died in battle, or in an accident, or from some ravaging disease? In a few days, they might even be able to find that out – if there was anything there, of course.

Suddenly she caught something hard in her fingers, and was snatched back to her present task. She looked down, peering into the murky water. It was a coin, black and obscured.

A great shout went up from the crowd. With a dreadful churning of motors, the crane had just taken the weight of the coffin. It swayed a little, swinging in its cradle, but seemed to hold, almost invisible in ropes and wrappings. Catriona watched with the rest, mesmerised, unable even to glance at Rob.

The crane paused, allowing the cradle to still itself. Then, effortlessly, the great machine raised the coffin bundle in the air and began to turn it, gently, in the direction of the lorry. The crane driver had judged the height to perfection. The cradle glided about an inch over the surface of the lorry, found its central space, and sank comfortably into place. There was a tremendous cheer and applause, and Rob and the crane driver exchanged thumbs-up signs, grinning proudly. Catriona breathed again, and the crowd began to disperse, a few cameras still clicking.

Catriona looked down again at the coin in her hands. This would be a useful discovery. It had come from the top of virgin soil under the coffin, so it would give them a terminus post quem, a point in time before which the burial could not have taken place. Nothing so useful as a Roman coin, she thought happily, and gently rubbed at the soil on its surface.

Only it was not a Roman coin. Catriona stared at it in alarm. It was another Scottish farthing, post 1280.

What was it doing beneath a Roman lead coffin? And how on earth was she going to tell Rob?

III

She tried to tell Rob several times over the next few days, but the man was altogether too excited. Besides, she had been left in charge at the dig site, and he had gone with the coffin to a warehouse-like building in Granton, down by the sea, owned by the National Museums, and appeared to be living there, for all he was ever seen anywhere else. Catriona had the difficult job of trying to keep the students interested in what they all saw as a rather feeble warm-up act to the main performance, trying to finish with the trenches they had opened on the hill and find something interesting to say about the bland geophysics results on the area around it. But there was not the same feeling of teamwork that there had been even before Alison's unexpected discovery, and only the most dedicated students were putting in much effort.

In the evenings she went to the warehouse in Granton, usually with three or four students cadging a lift, to see what was happening. The first day had not been terribly interesting: they had spent it taking photographs, establishing the environment to the conservators' satisfaction, testing and examining the leadwork, and recording calculations of weight and size. The evening had been spent, to the students' delight, arguing over the contents and setting up lifting equipment and lighting for the opening, an event to be attended by many of Edinburgh's great and good on the other side of a glass screen. Rob and his cronies, the Romano-British experts from the National Museums, interrupting and talking over each other in their excitement, spoke ceaselessly and Catriona could not find any point in their conversation to bring up the subject of a small Scottish farthing, circa 1280, logged and deposited at the archaeology department on the other side of the town. But she had to tell him before the press and public descended next day: she had to prepare him for whatever might or might not be in that coffin, put there perhaps thirteen centuries after whatever Rob was expecting.

In the end, she caught him as they were all leaving the warehouse, locking up for the night.

'Rob,' she said, looking more solemn even than usual, 'come for a drink?'

'Oh, come with us, Catriona,' he responded, gesturing to the few museum staff nearby. 'We're going up to the Ceilidh House.'

'Rob, I need a word in private,' she insisted, pushing herself to go on. It would be too easy to give in and let him find out about the coin the hard way. He stared at her, his mouth still grinning, eyebrows high and questioning. His face seemed to say, 'Nothing you can say can bring me down now, nothing at all!'

'Come on, Robbie,' said one of the museum conservators, 'if I don't' have a few pints I'll never sleep tonight.'

'Coming?' he asked Catriona, putting out a hand to take hers.

She went wordlessly then, her brain singing in confusion, and found that she was to take two of the students she had brought, Rob, and a large curator up to the pub off High Street. There was nowhere to park near it, not and find your car hadn't been impounded when you came out again, so she dropped off the students and the curator and drove with Rob up to the department to park there and walk back, a matter of five or ten minutes on a fine night.

Catriona manoeuvred neatly into the tight little carpark and they left the car, walking back to South Bridge down the dark side street. Rob's hand reached protectively for hers again, and when she looked he was still smiling: he seemed to have done nothing else for days.

'I don't reckon I even need a drink,' he remarked, 'I'm still high – on lead fumes!' He laughed. 'You know, even if it's empty, even if it's empty I could almost be satisfied, couldn't you?' He squeezed her hand. 'She's a beauty of a coffin, isn't she? A real beauty!'

A passerby, hearing this, stopped and stared as they went by, and Rob and Catriona, catching each other's eye, laughed out loud, the noise echoing off the shuttered shop fronts.

'We must be out of our boxes to do this kind of work!' said Rob, recovering. 'Even Chief Inspector McAlester doesn't spend as much time with the dead as we do.'

'He's been spending a lot of time with them recently, though,' said Catriona thoughtfully. 'Perhaps we'll turn him into an archaeologist yet.'

They had reached the door of the pub. Warm smoky air and beer fumes rose from the depths but there was no one in sight: their friends had already been absorbed into the fug. The only people around were on one of the city's hotly competitive Ghost Tours, this one led by a diminutive and pale woman, and escorted by a tall cloaked figure with its hood pulled over its face. They paid no attention to stray customers heading late into the Ceilidh House. Rob turned to Catriona and ushered her in comically, down the stairs before him, still elegantly attired in shorts, teeshirt and today's quota of mud. At the crowded bar they looked around but the pub was large and full of unexpected corners, and they still could not see their fellow archaeologists. Rob ordered a couple of pints and some crisps, and then turned to Catriona.

'So, what was it you wanted to tell me?'

They were pushed closer by the crowd, their hands side by side on the bar, each breathing the same air. Catriona inhaled deeply.

As soon as she mentioned sifting the earth from beneath the coffin, Rob seemed to sense at last that something was wrong. When she had told him her story, he was silent for a moment in the noise of the bar, propping his forehead on his hands, thinking through the implications – or just coming to terms with the idea, the horrible fact that his precious Roman coffin had been tampered with.

'It's not thirteenth century,' he said at last, beginning by stating the obvious. 'We know it's Roman lead, and it's a Roman pattern. So what are we looking at? Worst case scenario here.'

'Someone looted it and reburied it around 1300,' said Catriona flatly.

'And threw the bones back in after it. Why didn't they take the lead itself?'

'Too heavy,' Catrion suggested.

'So at the worst, we have a perfect Roman lead coffin and a Roman skeleton – and an early Scottish farthing for luck!' He turned back to Catriona again, eyes glittering. 'I don't see how we can lose!' And completely reinvested, he snatched her into his arms with an ungraceful bump, and hugged her close until the barman's pointed throat-clearing told them their beers had arrived.

No one went to the dig the next day. All the students, along with Catriona and the selected guests and press gathered in the blue warehouse in an area of semi-darkness around the brightly-lit room-within-a-room where the coffin lay on a long white bench. It could have been made yesterday, Catriona thought, the soft silver grey box with its simple pristine pattern.

The conservators, along with Rob and a museum curator, were already inside, wearing overalls, masks and hoods. Like police officers at a crime scene, they were less concerned about contracting some long-dormant infection than about contaminating the contents of the coffin with hair or breath of their own. The curator checked the lifting equipment and then addressed the audience via a microphone, his voice crackling when his mask got in the way.

'We'll lift the lid of the coffin just clear of it and swing it down here,' he pointed to the other end of the narrow bench, just long enough for coffin and lid end to end. 'When you're ready, Gordon,' he nodded to one of the conservators. The conservator gave a final check to the clips attaching the hawsers to the coffin lid, and set the little crane in motion.

Excitement fizzed in the little glass room, and outside the audience were transfixed. Cameras nattered like enormous mice crunching cream crackers in the shadows. The curator, the conservators and Rob huddled around the end of the coffin that would be exposed first, allowing the audience only a partial view. Catriona strained to see, and jumped with the rest of the audience at a loud gasp over the microphone. Restraint abandoned, the guests surged forward and pressed against the glass.

The coffin lid, moving slowly and smoothly away from its resting place, showed first the scuffed, dark toes of a pair of leather boots, stuffed hard against the foot of the coffin. As they appeared, it could be seen that they covered slightly flexed ankles, then became wide and floppy around the calves. A conservator pointed – the corner of some coat or cloak was flicked over one boot, the fabric dense and dark with age. The lid moved on: Catriona could feel her heart whacking at her ribs. A pair of bony knees edged into view, bent slightly upwards, and thighs with some kind of rough surface then hidden from view by the edge of a short skirt – a tunic? Or a shirt? There was another sudden intake of breath from the horrified audience as a hand appeared, brown and leathery and almost like a glove, except for the blackened fingernails. There was a belt now over the tunic, and an elbow … there was the second hand, just like the first but making a loose fist near the man's chest, just by some damage to the tunic. The cloth was ripped and crumpled where the body had shrunk. Then they were at the shoulders, the loose collar of the coat, the wide neck of the tunic, the wrinkled, tanned, throat, and at last the head.

One or two of the guests hurriedly turned away, reaching their limit. Catriona continued to stare, mesmerised, knowing she would see this face again in her nightmares.

Aged a blotchy, sunburned brown like the rest of his flesh, the man's face was long and drawn. His jaw had dropped open and the skin had pulled back from yellow, vulpine teeth, gaping about the dark ghastliness of his mouth. His eyes were open, dry and brittle, but seemed to stare at her as she watched, staring from somewhere far away, from the other end of sanity.

The crane came to the end of its reach and stopped with a grunt. The conservator operating it came back to life and used the levers to lower the lid gently on to the bench. No one really noticed him.

After a long pause, the curator drew breath noisily, and cleared his throat.

'Well, ladies and gentlemen,' he began, his voice slightly squeaky, 'as you can see, excellent tissue preservation, as we sometimes get with lead coffins. Ahm …' He looked back down at the body, and then at Rob. Rob shrugged weakly.

'It doesn't look like a Roman to me,' he said, loudly enough for the microphone to pick it up.

'No, I'd quite agree,' said the curator, looking relieved behind his mask. 'What would you say, then?'

'I'd say a Roman coffin reused in about – oh, it's not my period, but say thirteenth to fourteenth century?'

'That looks about right,' the curator agreed hastily. 'Well, show's over, for today, ladies and gentlemen. We'll be keeping you posted about any further discoveries we make, okay? There's plenty to be working with here – those boots, eh?'

Rob waited until the audience had begun to move off, then caught Catriona's eye. Above his mask, one eye very deliberately winked.

IV

Beyond the looped-up door cover, Nicholas Eliot could see a steep, rocky green bank, and a rectangle of lead-grey sky. There was not much to it, but it was the first time that Brother Mungo had left the door cover up, and Eliot feasted on the sight as though it had been the gardens of Paradise.

He had lost count of the days since he had woken up. He did not remember ever feeling so weak before in his life, and he drifted in and out of sleep hardly noticing the difference between them. Sometimes he forgot what the monks had told him: sometimes he remembered things they said they had never told him. They said they understood: he had been ill, they said, terribly, terribly ill. They had been sure that he was going to die, and he ought to know the last rites off by heart, so many times had they read them over him. They laughed at this: dying held no fears for them, and they saw no reason why it should for him, either.

Today was a day of great significance. Not only was it the first day he had been able to see outside, but it was the first day he had felt strong enough, sitting up, to be able to feed himself, and Brother Mungo had been able to sit by the fire as they all had their midday meal together. It was mutton and cabbage broth, and it tasted old: the brothers believed in making all they could of the sparse supplies they had.

Brother Mungo had told him about their life on the island, about the few sheep that clung to the beaten grass, the struggle to grow a few vegetables in the lea of the hill in which their hut and chapel stood, the fish to be caught for Fridays and the gulls' eggs for feast days, and the chapel itself, built lovingly of stone, so tiny that the three brothers could warm it themselves with their breath, even during the bitter night offices. It was a way of life that repelled Eliot. He was no lover of luxury, he told himself, though a cup of good wine would not go amiss just now. But he did like his comforts. If you were born and brought up on a miserable island like this surely it was your bounden duty to your Creator to get off and better yourself. And if you weren't born here, then to choose to live here was a perversion, a base lack of gratitude for the gift of the pleasures the world afforded.

'Hallo, there!' It was the irrationally cheerful Brother Peter. They were all like this, Eliot had discovered. 'You all right with the door open? Not taking a chill?'

'I'm grand,' growled Eliot. Nothing deterred, Brother Peter advanced into the room to fetch a burned clay pot.

'What about that coat that's over you, then?' he went on. 'Is it too heavy for you? It weighs half a hundredweight!'

'It's not a problem.' Eliot gripped the edges of the coat defensively. He knew it was his. His memory of the few months before his arrival here, which was fragmentary at best, brightened a little when he looked at the coat. He saw in his mind little pictures, like ones he had once seen in a book, of himself selling a fur to an old woman, a bolt of cloth to a man in an apron, a piece of salt beef to a cleric, then stitching, stitching the coins he had received into this coat. He could feel the coins in the lining between his fingers: it must be true.

'More water?' asked the irrepressible Brother Peter, smiling at him, twisting the clay pot in his hand.

'No!' snapped Eliot. Brother Peter made a humorous shocked face, and left the hut. Eliot breathed a sigh of relief.

When would he be well enough to leave? Well, he supposed reasonably, some time after he was well enough to get up. And the sooner he tried to do that, the better.

He tried shifting on the bed, wriggling his legs round under the scratching blankets. They seemed reluctant to move much, and he thought he ought perhaps to use his arms more. But his arms had no strength. They felt stiff and awkward. He felt one of them through the sleeve of his shirt. My, it was thin! He must have wasted away here! He pulled up his sleeve for a closer look.

His cry brought Brother Peter and Brother Mungo pelting back, flinging themselves through the door. As their eyes adjusted to the light, they found their reluctant guest with one sleeve up, staring aghast at his own arm. On the pale skin, from halfway up the upper arm to halfway down the lower, was a large, greyish, swollen blotch.

'What,' gasped Eliot at last, 'what in the name of the Holy Virgin is this?'

Brother Mungo was the first to recover. Tutting at the blasphemy, he went over to the bed and crouched down to Eliot's level, taking the scarred arm and turning it a little towards the light.

'It's gone down quite a lot,' he remarked, then met Eliot's eye. 'We told you you had been ill. This was one of the signs. They were much more swollen before.'

'They? You mean I have more of these?' Eliot demanded. Brother Mungo rose, looking benevolent. Eliot wanted to punch him.

'Oh, yes,' said Brother Mungo. 'There are several on your legs, one on your back, and of course the one on your neck and face. Not all as large as that one, of course.'

'My neck and face ...' Eliot remembered how stiff his neck had felt when he had first woken up. He felt it gingerly, touching the edges of another blotch. 'What was wrong with me? Will they go away?' His voice was less certain now, and even in the dim light the monks could see the fear in his eyes.

'We don't know,' said Brother Peter. 'We don't know what it is, or whether or not they'll go. They've gone down, certainly.'

'We thought it was the plague,' admitted Brother Mungo. 'We thought you would infect us all. We had to signal to the people on the mainland not to come over last time, in case it spread.' His voice was solemn, and then he brightened. 'But here we are, and not a thing wrong with us!'

'So what *is* it?' Eliot asked again.

'We think you might have been poisoned,' Brother Peter said cheerfully. 'But a few weeks here of rest and clean water and wholesome food, and you are really much better. The fever was fierce, though! I tried to see if we really could cook eggs on you, but they kept rolling off, and Brother Anselm had to put a stop to it.' He sighed happily, and reassured that their patient was now as fully informed as they could make him, they returned to their labours outside.

Poisoned ... Could he have been poisoned? There was a time he would have thought the whole idea laughable, or at worst a mistake, but just recently ... The trouble was, he could not quite remember. He had a feeling of urgency, that was all: a tremendous hurry to get somewhere, or maybe to leave somewhere? It was usually to leave somewhere, he thought, often with very little notice indeed. But then, he couldn't possibly owe the monks money, could he?

He squirmed in the bed and lay back down, leaving the covers about his waist and his bared arm visible. It was all a mystery, he thought. Clearly the monks were in no hurry, but why was he?

V

'Oh, this is just incredible,' said Gavin in disgust. He folded his freckly arms on the top of the steering wheel and peered forward under the sun visor. Tom rubbed his stinging eyes with his fingers. Two more cases of SAIDS during the night: two more deaths by dawn. Against all the odds, the little girl in the Infirmary was holding on to life, if not consciousness. They were the nearest research station to this miracle, and it seemed almost as if the prize, the glory of finding the cure, was being handed to them on a petri dish. When Gavin had come to pick him up this morning, they had both been in high good humour, if exhausted as usual. Gavin had joked about the meandering police investigation into the break-in, and Tom had made some macabre but fairly witty (he thought) remarks about bugs that preferred incarceration, and they had been laughing as they swung round the corner into the little road that led to the Establishment. It was then that they saw the demonstrators.

'No Aids for SAIDS,' read one of the posters. 'Don't Spend Our Money on Criminals' said another. 'They Deserve It: Our Children Don't,' said a third, a little ambiguously. After all, Tom thought, even criminals must be somebody's children. There was a bit of chanting, too, though the whole thing had a rather unprofessional air. But there were forty or fifty of them, and they had the gateway to the Establishment completely barricaded.

'This is unbelievable,' repeated Gavin, and undid his seatbelt. He reached for the door handle.

'Ah, no, Gavin. I think we should just go away and call the police,' said Tom, not wishing to see Gavin beaten up this early in the morning. Gavin was not noted for his diplomacy.

'No way,' said Gavin, and opened the car door.

The demonstrators noticed them. To Tom's eyes, they all seemed to see the car simultaneously, like animals scenting them. Tom sensed Gavin, skinny and angry, touch the car door again as if for reassurance. The crowd moved, edging forward, its motion amoeba-like, edges wavering. And then, amidst them, like a cancer in a cell, Tom saw him: a tall figure, clad in a black robe, the hood pulled down over his face. In one hand he carried a noose. In the other, he held high a placard. It read: 'The Death Penalty has Returned.'

Tom shuddered violently. He fumbled for the door catch, though whether he was going to try to seize Gavin or to run away even he did not know. The crowd were edging towards them.

Then suddenly there was the sound of another car behind them. He jerked round. It was George Mackay in his BMW, a look of absolute astonishment on his face.

He looked so helpless that Tom was finally driven to action. He found himself opening his car door and stepping out into the slow motion tableau before him, feeling as if he were moving much faster than anyone else. He seized Gavin's arm with a surprising lack of difficulty and steered him, as if he, too, were mesmerised by the hooded figure, back the few feet he had come to the driver's door. Tom opened it and pushed Gavin inside, a little more violently than necessary. He nudged Gavin's feet with his own foot till they lifted into the car of their own accord, and slammed the door.

'What's going on, Tom?' George called over, still sounding shocked.

'Get back in your car, drive down the road a bit and call the police,' said Tom, sounding more decisive than he felt. 'We'll be right behind you. Won't we, Gav?' he added firmly, getting back into the car.

'Aye, I suppose,' said Gavin eventually, and started the engine. The two cars reversed around the corner and out of sight of the crowd.

Tom shook his head to clear it. He realised he felt a bit sick. For pity's sake, all they were trying to do was to cure a disease. Why couldn't people let them alone to get on with it?

VI

'It's just lovely,' remarked Adrian, the departmental head, with luscious emphasis. He wore a slick black suit that had never seen a dig site, and a white collarless shirt, not unlike his namesake the magpie cat, and he was reading a list of the items found in the Roman lead coffin, and licking his lips. Some of the objects lay in open boxes on the table in front of him, set into specially cut foam and nestling in waves of bubblewrap and polythene bags. 'The wee dirk's just gorgeous.'

'Apparently it's German,' Catriona said helpfully. She had brought the boxes from the museum warehouse for writing up. 'And the curator thought the belt and boots were Italian.'

'My, quite the cosmopolitan dresser!' said Adrian. 'Have they found any designer labels yet? He maybe shopped in Glasgow.'

Catriona nodded slowly.

'I'll tell them to look out for them. The coat and the satchel are the most interesting, though, I think. The conservators say the coat has salt deposits all over it, and the satchel has, too. In fact, in general it looks as if the man fell into the sea.'

'And didn't change his clothes before going to Roslin? What was he, a knight in a hurry on his quest for the Holy Grail?'

Catriona smiled this time. Adrian had not been the only person to suggest that a dig at Roslin might produce the Holy Grail: quite a number of people seemed to think it was still there.

'Maybe. He wasn't dressed in a very knightly fashion, though: the dirk was the only weapon, and altogether his clothing is typical of, say, a trader of the period, perhaps operating here with overseas contacts, or perhaps travelling abroad himself – which might explain the sea water.'

'Maybe he drowned!' suggested Adrian suddenly, wide-eyed.

'I hope we'll find out, soon,' Catriona replied. 'Rob is at the post mortem just now.'

Dr. Eastleigh wrinkled her nose as she drew the protective sheet off the corpse's face. Rob gave a short laugh.

'Aye, a nasty look he's got there!'

'Horrible,' agreed Dr. Eastleigh. She had come from the Infirmary to do the post mortem in situ, so that conservators could attend to the removal of the clothing at the same time.

'We're calling him Alf, if it's any help,' Rob went on. 'Don't know why, it was the students' idea.'

'They're all heart,' agreed Dr. Eastleigh, and clicked her Dictaphone. 'Subject is … approximately a hundred and sixty centimetres tall in death, still clothed. On first inspection, lower limbs are slightly flexed and appear sound, upper limbs left flexed and right straight, appear sound. Visible flesh somewhat desiccated and much discoloured.'

The procedure was a lengthy one. Alf's boots and coat had been removed already, but the woollen hose covering his legs had required a certain amount of soaking and the conservators could only now begin to peel it back from the emaciated legs. The photographer and the medical artist worked away around them, and Rob, not entirely a stranger to these procedures, watched with interest, propped against a trolley.

'The legs are flexed, we think, because he was a bit too long for the coffin,' he said, as Dr. Eastleigh examined the knees and ankles.

'There doesn't seem to be any long-term trauma,' she agreed. 'The muscles were a bit thin, but he might not have had a very active life.'

The conservators, with careful cuts, were removing the tunic now. It seemed once to have been unbleached, but now was dark with various stains. The angle of the arms, now rigidly fixed into their odd positions, made the job awkward, but at last with the conservator's infinite patience they eased it free, only to find a shirt underneath.

'A fine one, too, by the look of it,' Rob said, coming closer for a moment. Joanne Eastleigh grinned.

'I wouldn't fancy it, myself.' She bent down suddenly. 'Look,' she said, 'the shirt is damaged in the same place that the tunic was. Now, that's a suspicious-looking rip, if ever I saw one.'

Rob's eyes lit up.

'A knife cut?'

'Maybe, maybe. We'll see when the shirt comes off.' Dr. Eastleigh backed off again to let the conservators do their work.

'Funny, we found a knife in the coffin, but it fitted his own scabbard.'

'But it was lying loose?'

'Aye, down by his knees.' Rob pondered a moment. 'Tossed in after, maybe?'

Dr. Eastleigh frowned, prodding the wound with careful, gloved fingers.

'Well, they do say down in Leith that the best way to get yourself stabbed is to carry a knife yourself.'

VII

Tom Buchan was beginning to think of uses for knives, too. He had a hit list at the moment: the people who had broken into his laboratory were at the top of it, but just now his boss George Mackay was running a very close second.

'But my dear Tom, we can't replace the equipment with just any old rubbish!' George was saying patiently. They, along with Gavin and Willie, the lab assistant with the permanently morose expression, were waiting in the canteen for the arrival of Chief Inspector McAlester to tell them the latest news on the break-in and the protests. They had all had too much coffee.

The past few days since the demonstration had been unexpectedly, almost magically, successful. The demonstrators had mysteriously vanished. And then, almost by accident, working in a somewhat makeshift space within their old laboratory, they had finally had some kind of breakthrough. They identified a minute cell in blood taken from the grey swellings on the bodies of the SAIDS victims which was not normally present, a curious cell shaped a little like a Greek letter zeta, which seemed to attach itself to normal cells like, as George Mackay put it, a monkey on a tiger's back. They double-checked their findings, and George Mackay ordered champagne which they all drank on the lawn, the bubbles going straight to their heads in the warm sunlight, on ill-nourished stomachs. Excited, they asked for samples from the swellings on the little girl. She was miraculously still alive five days after infection, and scientific centres all round the country were clamouring for her blood: fortunately, the Establishment had a good relationship with the Infirmary, as well as having an immediate need to examine the samples.

But before they could arrive, disaster struck yet again. It was Gavin who was working at the electron microscope when, as he said later, the wheels fell off. The power slowly died out of it in a long, unhappy sigh, and no magic the maintenance men could work could resuscitate it. And what they were going to do in the meantime was what was agitating them now, slumped around the table in the cool canteen.

'I still say we should go for whoever can get us the machine fastest,' said Gavin sulkily. He was acting as though he expected to be blamed for the death of the microscope, though no one had said anything to him.

'The best ones are German,' said George. 'And we should not skimp on important equipment like that. Anyway, no one will be as fast as we need them to be.'

'Couldn't we borrow one for the time being?' asked the lab assistant, chewing his moustache dismally.

'And what would they say to us? Oh, aye, lads, chuck it in the back of the van and bring it back Thursday? They're bloody enormous!' snapped Gavin, going red. 'It's not as if I smashed a magnifying glass, is it?'

Tom, however, had been thinking. You could not, practically, borrow an electron microscope for a few days, but you could, if you knew the right people, borrow time on one. And Tom was fairly sure that between them, they knew the right people.

'Look,' he said, 'we're stuck here. Why don't I go up to the University this afternoon and see if one or two places would give us a go on theirs? And you could ring around, too, see if somewhere else would give us a hand. They're hardly going to refuse, are they?'

'Hmm,' said George, for once unsure of himself. 'Nevertheless, it is a good idea, Tom. Why don't you go ahead and see what you can do? You may find willing co-operation on all sides. And when we seem so near to making a breakthrough, it would be terrible to have to stop now, just because this place seems so jinxed.'

'The whole bloody project is jinxed,' muttered Gavin, but Tom was already making a mental list of possible places to beg a little time on an electron microscope.

'Chief Inspector McAlester and Constable Williams, Dr. Mackay,' announced the receptionist, and showed the police officers into the canteen. George Mackay rose and greeted the officers like favoured guests, one of his better tricks.

'Tom, fetch the officers some coffee, would you?'

Tom blinked at his boss, but began to rise.

'No, no,' said the Chief Inspector, flapping his hands. 'Although a glass of cold water would be lovely.' The constable nodded agreement. The weather outside was still oppressively hot, and the officers were clearly basking in the cool airiness of the canteen.

Tom fetched two glasses of cold water. By the time he had returned McAlester and Mackay were already deep in discussion.

'There is no evidence that any of your immediate competitors was behind any of this,' McAlester was saying with unexpected authority. 'We are, however, still looking into the possibilities of protestors trying to sabotage any chance of finding a cure for SAIDS.'

'But that seems ridiculous,' said George Mackay. Gavin met Tom's eye.

'I'll believe it,' he remarked darkly.

'And anyway,' added McAlester, 'all your competitors have had similar problems.'

That was news. The Establishment staff stared at the police officers.

'Oh, yes,' McAlester said, 'it's quite true. Though of course they are all keeping it fairly quiet.'

There was silence for a moment, while they contemplated this information. Tom was aware of the vending machines humming. A gradual feeling of diminishing isolation came over him.

'Ah,' said George Mackay at last. 'That does put a different complexion on it, doesn't it.'

'Campaigners. I knew it was,' added Gavin.

'So, we'll have to have the security tightened again, I suppose,' said Willie the lab assistant, mournfully, looking around him for confirmation. Tom nodded at once. His whole instinct was to protect the work he was trying to do. He glimpsed it for a moment in his mind, foetus-like, held desperately in his protective hands, and then he saw in his imagination the tall, hooded figure with the noose, and knew he had to guard his work with his life, if necessary. He rubbed his forehead: he was definitely not getting enough food and sleep. He did not notice the anxious expression on McAlester's face until the police officer coughed gently.

'There is one small problem,' he said. 'You pointed out, Dr. Mackay, that the fire door through which the intruders made their entry has an alarm connected to it. Well, it had, but when the door was opened it hadn't.'

'The wires cut, I suppose,' said Gavin, blackly satisfied now that he had been proved right. George Mackay nodded.

'Ah, no,' said McAlester, almost embarrassed. 'No. You see, that in itself would have triggered something – it is a very good system, I believe. No, the particular part of the system covering the fire door was switched off. From the inside.'

VIII

Dr. Eastleigh finished washing her hands as the artist and photographer and conservators dispersed, and the mortuary assistant gathered up instruments and samples. The body of Alf, the man from the coffin, lay for the moment face down on the metal bench. It was a relief not to see his staring eyes, thought Rob, with a shiver.

'So all the rest is lab work, then,' he remarked.

'Pretty much,' agreed the pathologist. 'But it looks as if the stab wound killed him. No other apparent injuries, no rope marks on the neck or holes in the head.' She smiled brightly, drying her hands.

'A Middle Ages murder victim, then,' reflected Rob.

'Have you thought what you're going to do with him yet?' Dr. Eastleigh asked.

'Well, we'll want a sliver of tooth for the forensic dentistry unit down south, and –'

'No, I mean, when you've finished with him. Is he going on display or being reburied?'

Rob made a face.

'Hadn't thought that far ahead,' he admitted, staring at the corpse. The mortuary assistant had switched off some of the more direct lights, and now he pulled gloves on to turn the body again before putting it away. Dr. Eastleigh went to help, pulling out a fresh pair of latex gloves for herself. Rob watched, but suddenly yelled.

'Hold on! What's that?'

Frozen in mid-lift, Dr. Eastleigh stared down at the corpse. There appeared to be nothing remarkable about it.

'There,' said Rob, coming closer. 'It's the different lighting – I didn't notice it before.'

He pointed. The skin on the back of the neck, in one irregular patch, looked different from the skin around it, and seemed to be raised a little from it. They all peered more closely. It was possible, even, to believe that this raised skin was just a bit darker than the rest.

'Some kind of post mortem effect?' asked Rob.

'Let me see the rest of him again.' The two men stood back quickly at the tone of her voice and she scanned the rest of the corpse, now free of much of the clothing he had been found in. Where it had been, the flesh was not quite so leathery.

'Look,' she said, 'there on the left arm. And on the legs, and maybe … hard to tell … one on the back.'

Rob stared, first at the corpse, then at her. Her eyes had grown hard, calculating. Then she said abruptly,

'Give me the lab samples. Rob, come with me.'

IX

Shona Larssen was in every possible kind of pain. The tests the doctors had talked about when they had brought Vicky in, they had included a lot of blood sampling and her arms felt as if she had been lying on a bed of nails. Then she had had to watch them doing the same thing to Vicky. Granted, this probably hurt her more than Vicky: the wee girl was still out of it, not even reacting to Shona's voice, however hard Shona pretended to herself. And now there was the pain of shame as well. The nice nurse had come and sat on the other side of Vicky's bed, holding a clipboard, and asked Shona a whole great list of questions about Vicky, about Shona, about their lives and their family and friends, and at last, not meeting the kind gaze from above the mask, Shona told him everything. She told him about the police, about the trial, and about the charges, as far as she understood them. She told him about the day of the verdict, and how her body seemed turned to her mothers' suet pudding when the jury said 'Guilty'. And she told him about Sinclair House, the smart private prison, the weekly visits and the long bus journey and how well Vicky behaved each time, and how Andy could sometimes give her biscuits from the kitchens, and now he knew all about it. And then, after a few questions about what Vicky did on these visits that could possibly have brought her into contact with the disease, he asked a strange thing.

'And does your husband love Vicky?'

It'll be about kissing her hello and goodbye, she thought, saliva and all.

'Yes, he does, of course he does,' she said.

'Then,' said the nurse, with infinite kindness, 'what about letting him know she's in here?'

X

In a laboratory in the midst of the small village that formed the Infirmary, not far away, if he but knew it, from where Vicky Larssen was still fighting for her life, Tom and Gavin had inveigled themselves some time on an electron microscope. It was not quite as flash as the one

George Mackay thought appropriate for his Establishment laboratory, but it did its job, which was all they required, and even now they were setting up and sorting their slides and consulting with the lab technicians about the best way of getting what they wanted. Tom had also asked, informally, for a sample of the child victim's blood: he knew Gavin would sulk if he wasn't in on the first examination of it, but Tom was the one with the connexions here and Gavin was still brooding over the disasters at their own lab, and his mind was not entirely on the job.

Inspector McAlester's statement about the break-in being an inside job Tom had pushed to the back of his mind. It was not something that could be considered. There were three research teams at the Establishment, working on different things: there was a receptionist, a few canteen staff, three or four security men working some intricate pattern of hours, George's well-polished P.A. Annette, and of course George himself. That amounted to about twenty to twenty-five people, and he knew them all: far too small a number to start speculating, or working life would become impossible.

The thoughts he had been trying not to think were scattered by the sound of a voice in the corridor. It was the kind of voice that instantly put his hackles up – loud, authoritative, and with a kind of flagrantly regional accent that sounded almost assumed. From Gavin's expression, Tom could tell he was feeling the same way.

'We picked you up, Catriona, because I *have* no idea what's going on. Joanne Eastleigh won't tell me until she's sure. *I* don't know what she thinks she's found.'

There was a pause: whoever was with the man was evidently more quietly spoken. He assumed they would go past the lab in which he and Gavin were working, but in a moment the door creaked further open, and in they walked.

The man was as tall as Tom and wiry, with a scruffy beard and the kind of smug look on his face that had Tom's fist curling. He was about to turn back to his slides, but then he heard Gavin mutter basely,

'Oh, my, very nice.'

Tom regarded him.

'I don't go for beards, myself.'

'Not the man, you prat. Look!'

Tom looked, and the man's quieter companion appeared from behind him. She was blonde, not Tom's preferred colouring, though she had good legs. She shared with the man the same outdoor, roughened look, making Tom feel very indoor and grey, and he noticed she had what looked like soil under her fingernails. A gardener, perhaps? But what was she doing in a medical research laboratory? She had not noticed him and turned back to the door as if looking for someone else, and he saw that her blonde hair was wound in a thick plait almost to her waist. He nearly laughed: from the back she could have been a leggy schoolgirl, if schoolgirls still wore plaits.

He realised he was staring, and looked back at Gavin to find a lasciviously dreamy look on his colleague's face.

'A word of advice, Gav – it's cooler to keep your mouth closed. And you're a married man, remember?'

At that, Gavin grunted and returned to his slides, but Tom could not resist another quick look at the couple. The pair seemed a little lost, and he was about to go over and ask them, in that brisk voice which the British use for suspected intruders, 'Can I help you?' when Joanne Eastleigh came in and appeared to gather them under her wing. Tom knew her slightly: she was a pathologist, and he wondered what she had to do with these strangers. Beside them, Joanne looked even neater than usual, clipped and clean. She nodded at Tom with a small, hassled smile, and he turned back to his work, feeling dismissed.

The work was mechanical, if fiddly, and required little in the way of brain power. He found himself almost unconsciously eavesdropping on the conversation between the bearded man, who had a loud voice anyway, and Joanne Eastleigh. The blonde woman did not say much, though he strained to hear her voice, scowling at anything Gavin said. Joanne was talking through, in a sketchy manner, what she was doing with some samples she was setting up on slides for the other electron microscope in the lab: Tom thought she probably wasn't making much allowance for the non-scientific background of her companions, but she seemed to be in a tearing hurry.

The lab technician helping Tom and Gavin finished his side of the operation at the same moment that they did, and Tom abandoned his inconclusive eavesdropping to peer down at his samples and concentrate on them. For a little while, he shut out everything except the view down at the slides, the strange, Miro-like arrangements of light and dark and, again, almost imperceptible, the curly little cells of the SAIDS infection attaching itself to the white blood cells of one of the earlier victims. The infection seemed to send its cells to strangle the victim's precious white blood cells, trapping them in its tendrilly embrace, stopping them from fighting any infection. It explained a good deal about how the disease presented itself, the immuno-deficiency aspect of it, but there was still so much to learn …

He left the double eye piece for a moment, suddenly realising he had been breathing very deeply. He felt a bit dizzy as he reached to adjust the other slide he had had prepared, the one with the sample of blood from the little girl who was still alive.

'Dr. Buchan! Tom!'

He looked around, bleary-eyed and refocussing. Gavin glanced up, miles away. Joanne Eastleigh, a curious frown on her face, was calling to him from a similar position at the other electron microscope. Beside her, the man with the beard was looking puzzled and a bit sulky. The girl's face was quite calm, as she looked at Tom for the first time. She had startling blue eyes, he noticed, with dark lashes and a dark ring around the iris. He made a conscious effort to shift his gaze back to Joanne Eastleigh. 'Come and see this!'

'Now, wait a minute,' said the bearded man, putting out a hand as though to cover the microscope viewer.

'Look, Rob,' said Dr. Eastleigh quickly, 'I'm not sure. I'm not the expert. Tom here is, by chance: he should be able to tell us straight off.'

'And Tom is the expert in what, exactly?' asked the blonde woman crisply, still looking at him. A smile would have softened the question: she did not smile.

'I'm not quite sure which particular field of expertise Dr. Eastleigh is referring to,' he responded, trying to sound superior and coming out pompous. 'I am an epidemiologist, if that's any help.'

'I have no idea,' said the man called Rob, rather curtly. 'Do we need an epidemiologist, Joanne?'

'Yes,' said the pathologist firmly, 'we do. Tom, will you come and have a look at this?'

'If your friends are quite sure they want me to,' Tom said huffily. He truly did have better things to do – the blood sample from the little girl was just waiting for him to look down the viewer, and he was itching to turn and do it. But if Joanne really thought it would be something in his field - something this unlikely and frankly rude couple had brought in – well, he had waited for days to see the blood sample, and it wasn't going anywhere just now. And Gavin would relish seeing it first.

Rob the bearded man looked as if he was going to protest, but just as Tom thought it was a lost cause the woman said,

'Look, Rob, if Dr. Eastleigh has found something she feels she needs more specialist help with –'

Tom moved forward, taking his chance, and as Joanne Eastleigh edged away he put his eyes to the viewer and looked at the sample the strange couple had brought in.

For a moment he was confused. What was he looking at? Was there some possibility that he was viewing his own blood samples, the SAIDS ones, through this viewer?

There were the curly little cells, with their tiny strangling tendrils.

There were the white blood cells, throttled and useless. But there was something different here.

The damaged blood cells were not the only ones: there were healthy ones, too – or at least, not damaged by the SAIDS cells. And some of the SAIDS cells were – well, it was hard to say, since they were a strange shape anyway – but they looked deformed. Some of the curls had tightened about themselves, while others flopped useless and flat. It was what he had hoped to see, roughly, in the blood of the little girl, the leucocytes fighting back against the infection, but there was something wrong here. All these cells were dead.

Tom looked up from the eyepiece and met Dr. Eastleigh's eye.

'I've done the post mortems on the Scottish victims,' she said, evenly. 'I think I know the signs. Is there anything there that confirms it?'

'Where did this come from?' asked Tom. 'Is this one of last night's victims?'

'Last night?' said Rob, with disdain. 'Listen, lad: I don't know what he's a victim of, but this man didn't die last night. He died near on seven hundred years ago.'

'Seven hundred years ...' Tom sighed, not for the first time.

They were in Joanne Eastleigh's car again, heading for Granton. Gavin had gone to report to Uncle George on this shocking development. Rob had taken the front passenger seat as of right, and Tom and the blonde woman, now identified as Dr. Catriona Lindsay, were jammed in the back, a situation Tom might have appreciated if he had not been so stunned by what these people had just told him.

'But SAIDS is a new disease,' Tom had insisted. 'Like AIDS and Legionnaire's disease and ... and all those things they think come from monkeys ...'

Rob made a tutting noise from the front seat.

'I love the way scientists are so open-minded,' he remarked. Joanne gave a small impatient shrug.

'We don't know what caused it this year,' she pointed out reasonably. 'Whatever it was, couldn't the same circumstances have happened seven hundred years ago, too?'

'But why did it stop? What wiped it out?' asked Tom. His brain was still working far too hard for him to keep up with it.

'All the victims have died really quickly, haven't they?' said Catriona, speaking for the first time for a while. 'Maybe it just happened too quickly to last long. Isn't that why they say ebola isn't widespread? People fall ill too quickly and don't have time to wander about and spread it.'

'Good point, Catriona,' agreed Joanne Eastleigh.

'Ebola incubates in hours: we don't know how long SAIDS takes,' said Tom darkly.

'Anyway, it looks as if the knife wound didn't kill him,' added Dr. Eastleigh.

'Hey, what about this?' Rob bounced excitedly in his seat, and Dr. Eastleigh looked round in alarm, swerving. Rob laughed. 'Listen: the man has this weird disease, dark blotches, fever, whatever. What if someone knifed him to stop him spreading it?'

'He was too far gone, to judge by the blotches,' said Joanne authoritatively. 'I've done the P.M.s on the Scottish victims, I told you. They were all about as blotchy.'

'Do you think anyone would have gone close enough to a plague victim to stab him?' said Catriona. 'I mean, presumably this is a plague, one of the ones around about that time.'

'Don't know,' muttered Tom. 'What's an epidemic? How's it spread? Anyway, when was this dug up?'

'Over the course of the last week.' So that ruled out the possibility that this body was ground zero for the current epidemic. 'And how many infected bodies have been found?'

'Just this one,' said Catriona.

'Anywhere?' asked Tom, somewhat incredulous.

'That's right.' Rob was defensive, as if Tom were accusing him of missing something.

'How can we conclude anything from just the one corpse? I mean, how do you even know it's as old as you think it is?'

'It just is, all right?' said Rob, stubbornly. 'And it's pretty rare to find a well-preserved body from seven hundred years ago, so you just make the most of it, all right?'

'Bloody hell,' said Tom, falling back in his seat. 'What are the chances?'

There was a pause. Then Catriona asked,

'The chances of what?'

Tom looked at her, but only saw curiosity in her face.

'When you said earlier,' he began, 'that everyone dies quickly ... it's not entirely true. There's a little girl in the Infirmary at the moment – '

'I heard on the news,' said Catriona quickly. 'She's still alive?'

'So far,' said Tom, nodding enthusiastically. 'What I looked at after you asked me to come to see the body with you –'

Rob snorted: Tom's insistence on finishing what he had gone to the

Infirmary to do had not been seen as co-operative. Tom glared at the back of his head.

'What I was looking at,' Tom went on, 'was a sample of her blood. The thing is ... the thing is, there were unexpected similarities between her blood and your old boy's.'

'What kind of similarities?' asked Joanne Eastleigh sharply.

'I can't say. I mean, the Establishment wouldn't allow me to be specific. But from what I saw – you see, I think your man had SAIDS – but I think he recovered.'

'You don't see many corpses in your line of work, do you?' Joanne Eastleigh asked Tom, dropping back slightly as the other two led the way from the car park into the Granton warehouse. It was a huge, curving, blue plastic structure, looking like nothing to do with a museum.

'No,' said Tom, trying to sound relaxed. 'I've seen the bog bodies in the British Museum, mind you.'

'Mm. Close,' said Dr. Eastleigh, 'but perhaps not close enough.'

After this ominous remark, they followed the other two down a well-lit corridor and to a curious laboratory, curious more in the nature of what was being studied rather than the manner of studying, which was much as in Tom's own lab – before the break-in, anyway. Around the room in various forms of storage materials, were, amongst other things, paintings, a couple of swords, a caseful of stuffed squirrels and several elderly-looking documents. Rob and Catriona cast casual glances at these things, which were fascinating to Tom, and carried on to a heavy door which Tom recognised as the entrance to a refrigerated store. Rob called over one of the white-coated conservators, and said,

'Can we take another look at Alf, then?'

'Oh, aye,' said the conservator flatly, stopping short. He put his hands into the pockets of his lab coat.

'Well?' said Rob.

'Oh, very funny,' remarked the conservator. 'Like he's still there.'

Tom was confused. What had gone wrong? To see Rob's face, he could tell it was something potentially very bad indeed.

'Then where is he?' asked Rob slowly.

'Well,' said the conservator, 'I assume he's where you left him. And since I suppose you didn't want to be trailing around Edinburgh with a corpse, I suppose you left him at the Infirmary.'

To his astonishment, Tom saw that Rob was shaking.

'What –' he began, but Catriona had to finish it for him.

'What do you mean, at the Infirmary?'

The conservator's hands were bunching in his pockets. He was beginning to realise that this was no joke.

'The van came – came down from the Infirmary. We knew you'd gone up there with Dr. Eastleigh to look at some samples, so we assumed you realised you needed to look more closely at Alf, something or other you could do up there you couldn't do here, so we handed him over. It was your name on it.'

'Oh, my God,' whispered Rob, staring at him. Catriona had gone white.

'What did they look like?' asked Joanne suddenly. The conservator shrugged, all embarrassment.

'Well, they were wearing overalls with 'Edinburgh Royal Infirmary' on them. Blue, they were.'

'And did they show any I.D.?'

'Oh, aye. And they signed for the body.' He led them over to a logbook, where the last entry read 'Male adult body, ref. L2000.751, property of University of Edinburgh Archaeology Department, c.1300.' A departure time was given, and two signatures followed, that of the conservator and one which could have said almost anything.

'Maybe it really is up at the Infirmary,' said Rob, and Tom almost pitied him. 'Maybe it's all just some misunderstanding …'

'I'll call and find out,' said Joanne, efficient as ever. She slid her mobile out of her handbag and dialled the number, turning away to talk. It was hard to know whether or not to listen.

Rob asked the conservator to open the refrigerated store, anyway, and when the man gave him a quizzical look he said,

'I just have to see for myself, right?' in a voice on the edge of anger. Catriona moved a little closer to him, and put out her hand to touch his arm. Rob turned away, probably unaware of her approach. Tom watched as she hesitated, then dropped her hand back down to her side.

The conservator brought out the keys and unlocked the padlock on the store, hauling back the heavy bars. Inside were a number of boxes and crates on metal shelving, and on a table, bizarrely, a bearskin helmet, but nothing Tom could see over Rob's slumping shoulders was big enough to hold an adult body. Rob still walked inside, shifting some of the crates as if expecting to find his precious corpse hidden behind something a little bigger than a shoebox. Tom wondered whether or not he should just leave and get back to his own work, but it seemed heartless to abandon them all at a moment like this.

Joanne clicked her phone off with emphasis and turned back to Rob.

'No one knows anything about it,' she said at once, a sharp frown on her face. 'There was no request to come down here and pick up anything, and nothing has come in with any museum label on it.'

'Maybe it went somewhere else by mistake ...' muttered Rob. Joanne stared at him, disbelieving.

'A van that picks up the wrong thing and then takes it to the wrong place? Anyway, if they were from the Infirmary and wore Infirmary overalls, it would be hard for them to take it somewhere else by accident.' She looked at Rob, who did not seem to be taking it in. 'I mean,' she added, 'it's not as if they'd take it to Jenners, is it?'

Tom opened his mouth to make his excuses and leave, but Rob spoke first.

'I'm going up to the Infirmary to find it,' he said, somewhat defiantly.

'I've just told you, it's not there.'

'It can't not be there. It isn't here, is it? It's got to be somewhere! And as you said, the mostly likely place is the Infirmary.'

'I wonder ...' said Catriona diffidently.

'Oh, what now?' Rob turned on her, and she jumped. Tom experienced a sudden urge to give Rob a clip round the ear.

'I just wonder if maybe some of the students nicked him. You know – for a joke.'

'A joke?' echoed Rob.

'Well, there's that mummified body in one of the London colleges – maybe they thought it would have been good to have one of their own.'

'Of their own!' Rob repeated again. 'I'll kill the little bastards if I ever find that's true.'

'She could be right, though, Rob,' said Joanne. 'Sit back for a couple of days and don't make a fuss, and you'll probably find Alf on your desk in the Department, or something equally stupid. Probably with a traffic cone on his head.'

'Oh, for crying out loud,' snapped Rob. 'Is nobody taking this seriously but me?'

'We're all taking it very seriously,' said Catriona soothingly. She did look very upset. 'But why would someone have properly stolen him? Why don't we go back to the Department and take a look?'

'Good idea,' said Joanne Eastleigh briskly. 'And I'll take Tom back to the Infirmary – and we'll ask around again there.'

'Thanks,' said Catriona, after waiting for Rob to say something. 'Come on, Rob – I think I'd better drive.' She pushed him gently back towards the entrance. By the time Joanne and Tom had returned to the car park, Catriona was already reversing Rob's car out of the parking space.

'He's not usually that bad,' said Joanne, apologetically. 'This find means a great deal to him. I mean, he's usually a bit full of himself, but not actually rude.'

'Hmm.' Tom did not feel he knew Dr. Eastleigh well enough to go into his first impression of Rob Dean in any detail with her. 'Catriona seemed shocked.'

'Oh, she's always quiet. Don't know much about her.'

They did not say much on the return journey to the Infirmary. Tom had left his slides in the care of the lab technician, and part of him began to think about what he was going to do with them next. The other part of him was still dwelling, more than he would have expected, on the last curious hour. The look on Rob's face when the penny had dropped had been how his own felt when he and Gavin had discovered the break-in at the laboratory: if the man had been even slightly pleasanter he would have had all of Tom's sympathy. But it probably was students, anyway: Catriona was almost certainly right. After all, who else would nick a mouldy old corpse?

Back at the Infirmary, he found himself unable to desert Dr. Eastleigh as she made a few more enquiries about the possible appearance of an extra, unsolicited body. Everyone she questioned looked entirely innocent. He discovered that it would have been easy enough to lift a couple of overalls from the laundry, and that the Infirmary had so many that they were unlikely to be missed. The Infirmary was not far from the university buildings that included the Archaeology Department, and was slap in middle of the part of town in which most of the students lived in flats. Catriona's theory seemed more and more likely.

At last, he trailed Dr. Eastleigh back upstairs to her office, not far from the labs with the electron microscopes. Dr. Eastleigh waved him to a seat.

'Might as well see this through,' she said, with a thin smile. She picked up the phone and dialled a number, which seemed to be the university's central switchboard.

'Rob Dean, please, in Archaeology.' She waited. 'Oh, hallo – oh, Catriona! Any luck at your end? ... What?'

For once, Catriona seemed to be quite articulate. Tom waited, straining to hear any of the conversation. Joanne sat with her mouth open, her eyes wide.

'Well, yes,' she said at last, clearing her throat. 'I suppose you can't yet ... well, fair enough. No, no, we'll meet you there. I'm sure he would. Wait a tick, he's just here.' She put a hand over the receiver, and took a breath before she looked at Tom.

'She wants us to go to the department. Apparently ... apparently Rob has disappeared.'

3 – FLIGHT

I

The day he first went outside, the wind was like a slap on the face with a wet cloth. It took his breath and thrust it back down his throat, making him stagger back with his mouth open. Brother Mungo and Brother Peter held him at each side, faces anxiously close to his, seeing if he could cope. He deliberately kept all his struggle out of his expression.

'It's such a lovely day,' Brother Peter said encouragingly, but all Eliot could do was give a harsh laugh. What Brother Peter seemed to mean was that it was not actually raining, though the air was damp. They had walked him gently across the little hollow where the chapel and hut huddled, and now they spread one of his blankets on a rock, weighed it down with stones, and settling him on to it, wrapping his extraordinarily heavy coat about him. Then they left him to recover his breath while they set to work in the little garden. Brother Fillan emerged from the tiny stone chapel with cleaning cloths in his hands and waved them cheerfully at Eliot, clearly pleased to see him up and about. Then the wind snatched the silly man's hood and upended it over his tonsured head, and his brother monks paused in their tilling to laugh heartily. It made Eliot sick.

He turned away from them, pulling his coat tight over his shoulders, fingering the hard metal circles in its hems. They seemed unreal. When he unpicked it all finally and pulled them out, would they be coins at all?

From where he sat, the sea seemed very close. They were some height above it, but the May Isle was so tiny that it seemed just a fleck on the grey ocean. The brothers had told him they were only a few miles from the Fife coast, but here he could see nothing of that. He reckoned he was facing roughly south west, maybe towards the firth of the Forth. He wondered where he had been washed up: this side seemed unlikely.

He tried, for no particular reason, to see the scene about him the way Brother Mungo had described it to him yesterday evening, when they had first discussed the possibility of his expedition today. Brother Mungo had talked of the cliffs, noisy with seabirds, the individual stones pushed together to fit by the immense hand of God who had then coloured them like an Italian mosaic in beautiful, golden lichen and velvety green, some of it strewn with flowers, or left them a tawny brown, or splashed them with the birds' guano which even in itself was beautiful, a still, bright echo of the splashing foam below. And above the cliffs, the birds wove their dance: the gulls with their lazy, skimming sweeps, the puffins with their busy clipped darts, the hunched cormorants, all under a sky of unbelievable breadth and height, the towering clouds never the same for long. Below the cliffs, the spiky sea, grey and green and blue, flecked with creamy white. And for a moment, Eliot could almost see it for himself, could almost feel the enchantment of the island in the hesitant sunshine, but then the focus he had struggled to shift clicked back like a door latch and all he could see was barren rock and bleak sea, and the gusty dampness of the wind on his face. The noise of the wind and the waves and the endless pointless shrieking of the gulls was almost unbearable. He wished he could walk about a bit, get the blood moving. He was still recovering far too slowly for his liking.

He had grown used to the sight of his own grey, blotchy limbs, used to his own continued weakness and dependence on the monks, and all too used to their tedious diet. He wanted to go home, and though he had no specific idea where that might be he was sure it was somewhere warmer, drier and with more interesting food. The promise of seagull eggs did nothing to encourage him to get his appetite back.

But then, was home the same place as the place towards which this feeling of urgency was driving him? For that had not diminished, all the time he had been here.

He sighed. He would leave the island as soon as he had his strength back. But then where would he go? He had no business in Scotland that he knew of, but he must have been heading here for a purpose.

Frustrated, he pushed himself to his feet and began to walk, very slowly, across the hollow. The monks had given him thick sheepskin slippers of some sort, saying his boots were too heavy just yet – he felt like a baby. Not used to them, he stepped on to a sharp stone and before he could stop himself he had let out a yelp. At the sound of him Brother Peter looked up, gave a shout and leapt to help him, but Eliot pushed him off, wobbled a bit, and carried on. Brother Mungo, seeing where Eliot was going, drew Brother Peter back and watched Eliot's painful progress. He was making for the chapel.

Brother Mungo would have been disappointed if he had thought that Eliot's momentous walk had been stimulated by anything the least spiritual. Eliot merely wanted to see if he could push himself to walk a set distance to a visible goal, and he was too much of a coward to try to leave the hollow and go too far from ready assistance. But by leaning slightly into the wind, and setting himself a slow, but rhythmic, pace, he passed where the brothers had been working and pushed on, stumbling on the uneven, close-cropped grass, his coat hanging heavily down as his arms stayed half-raised in front of him, ready to save him if his balance went entirely. His eyes were fixed on the rough grey stone of the little chapel, as if some connexion between it and them could draw him onward when the rest of his strength failed.

There was a large, rounded stone by the chapel door: with a final lunging step he grabbed it and turned himself to sit on it, panting and gasping. He had done it. When Brother Mungo and Brother Peter called out their congratulations, he permitted himself a gratified smile. At last he was making progress.

He sat there for a little, eyes closed but bright with stars, feeling the wind cool the sweat on his face and the tingling in his limbs and feet. The brothers watched for a moment, then Brother Mungo nudged Brother Peter and they turned back to their work, smiling happily.

When at last he opened his eyes again and looked about him, he realised that he was in a small graveyard. There was no formal division between it and the cultivated lands the brothers were working, but then there were very few graves. One, well-settled and thick with grass, was cosily tucked against the chapel wall. It was marked with a cross formed of fist-sized rocks laid over it in lines. The other four were in a row slightly further away, bleak, bare and unmistakeably recent. A chill ran down Eliot's back, the drying sweat damp again. He stared at the four graves, and thought of the small hut the brothers lived in, and what they had told them of their life on the island. No mention had been made, he was sure, of recent deaths, particularly all in a group like this.

'I see you are paying your respects to your friends. A worthy task, for your first day out.'

Eliot leaped on his rock. Brother Fillan had returned from the hut and stood beside him, also gazing at the graves. Eliot wondered how Brother Fillan managed to stay so plump, on the muck they ate here, then realised what he had just said.

'Friends? My friends?' he queried.

Brother Fillan looked down at him as if trying to judge something, then squatted down comfortably beside Eliot's rock.

'Have you no recollection at all, then?' he asked casually.

Eliot shook his head, pursing his lips angrily. How many times did he have to tell them? It was as if they could not bring themselves to believe him.

'I remember very little. Of the journey on which you tell me I was shipwrecked, I remember nothing, neither means nor purpose.'

Brother Fillan showed no reaction to Eliot's tone of voice. He tucked his hands into his sleeves and nodded over at the new graves.

'The far two, by their dress they were sailors, I should think,' he said, with a bland absence of emphasis. 'They were very fair in colouring. I wondered if perhaps the crew was from Norway, or somewhere else in the far north. They were dead when we found them.'

He waited, but Eliot did nothing more than grunt. It was no use chasing memories: they came or they didn't, whichever they fancied.

'The other two were too richly clad to be sailors,' Brother Fillan went on. 'More richly clad than you, indeed. One was an old man, frail even in life. We found him on a little beach, tangled in some kind of tapestry, all life gone. The fourth was beside him. He was a young lad, and still alive.' His gaze flicked to Eliot, who did indeed look surprised. 'He spoke some few words, but whether he was wandering in his wits or spoke a tongue we did not recognise I do not know. He had had a blow to the head, perhaps from the mast falling – we saw it broken in the water. He was a fine-looking boy: I wondered if the old man was his father or grandfather, for the boy clutched at the old man's arm ... though he may have had no idea what he was doing, or where he was. We carried them all back up here, with you as well, and brought the two of you that had still been living into the hut, but the boy was already dead.'

He drew his hands out of his sleeves and pushed himself up, wincing a bit at the effort. The nearest grave seemed to draw his attention.

'Aye, a fine-looking lad indeed. A tragedy to some wealthy family, wherever they may be.'

'It makes no difference to me,' snapped Eliot, annoyed at what he saw as Brother Fillan's manipulation. 'However fine-looking he was, I cannot remember him.'

Brother Fillan looked at him sadly for a long moment, then he wandered away into the chapel, and left Eliot to face the challenge of how to return to the hut without losing any more dignity.

That night, they gave him the promised seagull eggs for his supper.

'You walked a long way today,' said Brother Mungo solicitously. 'I hope you haven't overdone it.' Eliot snorted. 'Well, we'll see in the morning,' Brother Mungo continued unabashed.

Eliot was tired after his exertions, and he wolfed down the eggs with little real regard for them. It was only later, as he tried to sleep, that the eggs truly made their presence felt. The bed could not be made comfortable. If he threw off the covers he was too cold, if he pulled them back over his shoulders he was too hot. And every time he closed his eyes against the dim light from the embers of the central fire, strange, nightmarish images flickered to life in his mind: figures huddled round a table, the glint of a knife in a moonlit street, footsteps behind him, running, running, a voice from a doorway - *You must do your duty* - a light at a window quickly extinguished. Then the same voice, more urgent, coaxing, *They know you now, so you might as well do it ... might as well do it ... might as well ... No!* The voice turned to a shout, a scream, a hideous male shriek. *No! No! No!*

Eliot sat straight up, panting. Had he himself screamed? He listened, trying to still his breathing. No, the others seemed all still to be asleep – he could not have disturbed them. The fire had died down completely: he was not sure if the tiny glow was really there or was simply the result of his efforts to see it.

Gradually the images dispersed from his mind, before he could even examine them and try to place their meaning. Nothing moved in the silence of the hut, only disturbed by Brother Fillan's inoffensive snoring. He lay down again, easing himself into some kind of comfort where his limbs still ached, and closed his stinging eyes.

He was back outside by the chapel wall, where he had sat that afternoon in the fresh air, only that now it seemed to be indoors. The brothers were nowhere to be seen: he was alone. He gazed at the four fresh graves, bare of grass, but the wind seemed to be rippling the loose earth on them as if it were grass. He watched, fascinated, and as he did so, the grave nearest to him stirred, as if the body within were turning over in its sleep. He waited. At one end of the gravecut there came a small upheaval, earth falling away from something – a fair, shining head, the hair ruffled by the soil, then shoulders and arms. A young man sat upright in the grave with his back to Eliot, then shook his head sharply and scrambled to his feet, carrying something in his outstretched hand. He turned towards Eliot, his fine clothing damp and stained, his face hollow, smiling directly at Eliot, but his eyes were ghastly, rotting and liquid. Eliot felt sick, but not afraid, and even in his dream he was aware that this was strange. Then he saw what the young man was carrying – it was a fine goblet, full – and he could even smell its heavy scent – of rich red wine.

At that he woke properly, screaming, and at last, at once, aware of what he had come to Scotland to do.

II

Tom had no idea what he was doing, trailing after Dr. Eastleigh. She was striding with her usual assurance into the High School Yards building where the Archaeology Department kept its discreet presence. If the objectionable Rob had really disappeared, was he expected to scour Edinburgh looking for him, while Catriona did some kind of helpless female act?

Anyway, what did Catriona mean, 'disappeared'? Did she mean that he had vanished like snow off a ditch? Been abducted by little green men and taken to the planet Zog? Or been so distressed by the disappearance of the body they had found that he had gone to fling himself off the Scott Monument? Tom doubted that one. Rob had seemed to set a high value on his own existence, and anyway there was no way yet of knowing whether or not Alf would reappear. Did she mean that he had run away to look for the body – in which case Tom was quite keen to see it too, for although he was not a pathologist he had seen photographs of the signs of SAIDS and was fascinated by the fact that they might still be visible after seven hundred years. And anyway, if it really was SAIDS – if it really was, it was incredible. And if it really was SAIDS, and it had been cured – if the man had really recovered – well, he would sort of like to look into the face of a man who had recovered, even if the man was dead. Even if the man couldn't tell him how to find the cure himself.

And that was the point, that was why he shouldn't really even be here. He had work of his own to do, important work, on which lives depended. He scowled at Joanne Eastleigh's back. The trouble was, Dr. Eastleigh was not a woman you could say no to.

He had not been in the building before, and thought it seemed odd: there were several dark departments crammed together in a yard below street level, with tight little entrances and curious archways. He thought he caught a glimpse of some improbable sign to do with writing indexes, before Dr. Eastleigh turned a corner and they were into the glass entrance of the Archaeology building. It reminded him more of school than of university, and he felt sheepish as his rubber soles squeaked along the silent linoleum corridors and up white stairs. When they reached the swing door into Archaeology's part of the building, however, there was a little more sign of life. A conversation seemed to be being held between one room and another across the passage, and one of the voices was Catriona's. As they approached, she appeared suddenly in an open doorway.

'Oh! It's you!' she said in surprise.

'What is going on, Catriona?' Joanne Eastleigh asked sternly. 'Where is Rob?'

'We don't know,' she said, her high forehead wrinkled anxiously.

'Of course we do,' said another voice. Tom sighed: another archaeologist, presumably. This one had what Tom thought he recognised as an Armani suit, as in black silk, with which he wore a pink shirt and slicked-back hair. Earth would never have been tolerated under those perfect fingernails. Joanne turned to him in relief.

'Professor Hervé,' she said, and Tom could not help drawing comparisons with their own Uncle George, 'where is Rob?'

'He's gone to the dig,' said Adrian, smiling creamily.

'To the dig?' said Dr. Eastleigh in disgust. 'Then there you are,

Catriona.' She was about to continue, but a purring from her handbag
drew her away with an apology to answer her mobile.

'Ah, how do you know?' asked Tom, diffidently. He had not taken
to Professor Hervé: he did not like Rob, either, but he thought Catriona
would have been sensible enough to check the obvious answer first.
Adrian Hervé saw him for the first time, and looked him up and down
with limited interest. Perhaps he took him for a student.

'Hmm. Well, Rob came running in, *slamming* the door back against
the wall, and straight in his office. And seconds later, he was off again. I
had meandered out into the passage to speak to him but he ran straight
past me. "Where are you off to now?" I asked. "To the dig," replied he,
in a very offhand manner. Then something about a wife? Or a life? I
assume he must have one or the other, at least. And in a moment I heard
his car start outside and away he went. He must have passed you,
Catriona, if you were here too.'

'I was in the loo,' she said briefly. Tom looked from the professor to
Catriona. She met his eyes defiantly, chin up. 'I think there's more to
Rob's disappearance than that,' she went on, looking as if only anger
were keeping her from tears. 'What did he mean, "life"?'

'He's at the dig, Catriona. Go and see for yourself. There's no place
in science for swooning and weeping, you know!'

Tom blinked, waiting for some kind of explosion. Catriona flung the
door behind her open wide, and pointed into the room.

'*Look* at that whiteboard!' she enunciated. Adrian regarded her
cautiously for a moment, as if he too expected an attack, then he looked
past her into the room. Tom also tried to see, but in the end the three of
them had to shuffle into the small study to examine the whiteboard on
the wall. It was large, mostly clean, with a few remnants of words or
numbers around the edge where it had been sketchily wiped. There was
nothing in the least remarkable about it: Tom had seen hundreds like it
before in labs and lecture rooms.

'You *know* he never wipes the whole board. Once a term, that's all,
if that. The rest of the time he only wipes the bit he needs at that
moment, then uses it. Someone else has been in here.'

Tom, who had been inclined to believe Catriona's interpretation of
the situation rather than the effete Adrian's, came back to earth with a
bump. A small nervous part of him was rather enjoying the sight of her
attacking Adrian – she was like a Valkyrie, he thought fancifully – but if
she were saying that Rob had disappeared and basing her conclusion on
an inadequately cleaned whiteboard, he for one was wasting his time
here. Adrian seemed to think so, too.

'Catriona, will you do me a favour?' he said, with an edge of steel in his voice. 'Will you go and check the dig first, before you call the police?'

'Why did he say he was going to the dig?' Catriona asked, off on another tack. 'What did he see here that made him go?'

They all looked about the room, Adrian clearly close to exasperation. Tom could see why: the place was in chaos. Books and papers were everywhere, on shelves, desk, chairs and floor. A pile of what looked like dissertations sat with a marks sheet on top, untouched. A plaster cast of a skull, wide-browed and lacking a jawbone, rested on top of the radiator, and boxes of slides and several baize-lined trays of minor artefacts nestled on the desk, wound about with the flexes of telephone, computer, printer, and two anglepoise lamps. On the walls, along with posters, hung a great convex Roman shield made of cardboard and painted vivid red and gold: on the floor lay a tray with a small kettle and three filthy mugs on it, one of them tipped on its side spewing coffee dregs. It was not what you would call an orderly room. If someone had left a note here for Rob, it would have been difficult even for Rob to spot it, let alone them.

'And you didn't hear the phone ring?' asked Catriona. Adrian sighed.

'No, I didn't. But I did hear him say he was going to the dig,' he added, as though to a slow child, 'so I think that might be the best place to look for him, don't you?'

Catriona ignored his tone.

'It must be for Alf,' she said to Tom. 'Someone must have told him that Alf was at the dig.'

'Maybe the message was on the whiteboard,' said Tom suddenly. He had been thinking out loud, and instantly regretted it – he would probably find himself dragged out to this dig, wherever it was. Catriona looked back at the whiteboard, and they both studied the fragments of writing at the edges more closely. Some looked very old. One of the more recent stood out in green marker pen at one bottom corner of the board: '5PM'.

'That'll be it,' said Catriona urgently. 'They'll have given him a time. What time is it now?'

Tom looked at his watch.

'Twenty to five,' he replied. Adrian added,

'Time for all good little archaeologists to be thinking about going home, Catriona dear!'

Tom tried not to smile – the man had a deathwish, clearly. He straightened his face as Catriona turned to him.

'Will you and Dr. Eastleigh come with me?' she asked. 'You'll have to see Alf, anyway.'

Tom was about to shake his head when Joanne Eastleigh, finally clicking her mobile shut, said,

'Sorry, Catriona, no chance. That was my childminder – my daughter's had some kind of accident. I've been trying to talk her through what to do but I'll have to go.'

'And I really need to get back to my lab,' added Tom.

'At the Infirmary?'

'No, down at Roslin.'

'But the dig's at Roslin! I'll give you a lift.' Catriona gave a last, quick look at Rob's office, and felt for her car keys in the pocket of her shorts. Tom could hardly refuse the lift: buses at this time of the afternoon were not two a penny, but he told himself firmly that he would not – could not – become any more involved in this farce. Disappearing bodies and vanishing archaeologists: he had almost forgotten the fact that the body that had disappeared seemed to contain traces of the SAIDS virus.

III

'Andy!' Shona leapt from her seat by Vicky's bed. Her husband had entered the little room almost silently, followed by a self-effacing prison officer in a mask like the nurse's. The prison officer looked about carefully, noted the complete lack of windows, and unlocked Andy's handcuffs with a quick twist. He withdrew, closing the door behind him.

Andy Larssen's bright blue eyes were nowhere near his wife, even as she hurried round the bed to hold him. They remained on his little daughter, lying tubed and wired in the bed. Her favourite teddy sat on her pillow, looking peculiarly content. The nurse had driven Shona home for an overnight bag, and she had brought the teddy back at his suggestion.

'How long has she been like this?' asked Andy. Shona looked up at him, and backed off a little, unsure of herself.

'Since Monday, sweetheart ...'

'Why didn't you tell me sooner?'

'Och, Andy! I thought ... I didn't want to upset you. I didn't think they'd let you out, anyway. I thought – well, it's all gone so quickly ...'

'So quickly ...' he repeated, his eyes still on Vicky. 'You think it's my fault, don't you?' he added softly.

'No! No, it didn't need to be – anyway, it could have happened to anybody.' In fact it had not occurred to her to blame Andy in the least: she had been too busy feeling ashamed of the fact that he was in jail.

She watched now as he took the seat opposite hers. Clearly there was to be no more discussion of it now, whatever the truth might be. His blond hair flopped over to shield his gaze, but it was focussed absolutely, as he was, on Vicky.

IV

He was panting, and Brother Peter hesitated, allowing him to choose whether or not to stop, but he shook his head fiercely and pushed on. His long boots felt strange on his feet – he had not worn them since the shipwreck, and they were stiff and salty which annoyed him. He had paid a good deal to have those boots made, in Firenze.

They reached the end of the little hollow, where they could see the patchwork headlands beyond, and he allowed himself to pause briefly.

'So the man in the inn,' said Brother Peter, with tentative encouragement, 'the man in the inn in Boulogne ...' he breathed the word as though it spoke of exoticisms far beyond his imagination. Eliot sighed impatiently.

'He said he was a spy. A Scottish spy.' He glanced at Brother Peter's astonished face. 'Well, of course I didn't believe him – who would?' Apart from Brother Peter, he added silently to himself. 'And he told me a few things. He said he knew something – something vital to Scotland's safety – but that he had no way of taking it back to Scotland himself. He was being watched, he said, and his mails were being tampered with whichever way he sent them. He was sure that if he tried to travel over himself he would never survive the journey.' Eliot was growing cold, and he had his breath back: he turned abruptly and forced Brother Peter to return with him, marching back to the other end of the hollow.

'So did you come back for him? On his behalf, I mean?' asked the young brother.

'Aye.'

'But why, if you did not believe him?'

'Ach!' Eliot was silent for a moment, angry with himself and his circumstances on so many levels that he was hard put to know what to be angry at most. He shouldn't have believed the man, he shouldn't have done all he had for him, but having done it he shouldn't have stayed in that plaguey village in Norway, and he shouldn't have trusted his life to that pathetic barrel of a boat, and he shouldn't be taking so *long*, Holy Mother, to fight back to health! And if he had to be stuck anywhere, why did it have to be with these wretched monks?

Brother Peter coughed politely. Eliot scowled.

'I did not believe him because he seemed to me to be talking nonsense, the kind of nonsense some men come out with after a few tankards of strong ale. And if he'd been drinking French ale for as long as he said he had, it's a wonder he didn't come out with worse,' he added sourly. Brother Peter laughed. Eliot was surprised. He had not made a monk laugh before – not deliberately, anyway. 'But he kept trying to involve me – kept trying to enlist my help, and in the end he even said that since he had been spending so much time in my company I might as well do it, as the English forces would assume I was involved anyway. Of course I laughed at that one: I've heard all the tricks from London to Constantinople and that one is as old as Methuselah. But it was a bit more convincing when he got himself killed.'

'Oh michty,' said Brother Peter, taking his hand from Eliot's arm to cross himself briefly. Eliot took a few proud steps unsupported, but was glad enough when Brother Peter returned like a watchful parent and held him again. 'Were you there?'

'I was – or I almost was,' said Eliot. Now that he had begun to talk, he could not say he was not enjoying having such an attentive audience. 'We were walking back to our inn late one night, with a link boy for a light. I stopped in a doorway to – to relieve myself. I heard a struggle and a scream, and the light went out. There were footsteps of three or four, maybe even five men, and the sound of metal in scabbards. I leapt out, but they were gone' (it sounds better, he thought, than the truth about hiding in that doorway trying to lace up my breeks while that stupid spy screamed and whined) 'and my acquaintance and the link boy were both dead – run through with sharp blades.'

'But – how could you tell?' asked Brother Peter, his eyes wide. 'You said the light had gone out.'

'True. True enough – the back streets of Boulogne are black as pitch at night. I felt them, if you must know.' Eliot tried not to think much about that as he said it: the stumbling, the fumbling, the smell, the sticky darkness horribly warm. Brother Peter was suitably impressed. 'There was nothing I could do for them but see them safely buried – and, at last, to undertake what he had asked me so many times to do.'

'So you leapt on to the next boat for Leith, and were blown north!' said Brother Peter, trying his best to sound cosmopolitan. Eliot gave him a thin smile.

'It was not quite that simple, Brother. Strangely, I saw no great advantage to Scotland or me in having a knife in my belly.' Brother Peter was not the least abashed, and grinned happily. 'I had been going to head south from Boulogne, for I fancied some warmth in Spain, perhaps, but instead I went north, and took my time, not drawing too much attention to myself, selling off my goods and – and leaving the money with trustworthy friends on the way.' He had no particularly wish yet to mention his over-heavy coat, though the monks must have guessed. 'The Baltic states were my goal. I have traded there for years, and know their languages and people. They are a sea-going race, and I knew there would be many there capable of bringing me to Scotland. It turned out to be more difficult than I had thought, though, and some of the villages where I had heard of people buying passages before with ease seemed reluctant to take to the sea. I had to bribe this lot.' He jerked his head savagely towards the chapel and the sailors' graves.

'And where were you heading?' asked Brother Peter. 'Not the May Isle, anyway, I am sure of that!'

'No, not the May Isle,' agreed Eliot. They had reached the other end of the hollow, and he had to take a moment to sit on a stone. Even his arms were weary from the walking. 'I had hoped to head for Leith. I did not know – it is many years since I have been in Scotland. I did not know how the land would lie, or where I might find the Guardians.'

'The Guardians!' Brother Peter sat abruptly beside him, mouth open. 'What do you want with the Guardians?'

Eliot rolled his eyes. Brother Peter had led a sheltered life.

'Do you not think that if there was a threat against Scotland,' he said with what he thought was remarkable patience, 'the Guardians might like someone to tell them?'

'Oh, aye.' Brother Peter giggled at his own stupidity. 'Come on, then, let's get you back in out of the cold.'

'No, I must make one more crossing of the hollow,' said Eliot, pushing himself to his feet. 'I must be fit to leave within the week. It may already be too late.'

'You're a bitty too late if you're looking for the Guardians,' said Brother Fillan in mild surprise. There were gulls' eggs again for supper but Eliot declined them, eating mutton broth with more enthusiasm than before.

'Why's that?' asked Eliot, not looking at him.

'We havena had any Guardians now since the Red Comyn surrendered to Edward of England – was it last year?' he asked himself, then nodded. 'Last year.'

'And the other Guardians?'

'Well, he and Bruce are still alive, of course.' Brother Fillan was the island's political expert. Eliot rolled his eyes in despair, then blinked in the rancid smoke of the mutton fat candles. Brother Fillan watched him kindly.

'When did you leave Scotland last, eh?'

'Oh …' Eliot tried to remember. 'I left the year Edward of England put John Balliol on the throne.'

Brother Fillan nodded agreement.

'I have nothing against the man, but the way it was done …'

Eliot grimaced.

'I owed money,' he said sullenly, and returned to his broth.

'Well, Balliol shilly-shallied about a bit till the Battle of Dunbar – that must be nine years ago now, or near enough. We were beaten there – ' there were groans and head shakings from the younger brothers – 'and then that was Edward back in charge. I hear tell Robert Bruce asked him for the crown then, but Edward had no intention of letting us have a king at all. So off he goes back to England and leaves a few of his pals in charge, but there was never what you'd call peace, was there?'

'Never,' said Brother Mungo glumly.

'So then this fellow Wallace comes along,' Brother Fillan continued, pushing away his dish with plump fingers. Eliot looked up.

'Aye, William Wallace. I've heard of him, but I'd like fine to hear more.'

'Then Peter's the lad to tell you of him,' said Brother Fillan generously. Brother Peter's eyes glowed.

'I would have been about ten,' he said, trying to adopt Brother Fillan's authoritative historical tone. 'I was a lad biding not far frae Lanark, in a wee village there. All the news was that a young quine by the name Marion Braidfute had been done to death by the sheriff, an Englishman by the name Haselrig. Anyway, this was bad enough but the next thing we knew this young fellow Wallace, a knight's son but no the eldest, ken, he had some interest in the girl and ups and kills Haselrig, although mind you there were some that said there was a deal more to it than that and Haselrig's death was some kind of signal, for it was like Wallace just went wud then entirely against the English.'

'It was a wise madness, then,' said Brother Fillan again, 'for he had them here there and everywhere. He was like a terrier at their heels wherever they went, and of course the more that he succeeded, the more men joined him, and he dispatched the English altogether at the Battle of Stirling Bridge the next year.'

'Victory!' cried Brother Peter. Brother Fillan gazed at him solemnly. Brother Peter blushed, and went to poke the fire.

'Then they made him a Guardian,' Brother Fillan went on, turning back to Eliot. 'They might even have made him king, but the great lords didna fancy any more competition for that role – the Bruces and the Balliols are busy enough fighting each other for it, without bringing in some knight's son. Anyway, soon they had enough to worry about, for

Edward went tearing back to England from the Low Countries and up here quick as you like. Mind you, his army was nothing much, forever squabbling, for the Welsh and the English have never had much in common.'

'Aye, if he'd stuck to his cavalry we'd have had him,' said Brother Mungo, more gloomy than Eliot had ever seen him.

'True, true,' agreed Brother Fillan, more philosophical, 'but it was the English longbow that did for Wallace at Falkirk.'

They all nodded solemnly, and Brother Peter gave the fire a weary poke.

'So Wallace is dead?' asked Eliot, trying not to sound too interested.

'Och no, bless you! It would take more than an English longbow to kill Wallace – by God's grace,' Brother Fillan added hastily. 'He stepped down as Guardian, true enough, and Comyn and Bruce took over jointly – not that that lasted long, either. What a pair to put together! It's like yoking a fox and a wolf.'

'Aye, there's no love lost there,' agreed Brother Mungo, brightening. 'Bruce gave it up last year, not long before Comyn's surrender.'

'But what happened to Wallace?' demanded Eliot.

'Och, he went to the continent,' said Brother Mungo, 'looking for support. He even had a wee word with the Pope in Rome.'

'That's what I heard,' said Eliot, nodding. He leaned forward on the bench, fidgeting with the edges of the scar on his neck. 'But he's back, aye?'

'Depends who you believe,' said Brother Peter shortly.

'Some say he's in Norroway,' said Brother Fillan. 'Others that he's down by Dumfries, fighting with John Comyn and Simon Fraser. There's one or two say he's dead. But there's one man who won't believe that – and that's Edward of England.'

'The man's obsessed,' Brother Peter broke in, ignoring Brother Fillan's reproachful look. He jumped up and began to pace. 'He'll no rest till he sees Wallace dead before him and Scotland his forever. He's no right in the head!'

V

'So, ah,' Tom began once Catriona was clear of the staff car park. 'This dig – that's an archaeological thing, right?'

'That's right.'

'This dig at Roslin – don't tell me you're after the Holy Grail?' He grinned, but no grin appeared on Catriona's face. She did not look at him as she fought her way out into the heavy traffic of South Bridge.

'We were looking for Romans,' she replied. 'Alf was unexpected.'

'Alf?'

'The students' idea. It's best not to ask.'

He was not sure if that meant that she had not asked or if he ought not to. For a moment he thought he might just have caught the shadow of a grin on her face. He waited for enlightenment, but soon gave up.

'So he is how old, exactly?'

'Well, I can't give you his birthday, but he's from approximately 1300. So that's around seven hundred years old.' He reflected that he could probably have managed that sum on his own. 'We found him in a Roman lead coffin, though, and it looks as if the bones of the original Roman had been thrown in after him, so there is a bit of a mystery.'

She spoke absently, as though she had explained this so many times over the past week or so that even she did not listen any more. Outside the car, the terraces of Edinburgh's south side flickered past, donkey brown or sooty red, repeat patterns of Victorian tenements. Tom stared at them, trying to think of something intelligent to say or ask.

'So what was happening in Roslin seven centuries ago?' he tried. 'Was the famous chapel there by that stage?'

Catriona had been doing some reading.

'No, it's fifteenth century. The St. Clairs themselves weren't even there – the castle was started in the early 1300s, but not by them.'

'So what else was there?'

'Well, there was probably a settlement of some kind. But the interesting thing is that there was a battle there, in 1302.'

'The Battle of Roslin? Doesn't ring any bells.'

'No, I don't think it even has a name. Sir Simon Fraser is supposed to have defeated three divisions of the English army in succession. In one day.'

'Quite a day. So does that mean your corpse could have been killed in the battle, then?'

'He could, but I think it's unlikely. He had no defensive wounds – the knife attack must have been a surprise. He was not dressed as a soldier, he wore no cuirass or sword belt, and apart from the knife wound and the marks of – of whatever disease he might have had, he had no injuries or scars, and that would be unexpected in a man of his age if he was a regular soldier.' Now it was her driving that was absent: her mind was definitely on the man, on what he had been, on where and when he had come from. 'We think he came from abroad, just recently arrived: there was sea salt in his clothing and in his satchel.'

'What was he carrying in his satchel?' Tom was beginning to catch a kind of interest from her: this was not just a disease-survivor, but a man, a traveller. And if he was a traveller, had he caught his disease in Scotland, or furth of the kingdom?

'Papers, we think, and something that might have been some kind of tinder box.'

'And on the papers?'

'They're seven hundred years old and they've been buried with a mummifying corpse,' said Catriona sharply. 'They're a bit tricky to read.'

'Well, couldn't you even tell if it was the *Scotsman* or the *Daily Record*?' asked Tom, annoyed into sarcasm. Catriona looked at him, half-querying, half-hostile.

'We can tell an awful lot, if you must know,' she said coldly. 'He didn't exactly come out of the ground with a 'circa 1300' label tied to his collar. He was in his thirties or forties. His clothes had been in the sea but his boots were Italian, probably the north, possibly Florentine. His dagger was German. His coat was French, his hose were Spanish, and his shirt was Russian. He had good teeth and no broken bones and was probably a moderately wealthy merchant. We have sent off a shaving of tooth to the dental laboratory and soon we'll know by the strontium levels what kind of diet he had as a child, maybe even where he came from. We know he had a disease like jail fever – *your* jail fever, not the original one – and we know he was stabbed to death. And we can even deduce, from soil deposits on his heels, that he was dragged over muddy ground shortly before he was put in the coffin. There, now, how's that?'

'Pseudo-science and guesswork,' said Tom, deliberately annoying. These people paddled round in muddy fields for a living – he was the scientist here. 'For centuries you lot have been digging things up with about as much sophistication as a dog looking for a bone, and now you've suddenly discovered microscopes and carbon dating and you think you're nuclear physicists.'

'Oh, aye? And what were epidemiologists doing two hundred years ago while archaeologists were discovering the history of the Pyramids? Feeding their leeches?'

There was a sudden shocked silence: the row had come out of nowhere. Tom felt as embarrassed as if he had confessed his darkest secrets to Catriona – after all, they had only just met.

Catriona turned off the main road at a white gateway and showed a pass to a security guard, who bent down to examine Tom's face. The gateway was to some private research institute with which Tom did not remember having had any dealings, Elysian Fields. Very poetic, he thought, and wondered why Catriona was driving this way. Then they turned on to a well-worn dirt track, dusty in the drought. Ahead of them was an ancient tent, reminding Tom abruptly of Cub camp. There was a car parked beside it, an elderly Renault 18 in a kind of camouflage green. It seemed to be empty. Apart from that, there was nothing to be seen: the low hill, the flattish land by the river, the scrubby trees nearby, all bare.

'And this is where the dig is?' he asked, as inoffensively as he could manage.

'Yes, and that's Rob's car,' said Catriona, relieved.

'It – ah, it doesn't look quite what I expected,' ventured Tom, as they got out of the car.

'What did you expect?' They both sounded wary, not wanting to start off another row.

'Well ... holes in the ground, at least, I suppose.'

'They've been backfilled. And turfed over. We save the turves, and we try to train the students to leave things as tidily as they found them.' Tom looked about more carefully: there were indeed one or two suspiciously geometric yellowish patches on the earth.

'I see. So the dig is over?'

'That's right. We left the tent, with some of the stuff in it, till we could come back again with the minibus. I suppose Rob's inside.'

They walked over to the tent, aware of the running of the stream, the birds in the trees, their own soft footsteps – and the silence from the tent in front of them. The entrance faced away from them. They picked their way past the guylines and rounded the corner to find the flap flopping open. Catriona snatched it up and stepped inside, then gasped. Tom followed.

He had a horrid feeling of déjà vu. Everything in the tent had been upended, emptied and thrown about. A trestle table lay on its side, a map half-ripped off its surface. A theodolite, its legs skewed like an abandoned pantomime horse, sprawled nearby. A few crates lay on the ground, the files they had held spilled over the tarpaulin floor. Plastic finds trays had been smashed, and polythene self-seal bags and paper tags in various sizes were scattered about like autumn leaves.

'I take it it's not usually like this?' he asked at last.

'No, of course not,' she snapped. She moved forward.

'Careful!' he said. 'We'll have to call the police again.'

'I just want to see –' she stopped to peer over the fallen trestle table. 'No, no sign of Alf.'

'Or Rob.'

'Or Rob.' She looked back at him. 'What do you mean, "again"?'

'What?' Tom was too distracted by the horrible similarity of the scene, even here under canvas. The cool green light seemed the same as the indirect fluorescence of his laboratory.

'You said "call the police *again*".'

'Yes, we should. Sorry, our laboratory was broken into last week – it just brought it all back.'

'With all your work in it?' He nodded, and at once saw he had her sympathy. 'Who would do such a thing?'

'Protestors, we think. Thinking that SAIDS is a judgement on prisoners and we shouldn't be wasting our time trying to cure it.'

She tutted.

'Sick. Well, this is obvious, I suppose. Someone wanted the tools or thought there might be something else of value, and did a bit of wrecking.' She retreated to where Tom was standing. 'I've a mobile in the car, we can call them from there.'

'And Rob?'

'About that as well.'' She frowned, examining the tent again as if she could have missed him somehow. 'We should look at his car.'

'But we shouldn't touch it,' Tom added urgently. Catriona nodded thoughtfully, and went outside.

When Tom came round the corner of the tent, he found Catriona peering into Rob's car.

'So, any sign of him?' he asked.

'No. The keys are in the ignition.'

'Could he have found the tent wrecked, and gone to call the police from somewhere nearby?'

She frowned.

'Yes, that's a possibility,' she conceded. 'He would gone either to the gate, where the security man is, in which case we would have seen him, or he would have gone up to the main office of Elysian Fields. Their P.R. department is helping us with funding for the dig – they paid for a lorry and a crane when we shifted Alf in his lead coffin.'

'Generous,' Tom remarked.

'Mm. But if he called from their offices, surely he would have headed back here to meet them?'

'Maybe he's on his way. Is it far?'

'Just up there.' She pointed to where a footpath cut off the road they had left and disappeared in the opposite direction, between thick, well-trimmed hedges.

'I could go up and take a look,' he offered, 'while you call the police from here.'

'Oh,' she said, 'I'm not sure they'd like that. The Elysian Fields guys aren't keen on people just wandering around. We'd better both stay here where we're supposed to be, not get into any more trouble.'

He looked at her in surprise, but she was still frowning anxiously at Rob's car. She seemed to be miles away. He cleared his throat.

'Police, then.'

'Yes,' she said, and they walked back to her car at the end of the dirt track.

When she had made the call, she tossed the mobile back into the car and they sat a few feet apart on the grass beside it, staring at Rob's car, the tent, and the traces of the finished dig.

'Did you lose much work, at your lab?' she asked after a moment.

'A fair bit. It was redoable, but it all takes time, you know?'

'Hmm. Is that why you were using the electron microscope at the Infirmary?'

'That's right.' Well, not quite, but near enough. 'Calling in a few favours, trying to get back on track.'

'Tough.'

They waited about twenty minutes then, saying little. Tom's mind was half on his work, half on the unsteady pleasure of spending a while out in the sunshine in attractive company, at least. Catriona, despite her obvious anxiety, looked at home out here as she had not done in the lab: Tom watched her surreptitiously, seeing how she fitted in with her chosen landscape. For himself, while he was enjoying the novelty of his day out, he knew he liked the comforts of his lab too much to spend his working life out here. And what did you do when it rained?

This prolonged heat was extraordinary for Edinburgh. It had to end soon, and the quickening breeze flicking at the scrubby trees seemed to say that it would. But the sun was still hot on his face as he closed his eyes into its glare.

The police arrived discreetly, the unmarked car pulling up without a fuss beside Catriona's. Out of it respectively stepped and scrambled a tall young constable and Detective Inspector McAlester.

'Hallo, Dr. Buchan!' said McAlester with evident delight, so friendly that for a moment Tom thought that Columbo-like he must be McAlester's chief suspect for the laboratory break-in. 'And Dr. Lindsay! Isn't that just lovely, Constable?'

'Oh, aye, sir, very nice,' said the constable sincerely.

Tom, trying to assess discreetly how Catriona might be known to the police, found that she was doing much the same to him. The little hostile line had reappeared on her chin, and his heart seemed to sink.

'Nice to see you again,' he said with emphasis to the Inspector, shaking his hand firmly, trying to look like an upstanding member of the community.

'Oh, people don't usually say that!' said McAlester. 'For instance, what have you called us out for this time? I'm sure it's not for good news, anyway!'

'No, it isn't.' Catriona sounded unconvinced by Tom's show of comradeship with the Force. 'It's this tent – it's been broken into. And that's not all.' Methodically, she told the story of today's events, including the disappearance of the fourteenth century corpse and the apparent disappearance of Rob. From what she left out, Tom could only deduce that both the Inspector and his constable knew a good deal more of the excavation of Alf than he himself did, and a small flicker of jealousy surprised him. The constable, indeed, seemed to take the corpse's disappearance as a personal insult, and kept directing concerning glares at a particular hollow in the ground. It was by the river, and from what had been said earlier, Tom suspected that Alf had originally been exhumed from there.

'Whose is the car?' he asked at last.

'Rob's,' said Catriona. 'The keys are still in it, but he's nowhere to be seen.'

McAlester raised his eyebrows and pursed his lips, making a face of thoughtful concern. He surveyed the whole site for a moment longer, then ambled over to Rob's car and the tent. The rest of the party followed.

'Is anything obviously missing?' he asked, after a few minutes' quiet perusal of the car and the interior of the tent. Catriona peered in again, her eyes adjusting to the submarine light inside.

'No,' she said, after a moment's thought. 'Nothing obvious.'

McAlester turned a bleary eye to his constable.

'What do you think?' he asked encouragingly. The constable bit his lip.

'Possible sign of a struggle, sir?'

'Hmm,' said McAlester. Tom looked at Catriona, who had gone pale.

'You think he's been abducted, then?' she asked, her voice unreliable.

'Hmm,' said McAlester again. He and the constable exchanged looks. 'It's a possibility, although why anyone should do it ... Call forensic, constable, and we'll see what they come up with.'

'Are you going to look for blood?' asked Catriona suddenly, with a light of panic in her eyes. Deciding and trying to convince others that Rob had been abducted was one thing: clearly facing the reality of it was another.

'Oh, no,' said McAlester with a kindly smile, 'not necessarily blood. All kinds of things, left in all kinds of places.' He began, bizarrely, to sing the signature tune of *The Archers*: 'Every contact leaves a trace, every cloth a fibre!'

'You're not exactly Inspector Rebus, are you?' asked Tom, unable to help himself.

'Rebus? Don't think I know him,' said McAlester innocently. 'I might have known his uncle, though.' And continuing to hum, he began to make a minute inspection of the outside of the tent. The constable, notably not meeting anyone's eye, pulled out his mobile and began to dial.

VI

He left a week later.

The brothers held a special mass for him before he went, a prolonged version of one of their usual services. He attended with less reluctance than he would have a month before: he had to admit to himself, angrily, that he was scared almost witless of the dangers before him, and at this stage any assistance, any luck he could bring on himself was more than welcome. The brothers' enthusiastic singing did not help. They were very good, all three of them, and the music echoed ethereally in the little stone chapel in an otherworldly swirl of sound: he would have preferred something a little more down to earth, maybe even one of them singing off-key just to be a bit more human.

There was an awkward hour or so then, waiting for the boat to come over for him from Anster village. Brother Fillan solved the problem by spending the time in prayer for Eliot's wellbeing, with a word or two for his soul should it need them in the near future. That left Brother Peter pacing nervously up and down, and Brother Mungo struggling to think of any last minute advice, useful to a traveller who had not been home for ten years.

'You could try St. Andrews first, see if anyone there knows where Wallace is. There again, I suppose St. Andrews isn't the centre it used to be, and the chances are that Wallace is in the lowlands. Even when he was fighting he never went very far north: Andrew Murray did most of the recruiting up there, but the people didna take to him in the same way. Then he died, anyway. But if you go to St. Andrews then you're sort of off the track for the lowlands, and you might want to try Linlithgow instead, and at least then you're on the way to places he might be.'

Eliot eyed him, trying to be unnaturally patient with his hosts on his last day. He had already decided where to go: Edinburgh. He had a feeling about Edinburgh, a notion that he would find what he was looking for there or thereabouts, and even if he didn't it was a good place to lie low for a few days if he needed to get his strength back. He could afford it. He knew that his sense of urgency was still not matched by his energy, and it worried at him. If it came to a chase, or a fight, how well would he fare? As Brother Mungo babbled on, he told himself that it would be different if his life depended on it: he could run or fight then. And he had his knife, sheathed at his thigh, and he had used it before when he had needed to. It would be all right.

Last night he had unpicked some of the hem of his coat and taken out four gold coins. He gave one for the monks to Brother Fillan, who had demurred for some time until Eliot had become angry. He did not want to owe anyone anything, not at this stage. Brother Fillan had also unearthed from somewhere some silver coins for which Eliot exchanged two of his other gold coins, for discretion's sake. He had all the coins now in his satchel, wrapped in some of the papers the man in Boulogne had left. The papers were for Wallace, if he ever found him.

At last they could see the boat, lifting lightly over the waves from the mainland coast. It seemed to be moving quickly but still took an age to arrive. The men in the boat examined him suspiciously, particularly the scar on his neck, just visible between hair and collar. Eliot pulled his hat down hard and looked grimly back at them, which did not help. Only the young monks' cheerful enthusiasm seemed to reassure the boatmen, and as the monks themselves still looked remarkably healthy the men at last allowed Eliot freely on to their boat. He tucked himself in, hugging his coat around him, wrapping his satchel close to his body. The boat surged a little under him, and he felt a thrill up his spine. At last, he was moving again.

The monks, Brother Fillan along with them, waved energetically until he was out of sight. He did not wave back, but did them the honour at least of watching them as they became small specks of movement on the beach, nothing more than the woven net of seagulls around the uneven ridge of the island. The thrill remained with him, but there was a thread of fear in it, too. He was leaving somewhere where, despite everything, he had felt safe. Perhaps he should have felt more grateful towards the brothers.

The wind was with them as they bobbed towards the shore. All the same, it was a couple of hours before the boatmen took down the sails with a clack of canvas, and rowed peaceably into Anster harbour.

The harbour was bundled together out of irregular reddish stones. Eliot scrambled up the steps, declining the help of the boatmen, and paid them off unsmilingly. Then he turned and surveyed what he could see of the village. It was a sharp little place built on a steep hill up from the harbour, rig-style fishermen's houses with the nets drying over the outside steps. The sandstone and plaster walls had tiny huddled windows, secret in the sunlight that was splashing them with colour. Eliot appreciated the signs of civilisation, but this was only a taste. Soon he would see towns again, and even a city, if he was lucky. He breathed in the fishy air, adjusted his satchel under his coat, and set off, stepping carefully between the creels and the net weights, to make his way up and out of the village, on the road to the rest of the world.

It was nearly mid-day when he set off, as the boat trip had taken so long. He soon grew hungry, the fresh air making him feel energetic and sleepy at the same time, and he took an opportunity to sit by the side of the road after he was clear of the village and eat some of the provisions the monks had given him. If nothing else it would make his satchel lighter, for they had packed dried fish, hard boiled eggs, a piece of precious mutton and a loaf of bread. Their usual generosity annoyed him faintly, but he felt so far away from them now that the irritation was beginning to fade a little.

He allowed himself to doze for a few minutes after he had eaten, with the sun warming his face, then set off again, trying to curb his sense of urgency and pace himself. He did not want to be dependent again so soon, not on anyone. The day continued fine: the hedges were a cheery green, the trees a vibrant colour filled with birdsong, and the banks were sprinkled with primroses and other more obscure flowers of which Eliot knew nothing. Still, the sight was a pleasant one, the road winding about in healthy-looking farmland, and the glittering sea spread out to his left. His path led him along by the coast, keeping to where villages were many and hospitality might be easily come by. What he was following was the road that led to the best crossing of the Forth river at the Queen's Ferry.

The walking was easy enough while the weather stayed this fine, anyway. By nightfall he had passed Elie, and had rounded the rocky basin of Largo Bay. He came to a village at the far side of the bay where a broad river seeped out over a sandy shore, and by its description took it to be Leven. Here Brother Fillan had given him the name of the local priest as a kindly man and welcoming to travellers: Eliot was tempted to find an inn if he could and avoid any further debts to his erstwhile hosts, but by the time he had found the church, and seen little sign of an inn, he was exhausted. The priest was taller even than he was, and worryingly thin, not a good sign for a hearty supper. But the priest's sister turned out to be an excellent cook and brewster, and Eliot and the priest sat down, after prolonged thanksgiving, to a boiled fowl in herbs with bannocks and warmed ale.

The priest, questioned discreetly, thought Linlithgow might be the place to look for any ex-Guardians that might still want to admit to the title. Eliot took the suggestion without rancour. From where the ferry docked, he could go to Edinburgh first and on to Linlithgow if necessary.

He slept like a bairn in the priest's own bed, and rose refreshed to more bannocks and bacon. The priest, who had deduced perhaps a little of his purpose, said a blessing over him as he drew on his coat and satchel, and he departed, deeply grateful for once that he had not striven to find some fleapit of an inn.

He had started early and passed through Kirkcaldy before dinner time. He bought a couple of pies there to add to the remainder of what the brothers had given him, for it was a fair-sized village and he did not wish to be caught without food later for want of buying it now. This second day was as fine as yesterday, but the going was rougher now, the landscape wrinkled into sharper hills, and the drop to the sea a steeper one for much of his way. He ate his first pie outside a village called Kinghorn, and found an inn that would sell him a fill of ale to wash them down. He sat on a bench leaning against the front wall of the inn, satchel cosy as a cat on his lap in the sunshine, and succeeded very well, for an hour or so, in forgetting all about the spy in Boulogne and his informative death.

VII

Notwithstanding the fact that she had scarcely spoken to him since the police had appeared, Catriona offered to give Tom a lift, as promised, to the Establishment. He thought of walking, but decided that she would rather he refused, and anyway, he added to himself to justify his perverse argument, the wind was still discussing rain and he had no coat with him.

The police constable had taken a statement from each of them about the last time they had seen Rob and the state in which they had found the tent. Catriona's statement had been more lengthy than Tom's, going into details about Rob's apparent frame of mind and his personal habits relating to whiteboards and car keys. She also explained how they had seen the remains of the note on the whiteboard and assumed that Rob had an assignation of some kind at five o'clock. That set the constable scribbling: it meant that Rob had vanished within a very small window of time.

Tom had wandered off a little, not wishing to seem to be eavesdropping. Surprisingly, Chief Inspector McAlester seemed to take the matter of Rob's disappearance quite seriously. Tom had always thought that adults, particularly male adults, were considered by the police to have minds of their own and to be free to come and go as they pleased. But the circumstances here at the dig site probably changed that, the abandoned car and the wrecked tent.

He looked around the dig site. He had never been to an archaeological dig before, and was rather disappointed that this one had finished. The little mound looked a bit hacked about, and a small ruined hut had a scarified look, stripped bare of undergrowth, but the fresh green heads of young nettles were growing up secretly amongst the yellow stubble. The field then met a little meandering stream with muddy banks, and beyond that there was scrub-like woodland. It did not look as if the field was used regularly for anything much by Elysian Fields, whose neat dark hedges seemed to have been delivered ready moulded by the metre.

What had the mysterious Alf been doing here seven hundred years ago? Why had he been buried here? It seemed a bleak enough place even now, with the withdrawn presence of the various research establishments. What it must have looked like in 1300 he could easily imagine.

The police offered to leave a constable at the tent until they had finished with it, and to let the Archaeology Department know when they could come and take it down. They wanted to remove Rob's car themselves for further examination, and Catriona watched it go with some reluctance. It was as if she could not decide for herself whether Rob had been abducted or not, however hard she tried to persuade others. He might, after all, come back and think his car had been stolen.

There was not much more conversation in Catriona's car on the way to the Establishment. She drove in silence, her mind obviously far away, though she responded readily enough to Tom's directions. When they reached the final turn into the lane, he said,

'That's fine, here will do.'

She looked about in surprise.

'Where is it?'

'Just up the lane. There's no point in you going up there, it's a dead end and it's not far, anyway.'

She nodded, and waited as he freed himself from the seatbelt and gathered up his knapsack.

'Thanks,' said Tom awkwardly. 'See you, then.'

'See you.'

'I hope Rob turns up soon. I'm sure he will.'

'Aye.'

He stepped out of the car and turned the corner into the lane, then instantly turned back again. At the top of the lane, by the gate, there stood a tall, hooded figure at the edge of a small crowd. The demonstrators were back.

Catriona, about to drive off, saw his indecision and looked down at the passenger seat, as if to see what he had forgotten. He tried to catch her eye to shake his head at her, wave her on her way, but she did not look up immediately. He went back and leaned down to her open window.

'It's all right,' he said, 'it's just we had a problem the other day with some demonstrators and they seem to have come back. I'm just wondering how to get into the building.'

Catriona glanced towards the end of the lane. Fortunately where she had pulled in was not within the line of sight of the demonstration.

'Are they violent?' she asked.

'No idea. They looked a bit nasty the other day, but we didn't stay long enough to find out.' He straightened for a moment, thinking. He could walk down to the village and call the police – who would soon be asking to be put on a retainer, at this rate – or he could try to get round the back of the building some other way and go over the hedge, or through the fence ... he remembered all George Mackay's carefully chosen thorny plants, and the fact that he was wearing shorts and a cotton shirt, and thought again.

'What are you going to do?' Catriona asked.

'Call the police again,' he said at last. Catriona twisted over the back of the seat and pulled her mobile out of the pocket of a knapsack.

'Here,' she said. He took it and looked at it vaguely, until she snatched it back from his hand with a sharp sigh and dialled the number for him, then handed it back, muttering something about scientists which Tom chose not to hear.

A patrol car arrived quite quickly, two uniformed officers stepping out in a deliberate fashion and adjusting their caps as they walked up the lane and vanished out of sight.

'You could go now, if you like,' said Tom to Catriona. 'Thanks for your help.'

'You'll be all right?' she asked reluctantly.

'I think so, thanks.'

She started the car and left with a small acknowledging wave. He waved back, thinking that it was the closest they had come to peaceable communication all day. Then he tiptoed up to the corner of the rough hedge and peered cautiously round, to see how the police were getting on.

The demonstrators again seemed to be moving away relatively calmly under the direction of the police. They were manoeuvring their placards into the boots of cars they had left parked in the lane, with no raised voices or apparent protest. Perhaps, Tom thought, they were afraid of doing anything that might land them in prison themselves, which would render their protest against helping prisoners a bit embarrassing, if nothing else.

The cars were started and began to drive down the lane towards him, and he pulled back from the corner, moving away in mock nonchalance. He watched them go, thinking of nothing in particular, until he suddenly realised something. While he had been watching the police disperse the demonstrators, there had been no sign of the tall one with the hood. He wondered if the man was still lurking somewhere up by the gate, or even just inside it, out of sight of the police, waiting until they had gone. He found that he did not like that thought at all.

However much he looked about, he did not see any figures, hooded, tall or otherwise, as he made his way up the lane and through the gate. He let himself in and nodded to Eck the Door, now chatting with the police again, and went to see what was going on in his own lab. One bright spark, one of the other researchers to judge by the sense of humour, had constructed a printed sign for the door saying 'Demolition Unit – Bring Your Unwanted Equipment Here and Watch the Wheels Drop Off'. Tom left it there and unlocked the door, then swiped himself in with his card. Inside was much as usual, to his mild surprise. He went to his desk and unpacked the samples he had studied at the Infirmary, as well as the notes that he had made there. He sat down and methodically input them into the computer with its new monitor, and then stuffed the paper notes into a filing tray to deal with later. He looked about him, wondering what to do next. After a moment's thought, he opened a new document and listed what he knew about Alf and his possible illness, mentioning Dr. Joanne Eastleigh to approach in the future if necessary. The file seemed entirely inconclusive, and he called it 'Alf' for want of anything better.

He pushed back his chair and stared around the room. It had been such a peculiar day he did not feel like settling down to work just now, and yet he had put in very little time today. He looked for something that would constitute work but not actually be real work, something requiring little concentration.

On a bench further down the lab was a small heap of objects, looking unsanitary and out of place in George Mackay's bright white world. Tom hauled himself upright and went over to have a look. Beside the pile was a note from the forensic team who had searched the lab.

'Dear Drs.,' it began. 'These were found under furniture etc. and seem to be homeless. Hope useful.'

Tom turned to the pile, which consisted of buttons, a couple of used tissues, paper clips, a loose screw or two, staples and a few scraps of paper. Gavin had a habit, well-known to Tom, of tearing small strips of paper to use as bookmarks, and one or two of these were clearly his work. Tom picked one of them up in an attempt to identify where it had come from. It was evidently from the top right hand corner of a letter of some kind, a long strip showing the last few letters of each line of the address in a pleasant green italic typeface. It read '... Road, ... Devon, ... 5PM'.

It was not familiar to Tom, so was not one of the other institutes with which they often communicated. In fact he could not think of an establishment in Devon with which they communicated at all. But something about it made him think of something earlier in the afternoon, and as he thought about it he remembered himself back in Rob's deserted and chaotic study in the Archaeology Department, looking at the whiteboard. It was possible, he realised suddenly, that 5PM might not have been a time: it might well have been part of a postcode. And there were all kinds of other things it could have been. They had just jumped to conclusions.

He was fed up. There was no sign of Gavin, and he did not want to go looking for Uncle George. He decided to go home.

He knew there was a bus at half past seven or thereabouts, so he collected his post from the receptionist, told her with a grin that he had not been there at all, and headed for the bus stop, reaching it just in time.

On the bus he looked at his post. There was a copy of a journal along with a reminder about the subscription due; a couple of promotional leaflets for firms supplying lab equipment which George would never let them have anyway, and a letter addressed in block type in a plain white window envelope, with a second class stamp and an Edinburgh postmark on it, and nothing else. He checked the back: it too was blank. Curious, he ripped it open with his thumb, and pulled out a sheet of A4 paper, blank white on one side, and on the other a message typed in block capitals.

DEAR DOCTOR BUCHAN

THERE IS NO POINT IN GOING ON WITH YOUR WORK ON JAIL FEVER. WE WILL NOT ALLOW IT TO BE COMPLETED. WHAT HAPPENED TO YOUR LAB AND EQUIPMENT WAS NO ACCIDENT. WHAT CAN HAPPEN TO EQUIPMENT CAN HAPPEN TO PEOPLE TOO. STAY AWAY FROM WORK. YOUR COLLEAGUES HAVE RECEIVED THIS TOO. IF YOU COME TO

WORK YOU WILL BE ALONE AND VULNERABLE. STAY AWAY FOR YOUR OWN SAFETY. WE WILL BE WATCHING.

It was unsigned. On the stuffy, hot bus, Tom suddenly felt very cold indeed. In his mind, the hooded figure watched him, waiting for him.

4 - PURSUIT

I

When the alarm clock rang next morning, Tom surfaced only slowly from a deep and glutinous sleep. It took a few moments for the recollection to hit him: the anonymous letter had left a sick feeling in the pit of his stomach, and that returned immediately.

He had lain awake for hours in the night, wondering what to do. He felt like going to work and defying the threat, and then the next minute he wanted to ring the police and have them advise him. Then the next minute he would decide it was all a joke, probably Gavin's or that prat in Molecular who had put the sign up on the lab door, and if he rang around to find out if it was true that his colleagues had also received threats he would be a laughing-stock – or the joker would lie to him and all the rest would have received letters anyway.

But if it was genuine, what then?

The protestors had not looked violent, but perhaps that was the milder element of the organisation – he found that suddenly he believed in an organisation behind it. Before he had dismissed the protests as random and amateur, but now he sensed something more central and professional about the whole thing. He shivered. He valued his work, but somehow it suddenly did not seem worth dying for.

Dying! That was a bit over-dramatic, wasn't it? He kicked his way out of bed and went to find the letter and read it again. 'Stay away for your own safety.' It did imply that death was an option, but it was a bit unspecific. Did he want to risk it?

The crumpled bed looked unappealing, and he decided to go and make himself a cup of tea, finding his way through the flat without bothering to turn any lights on. The street lamps outside gave just enough light for him to manage. He put the kettle on and glanced at his watch – three a.m. He wandered over to the window, and peered outside at the street below.

He did not notice the figures at first, for they were standing in the shadows of a gateway across the road. It was only when one of them moved slightly that he saw them: three men in dark overcoats, and one tall one, right in the shadows, wearing a long cloak with a hood. Tom fell at the kitchen table, dragged out a chair and sat down. His legs were shaking.

He would have to call the police. But what would he tell them? Here, I've been sent this threatening letter which might well be a joke, and there's some guy in fancy dress hanging around outside my flat?

There were over a hundred flats in the street, and eight in his block alone. Even if the people across the street were watching anyone, they might not be there to watch him – they had not even glanced up, after all. And the police would not be best pleased to be called out at three in the morning to look at an anonymous letter that had, after all, arrived yesterday and would still be there in the morning. He wanted to speak to Detective Chief Inspector McAlester, anyway, and assumed the man went home for the night. At least to him he would not have to explain about the protests and the lab break-in all over again.

Well, that was he would do, then. He would wait till the morning, call work to say he would be late, and then call McAlester and explain it all to him. Or should he call Gavin first and ask him if he had received a letter? He tiptoed (ridiculous – as if they could hear him!) into the living room and peeped round the curtain there. He could not make up his mind whether he wanted them to have gone or not: if they had gone they could be anywhere, coming up the stairs or going to fetch reinforcements or anything. However, they were still in the gateway, apparently in fairly intense conversation, heads bowed, hands thrust in pockets. Tom slid away from the window again and padded back to bed, and only when he was about to lie down did he remember that he really wanted that cup of tea. He went back to the kitchen and made it as quietly as possible, then returned to bed and drank it in the dark, trying to think logically about the implications of moving the labwork entirely somewhere else. Eventually he must have fallen asleep, for when he swung his feet off the bed in the morning he stepped on the overturned tea mug, empty on the carpet.

'Ah, the curse of the common word processor!' sighed Detective Chief Inspector McAlester, clutching his brow dramatically. The note, now in a plastic holder, was lying on the table in front of them. Beside it was an identical one sent to Gavin, who had come with Tom to the police station.

'Aye,' agreed the constable. 'Used to be when they cut the letters out of newspapers and stuck them on. Much more traceable, and of course it kept the word count down. They just don't know when to stop, now.'

'So you think we should take it seriously?' Gavin asked, trying not to yawn. Tom, too, was on his third cup of police station coffee, and it was doing bizarre things to his stomach.

'It could just be another delaying tactic,' suggested the constable. 'You've had the break-in, you've had the protests, you've had machinery break down: this is just the next stage.'

'But none of it actually stops the work,' Tom protested. 'We still go on. It just slows us down.'

McAlester stared at him wide-eyed.

'I wonder if there's something in that,' he said slowly. 'I wonder if we should be looking more closely at the related attacks in the other parts of the country and see if someone might be orchestrating them for that very reason. I take it for whoever develops this cure first, there would be a lot of money in it?'

'Oh, definitely,' said Gavin. 'Money and kudos. Brilliant for the lab's reputation, and reputation means funding, and round and round we go. And funding means jobs, longer-term contracts for existing staff, that kind of thing.'

'That's a motive!' said McAlester, sounding slightly surprised to recognise it.

'It certainly is,' said Gavin sourly. 'But should we go into work or not?'

McAlester regarded the plastic folders anxiously.

'No,' he said at last. 'I wouldn't. Not yet, anyway.'

Gavin and Tom stared at one another blankly. Another day lost. If it was a delaying tactic, it was working.

They rose to go, throwing the polystyrene coffee cups into a plastic bin by the door. Chief Inspector McAlester was fumbling to open the door for them when a thought struck Tom.

'The other research establishments looking into SAIDS, the ones you've heard have been having trouble too,' he said. 'Were there any in Devon?'

'Devon?' McAlester rolled his eyes up into his head and pursed his lips, thinking back. 'Dorset, yes,' he said at last, frowning. 'Not Devon. We haven't heard of any down there at all, have we?' The constable shook his head. 'Why?'

'No reason,' said Tom, thinking it would take too long to explain about the scrap of paper he had found in the lab last night. He shrugged. Gavin gave him an odd look, and they left.

II

The first heavy drops of rain woke Nicholas Eliot as he sat outside the inn. They were so sparse that for a moment he thought that a bird had dropped on him, or simply that something had splashed him. He sat up looking about him, wiping the water off his face, confused by his surroundings.

Above his head was a window in the inn wall, giving light to the main room inside. When he had been in earlier to buy his ale, the room had been busy with dinner time custom, but now it sounded quiet. A couple of easy voices could be heard, by the sound of it the innkeeper and his wife, swapping gossip from the dinner hour as they tidied up inside.

'Andro says young Malcolm's thinking of selling his boat,' came the man's voice.

'Oh, aye? Pass me the clout, then. That's a strange thing, for Johnny thinks his Marian is to marry Malcolm, and I doubt he'd let her without the man has a living.'

The innkeeper laughed shortly, then said, as if suddenly remembering,

'Did you see that man came in in the dark cloak?'

'Oh, aye, I seen you talking to him. A stranger in these parts, was he no? What did he have to say for himself?'

Eliot pricked up his ears, wondering if they were talking about him. There was a thudding of falling leather tankards which covered the next few words, but then the man said,

'I was saying, he's the sheriff's new man. He's been around looking for survivors from some shipwreck he thinks happened a while ago.'

'A shipwreck? I've no heard of one in these parts recently, have you?'

'No since the winter. But apparently he thinks it might have been further north than here. Around Crail or Anster, maybe.'

Eliot felt a chill down his back. The rain was growing heavier, but he did not feel it now.

'Why is he seeking survivors, then?' asked the goodwife. 'And why all the way down here?'

'Some dark business, no doubt,' replied her husband. 'That sheriff has his notions of right and wrong that are neither man's nor the Holy Church's.'

'Hush!' said the wife, but she was chuckling. 'Did you tell him we'd keep our eyes open?'

'I did, and I might, but if I do see a shipwrecked man I might not necessarily choose to tell the sheriff's man.'

'Is this the only place he's looking? Because if it is, someone must have given him information.'

'Ach, I had the idea he was on the move, just passing through. He said he'd been up in Crail for a week or so, so I guess he's just heading along the coast, maybe down to the ferry or something.'

Eliot's stomach turned. If the man was just travelling the coast he could be avoided. Eliot could cut inland, take a shorter, if tougher, route. But if he was going to the ferry – and the only ferry was the Queen's ferry – he could cut Eliot off altogether. What should he do? The ferry was the quickest way across the Forth by far.

The innkeeper poked his head out of the low doorway and saw Eliot.

'You finished with the tankard, man?' he asked genially. It was dangling from Eliot's hand, his own lost in the shipwreck.

'Oh, aye, sorry. I fell asleep.'

'Aye, it's been fine up to now. You're no from around here, are you?' he asked casually, and Eliot swallowed.

'No, you're right,' he said, sounding artificially cheerful. 'I'm frae Falkland.' He picked a town well inland, important enough, with its fine Macduff castle, to attract a few visitors and make his answer plausible. 'I'm heading for the ferry and Edinburgh.'

'Aye, well, you've a clear enough road,' said the innkeeper, without suspicion.

'Aye, I've trod it before!' agreed Eliot. He handed over the tankard. 'Well, I'll be on my way, or I'll make no progress before night.' He stood up and adjusted his satchel under his coat. The rain seemed to have decided not to bother, and as he looked up a cloud passed away from the sun and the light fell warm about them. There was an awkward pause. He wondered if the innkeeper was trying to decide whether or not to give him a warning about the sheriff's man. Perhaps he was trying to decide whether or not to betray him. For himself, Eliot was trying to hold back an unnatural urge to thank the innkeeper for the warning he had already unwittingly given him. It must be some lingering influence from those bloody monks, he thought grimly – gratitude! He did not want to find himself involved in that kind of thing, not at this time of his life.

He sauntered off down the road, in the general direction, at first at least, of the ferry.

Navigation was a bit harder than he had expected after he cut inland, down the road and out of sight of the inn. The sun was clear, leading him west, but the roads never seemed to go towards it for long. He felt he was doubling back and being pushed towards the coast again, and wondered if all the roads in this part of the country led to the ferry. The sky was broad and aloof and he met few people: those he did meet he avoided speaking to where possible, so as not to attract attention to himself. When night fell, sooner than he had hoped, there was sign of neither village nor farm steading, and the few cottages he had seen he had drawn away from, afraid of being betrayed to the sheriff's man. The rain had begun again, softly drizzling, and he pushed himself on for as long as he could see the path in front of him. He lamented the loss of his bedding roll, now at the bottom of the sea: it seemed warmer and more comfortable now in its absence than it ever had when in his possession. He felt more sorry for himself than he had done since he had left the May Isle. With the very last of the light he half-felt his way to the damp hollow where hedge and ditch met, and wrapping his coat about himself and his satchel he made as small a bundle of himself as he could. The hedge was full of faint rustlings, but in a moment or two he found them curiously reassuring, and soon drifted into sleep.

III

Tom fell asleep on the couch in his flat, keeping his boots handy in case he had to leave quickly. He slept surprisingly soundly, and woke with a crick in his neck and a dreadful longing for a cup of tea. Before he left the living room, however, he took a quick look round the curtains and checked the street below. A woman pushed a buggy along, strolling to allow a toddler to keep up. The owner of the Indian grocer's on the corner stepped out to take the air, and an old lady with a tartan shopping trolley let herself into one of the stairs across the street. Tom regarded each of them with deep suspicion, and went to put the kettle on.

The kitchen cupboard was remarkably bare again, and he was almost out of milk. He decided to fortify himself with the tea first, and then make a cautious raid on Mr. Kumar's grocery. He made the tea and sat at the kitchen table with it, thinking of nothing much. In front of him lay the rest of the post that he had collected along with the anonymous letter. He picked up the journal and flicked through it, starting to read a couple of interesting-looking articles but not making much progress. He turned to the letters page, and struggled through one or two of the shorter ones, but it was still beyond him. He pushed the journal aside, and opened the motoring atlas he had been leafing through the previous week. He was thinking of cycling through Fife for a holiday – perhaps between contracts, at the rate this one was going. He turned to the right page, following the M90's thick blue line up from the Forth Road Bridge, wondering if he should take a train to some central point and cycle from there. His finger paused at Kinross Services as he pondered, and as his eye meandered about that spot, he suddenly saw the word 'Devon'.

That's odd, he thought. He moved his finger slightly. 'Crook of Devon', it said. Now what was more likely to be found in an Edinburgh lab: a letter from Fife, or a letter from the far end of England? This was something he had to think about. He finished his tea in a couple of gulps, and went to get his boots.

He had walked straight past the grocery shop before he had thought, and kept on walking towards the middle of Leith, head down and determined. The breeze whipped along the busy street, flicking litter into the air and dust into the eyes, but it was fresh after the unnatural heat and he relished it. He was in no hurry: he thought he might walk all the way up to Princes Street and buy his groceries in Marks & Spencer for a change.

Was the Devon of the letter in the lab really Crook of Devon in Fife? And if so, did it help at all? Only if it led them to the protestors, he supposed. He had never heard of any labs in Crook of Devon either – in fact, he had never heard of anything in Crook of Devon.

He strode past the little fruit shops and seedy video stores to the foot of Leith Walk, turned right and began the steady climb up to the east end of town. Leith Walk was broad and lined with shops on the ground floors of solemn Victorian tenements: side streets led off from time to time between more tenements much the same. The breeze rushed down the Walk, sweeping the wide pavement clean as he wove his way between trees in cages, bus stops, plump ladies in saris and elderly Ukrainians in caps, and a few early drinkers from the sailors' pubs. He loved Leith by daylight: it was a real port, a guddle of widely varied nationalities and backgrounds, full of the smell of fish and Chinese supermarkets and Italian restaurants and cigarette smoke and beer. He was just drawing in a long breath of this potent cocktail when someone walked out of a side street and straight into him.

'Ouf! Sorry!' he exclaimed.

'Oh, for goodness' sake, sorry,' muttered the other person, and he looked more clearly at them. It was Catriona Lindsay. She recognised him at the same moment.

'Oh, it's you. Sorry,' she added again, a little grudgingly. He nodded a greeting, as usual at a loss for something to say to her. She had covered those excellent legs in fashionable combat trousers, but she wore them in such a way that he felt inclined to look round for the rest of the troops. Her hair was still severely plaited.

'Do you live in Leith too, then?' he asked, shoving his hands into his pockets.

'Yes, just along there. What about you?'

'Just off Ferry Road.' He struggled to think of something else. 'Any word from Rob?'

'Nothing. I'm just going to the department now, after I've picked up some choc – groceries. You not working today?' she added hurriedly.

'No. We're having a bit of difficulty with the protestors,' he said, feeling defensive. 'The police have advised us not to go in.' Catriona raised her eyebrows. He had the impression she thought he was a coward. Well, wasn't he? 'What about your break-in at the dig?'

'No word from the police at all. But then, if they're dealing with your protestors and your lab break-in they'll barely have time to do anything about some unimportant archaeologists, will they?'

'I'll see you about, then,' said Tom huffily, and strode off.

He had reached the bottom of Leith Street before he even began to think straight again. He half-felt that he should have given a curt bow, like some offended eighteenth century pink. He had only been being civil, after all: if he had followed his inclination he would not have stopped to speak to her at all. And anyway, why did he always fell he had to say sorry to people who had, in fact, walked into him?

Grumbling to himself, he reached the top of the hill and marched grumpily on to Princes Street.

IV

'Maister! Sir, wake up!'

Eliot twitched in his hedge. A hand on his arm shook him a little.

'Maister, shift yourself!'

'How long has he been here?' came another voice.

'He was no here last night at dusk, onywyes. I'm sure I would have seen him.'

Eliot opened his eyes cautiously. It was daylight, and the world swam. He could see the blurry outline of a face, looming towards him and receding again.

'He's his eyes open, onywyes. Though I dinna ken if he's seeing us rightly.' It was the first voice again, a woman's voice, light and cheerful. 'He doesna look too well.'

'We'll have to take him inside, then, I reckon,' said her companion. A deeper voice: male. Another face floated near him. He felt himself shiver, and then found he could not stop.

'Chilled to the bone, I'd say,' said the man, and he felt strong hands reach around his shoulders, pulling him up out of the hedge, and all he could do was cling to his stomach where his satchel rested. They propped him between them – 'Monks!' he thought briefly, bitterly – and walked him, weak-legged, to a smallish building a little distance away. Vague movement around his feet and a harassed clucking suggested a chicken yard of some kind, and then he had to stoop suddenly to avoid the lintel of a low door. They sat him on to a recess bed beside a hearth, and he felt the soft contours of a quilt beneath him. After a moment, seated in the warmth, his vision improved. He was in a small cottage room, smelling of livestock and broth. A young man stood by the window where the shutters let in some daylight, and a young woman, swelling with child, leaned near to him, studying his face. She was pretty, he saw, with nut-brown hair and dark eyes. He tried to smile at her.

'What's your name, stranger?' she asked kindly.

'Eliot,' he managed, surprisingly easily. He was cold, still, but had not that dreadful feeling of weakness so much that had made him think he might be stranded here as long as he was on the May Isle. 'Nicholas Eliot. Who are you?'

'This is Jennet and I am Davie,' said the man, not unfriendly but cooler than the woman.

'You're travelling, then?' she asked. 'From the Borders, are you?'

'A long time ago,' he agreed, nodding, though it made his head swim again. 'I'm a merchant by trade.' He liked her: she had a round, happy face, and curved in all the best places under her brown gown. It occurred to him that these two could betray him to the Sheriff's man – or that Davie could even be the Sheriff's man – but the bed was soft, and the breakfast bannocks smelled good, and he hoped he might be invited to share them, regardless.

Jennet had the broth by the fire, and she filled a wooden bowl with it, sweet-smelling and full of vegetables and herbs. She handed it to Eliot, and he drew his spoon out of his satchel and ate it gratefully, soaking up the juice in the bannocks. Once he was settled, she served a bowl to Davie as well, and he sat on a creepie stool like a bairn and ate with evident appreciation of his wife's cooking.

When he had finished the meal, Eliot felt significantly better. He looked expectantly at his hosts, who were watching him. Then the man Davie rose, and said,

'You'll excuse us for a moment. I have a word to say to my wife.'

She did not look surprised as he took her by the hand and led her outside. Eliot could hear the vague muttering of their voices in the kailyard, though they seemed to be in agreement. He felt a sudden sharp pang of envy for this cosy domestic setting, the wife, the cottage, the family on the way: he knew he could never have lived entirely content, but there was still something about it that charmed him. Maybe one day, when he could settle down.

After a moment or two they returned, their faces set with a shared expression of determination.

'Sir,' said Davie, visibly shouldering the responsibility, 'the Sheriff's man was about yesterday asking about the likes of you, a tall stranger with a look of other lands about him.'

They're going to throw me out, thought Eliot. Oh, well: it was a grand breakfast, and they cannot take that back. And small blame to them, anyway.

'I fear he may come back,' the young man went on. He was almost young enough to be Eliot's own son: his face was raw with youth. 'But you are not well enough to travel today, maister, and so you are welcome to stay. Only bear it in mind that we may have to hide you quickly.'

Anxious in her cheeriness, his wife took Davie's hand, nodding her agreement, watching Eliot's face. He stared back at them, standing straight before him, the young man with his smooth, bright face, and the girl, plump with her child, ready to defy the Sheriff's man to help a stranger in need. The Sheriff's man could not be popular. He looked at them, and knew that for their sake he would have to be on his way.

V

Tom was even more edgy by the time he returned home on the bus, with several bags of groceries on the seat beside him and a sense that he had bought provisions for a siege. It was perhaps not surprising that Princes Street at lunchtime should be well endowed with men in suits, but every time he saw one Tom thought of the huddle of men outside his flat last night, and imagined he recognised their faces. The ones that followed him on to the bus were even more alarming. From the bus stop he scuttled, bags rustling, to his own stair and slammed the street door behind him, feeling like an idiot – but a relatively safe idiot. At the top of the stairs, back inside his own flat, he put the groceries away absently, his mind on the protestors when it could have, should have been on SAIDS. Resentful, he glanced down at the open motoring atlas on the kitchen table. 'Crook of Devon,' he thought, and picked up the phone.

Gavin must have been sitting right beside his phone: he answered halfway through the first ring.

'Hi, Gav, all right?'

'Tom?' Gavin sounded hassled. 'Is it something quick?'

'Can be,' Tom agreed. 'Do you know of any dealings we have with a firm or a lab in Crook of Devon, in Fife?' There was silence. 'Gav?'

Gavin breathed out through his nose, sharply.

'Why do you ask?'

'I found a bit of paper at the lab from there, I think. Or it might just be Devon. Any ideas?'

There was another pause.

'Sorry,' said Gavin, 'the wife's wanting to go out. It doesn't ring a bell. Look, is this something to do with the break-in?'

'I'm not sure. It might be.'

'Why don't we meet this evening? Say, the Ceilidh House at, ah, eight-ish?'

'Fine,' agreed Tom. 'Have a good day out. I'll let you go!'

'Thanks. Bye.' Gavin put the phone down.

Tom remained seated for a moment, puzzled. Usually when Gavin's family were agitating while he was on the phone, you could hear them. Sometimes you could scarcely hear Gavin. He hoped everything was all right in the Price household.

He looked at his watch. It was already four o'clock. He drummed his fingers on the table. He wanted to take another look at that bit of paper. If Gavin, when he saw it this evening, really had no idea where it came from, and he did not either – oh, and he should check with Willie, the lab assistant – then the paper might well have been dropped by the vandals, and subsequently shredded by Gavin.

He flicked through his phone book and found Willie's number, but when he dialled he only got an answering machine, speaking in Willie's lugubrious voice. Tom thought quickly, then said,

'Hi, it's Tom Buchan. Gav and I are going for a bevy at eight. Meet us at the Ceilidh House? Bye.'

He needed to see that piece of paper. He looked at his watch again – five past four. The protestors would never expect him to go into work at this hour of the day, so they would hardly be watching the Establishment. Would they be watching his flat? He wandered nonchalantly to the window and glanced down. There was one man in the street, wearing a suit and a raincoat and pausing to look at a streetfinder map. Tom was sure he recognised him. Still, the man was on his own, he should be easy enough to lose.

Full of confidence, Tom grabbed his knapsack and stuffed the journal copy into it from the kitchen table. He paused in the hall, and after a moment's thought took a padded plaid shirt from the coat rail, pulling it on as a jacket as he closed the front door behind him and trotted down the stairs.

The man with the map followed him to the bus stop, and waited as two buses went past. When Tom caught the third one, the man with the map followed him on, ushering an old woman on in front of him and stopping to ask the driver about the route. Perhaps he was puzzled, thought Tom: this bus was not a direct one to Roslin. Instead it was going up to the main bus station in St. Andrew's Square. Tom went upstairs, and the man remained downstairs, and the bus made its laborious way to Great Junction Street and began to climb Leith Walk.

Maybe it was because it was daylight, or maybe because it was harder to be afraid of a mediocre little man beside you at the bus stop than it was to be afraid of distant faceless men at night, but Tom felt less nervous and more excited by his situation. After all, this was a civilised country: what could happen to him in daylight on his way to work? They would not dare to do anything to him.

The bus station was concrete and dim and stank of diesel fumes. Buses hissed and roared under a high black ceiling, threatening any pedestrians that stepped out of line. Tom enjoyed a few silly moments dodging from stand to stand, confusing the poor man in the raincoat who soon disappeared into the crowd. Tom darted to the stand for the Roslin bus and waited five breathless minutes, nipping on to the waiting bus just as it was about to go. The driver scowled at him, but Tom felt particularly smug as he took his seat and the bus set off.

The journey was uneventful. He stepped off the bus at his usual stop, carefree, and walked up the empty lane to the lab gate. Eck the Door looked very surprised to see him.

'I was tellt you all had an away day the day, at one of they big conference centres,' he said distrustfully, as though Tom might be an illusion.

'Who told you that?'

'Professor Mackay himself.'

Good old Uncle George, covering up trouble as usual, thought Tom. He grinned at Eck.

'No one invited me,' he said. 'I'm only in to pick something up. I won't be a minute.'

He went down the corridor to the lab and let himself in. The silly notice was still on the door, and inside his notes on the work at the Infirmary remained in the filing tray on the desk. The samples he had brought back were obediently where he had left them: only the small pile of stray articles left by the scenes of crimes police had vanished.

He looked fruitlessly round the lab for a few seconds, then locked up and went back to Eck.

'Any idea who's been in our lab?' he asked casually.

'In it? I havena seen a'body. Except the cleaner, of course, this morning.'

'But she wouldn't take stuff off one of the benches, would she?'

'Ah, no way, Dr. Buchan, she'd know better than to do a'thing like that.'

Nevertheless Tom could think of no other solution, and the heap had looked very like rubbish. He sighed, and waving goodbye to Eck he left again. He was glad the risk coming here had not been as great as he had feared, for such a negative result.

It was past six: it had taken him an hour to get here, and if he walked down to the village chippy he could grab a sausage supper and eat it on the way back to town, and be at the Ceilidh House a bit before eight, time to get the drinks in before Gavin and Willie arrived. He was so blasé now about the threatening letter that he did not even look at the other passengers on the bus when it arrived, and munched his battered sausage happily, wiping his fingers on the chip paper. He walked from the bus station up North Bridge to the Tron Kirk and passed behind it to get to the Ceilidh House. It was barely dusk, and the High Street was lively with late tourists and pub goers, and on the newish little plaza at the back of the Tron the local café had tables out, making the most of the warm evening.

He was early, and did not feel like going into the pub just yet. He had bought a Snickers bar from the chip shop for pudding, and he pulled it out of his bag and unwrapped the end. He found himself a place on one of the long stone seats, and settled back to people-watch.

One of the city's ghost tours began to filter round the corner from the High Street, and late businessmen laughed together with brittle heartiness at a café table. As Tom relaxed, he saw a familiar figure come up from South Bridge and turned on to the plaza. It was crowned by a juvenile plait of blonde hair. It was Catriona.

'This city's getting awful small,' he said to her by way of greeting. She blinked, then looked resigned.

'The cure for SAIDS not so urgent as it was yesterday, then?'

'I told you – the demonstrators are making things difficult.'

'Oh, so you did. Sorry,' she added unexpectedly. 'I had my mind on my own problems.'

The ghost tour was coming closer, the diminutive guide pointing out some dim features high on the Tron Kirk tower. At the café table, one of the business men made a move to leave, pulling on his dark overcoat.

'No sign of Rob yet, then?'

'Adrian thinks he's in Fife. He thinks, on reflection, that what Rob said as he ran out was not 'wife' or 'life' but 'Fife.'' She sighed.

'And you?' Another business man had risen now, joining his companion.

'I spent the afternoon going through a Fife postcode book. Did I tell you, I thought maybe that 5PM was the end of a postcode, not a time at all?'

Tom opened his mouth to agree. Then something he saw behind Catriona made him freeze. The two business men were coming towards him, curiously focussed. And, detaching himself quietly from the back of the ghost tour, was a tall, hooded figure, wearing a black cloak.

'Oh, shit,' said Tom. Under the dark overcoats of the business men he thought – was he hysterical? – he saw bulges under the armpit, reminiscent of something in *Reservoir Dogs*. The ghost tour guide looked puzzled as the hooded man strode away from her. Tom tried to stand up. His knees seemed unsure. Then the nearest business man began to unbutton his jacket. Tom found his feet, and flew.

Catriona ran beside him, clearly not sure what he was running from but prepared to think something was dangerous. They broke out together on to South Bridge and headed for the top of North Bridge, at the other side of the traffic lights. The red man shone accusingly. They darted across, blared at by a taxi, and kept going.

'Look,' said Tom breathlessly, 'you're all right. It's me they're after.'

'Oh, aye, that's fine, then,' Catriona gasped. 'I'll just drop back and ask them if it's okay if I just go home.'

Before them, between the tall buildings, the broad, well-lit ramp of North Bridge opened up. Tom felt he was just going to roll to the bottom of it like a golf ball.

'Carlton Hotel?' said Catriona suddenly.

'What?'

'Hide in the Carlton. Call police. Can't touch us there.'

'Never get across the street.' He waved at the fast traffic. 'Life's not like the movies,' he added, as the option of the Carlton Highland slipped by on the other side of the road. He glanced back. They were holding their pursuers at a distance now, but what would happen when the adrenalin rush subsided? His heart was already walloping along faster than he liked. Then he had an idea.

Edinburgh's Old Town was full of little passages and long steep flights of steps, linking streets high and low, burrowing between precipitous tenements. Some were less salubrious than others, and the one he had in mind was one of the worst, but the Scotsman Steps were their only choice from here if they did not want to run all the wide, exposed way down North Bridge to Princes Street. They reached the Scotsman building even as he thought this, and he grabbed Catriona's arm and yanked her round the corner, into the entrance of the dark stair.

She gasped, but did not say anything as she followed him into the stinking darkness. Steps followed all too quickly behind them. But the advantage of this stairs was that it twisted round and round as it descended to Market Street below. The disadvantage was that it served as toilet and bedroom to some of Edinburgh's choicest down and outs. The smell was striking, and Tom's feet stumbled over empty bottles and damp blankets in his headlong flight. He ran heedless, mesmerised by the endless steps, until suddenly there was a bang, a sharp metallic thud that made his ears sting. It was followed by a whine, and Catriona gave a surprised cry and missed her footing. She fell against him, just at a corner: he managed to save himself on the wall ahead of him, grabbing Catriona with one arm to stop her tumbling past him. Then they were off again, and in a few seconds they were running out on to Market Street.

'Where, now?' he asked, almost to himself.

'Waverley,' said Catriona at once. The back entrance to Waverley Station was just along the street, and they flung themselves inside, finding themselves in a long, low corridor. At the far end were the stairs down to the main concourse.

Their pursuers must have had more trouble with the steps than they had had: Tom and Catriona hurled themselves all the way to the stairs before the men appeared at the Market Street entrance. These stairs were broad and easy, with only a few wandering train travellers to dodge. But their hunters were gaining again, and when Tom glanced back this time the men in suits were at the top of the stairs. He pushed Catriona ahead of him out on to the station concourse.

'What's the next train?' he demanded.

'Where to?'

'Anywhere.'

They looked up at the huge departures board.

'Look,' said Catriona, 'Platform 12 to Stirling and Dunblane.'

'Go for it,' hissed Tom, and they ran, slithering on the floor, down the side of the concourse. The train was waiting just around the corner, a morose-looking Scotrail official ready to blow his whistle. He jerked his head resignedly at Tom and Catriona, and Tom seized a door handle and pulled it open, shoving Catriona up before him. He slammed the door as the whistle blew and the train began to move slowly. They pressed their faces to the window. The two men in suits were flailing on to the platform, yelling at the Scotrail official, whose very shoulders had the set of a man who did not choose to be yelled at. The train gathered speed inexorably, and in a moment they found themselves prosaically looking for a couple of seats.

Tom threw himself down at the first vacant set of four, deeply regretting all those evenings he had avoided going to the gym. He wondered if he was going to have a heart attack, and it struck him how embarrassed he would be if such a thing happened in front of Catriona.

He tried to control his breathing, and pretended to stare out at the parallel lights of Princes Street so that he would not have to speak.

At last he decided that he was not going to die just yet, and he said,

'We should just have got a taxi at the station rank, and gone to the police station.'

There was no response, and he looked round at Catriona. She was clutching her arm, and had gone quite white.

'What's wrong?'

'It happened on the Scotsman Steps. I think ... I think I've been shot.'

Tom felt his jaw drop. Of course, the bang. How stupid – he hadn't even thought.

'How bad is it?' he whispered. He glanced around: the train was almost empty. Should he stand up and shout for a doctor?

Catriona looked as if she was trying to let go of her injured arm but could not quite bear to. Tom slid off his seat to kneel in front of her, scared stiff but desperate to see how bad the damage was. He pulled back the collar and shoulder of her fleece jacket, and gently, gently, peeled down the sleeve.

There was a lot of blood.

'Have you a hankie, or something?' asked Catriona, trying to pull herself together. Tom stared at her for what felt like seconds. Then he realised she was not going to cry, she just wanted something to stop the blood. He pulled out an unironed but fortunately unused large cotton handkerchief, and silently blessed his mother who gave him new ones every Christmas.

'Good, but probably not thick enough,' Catriona went on, faint but determined. 'I know. My hat's in my pocket. Pull it out and use it as a pad to stop the bleeding, and tie it on with the hankie. Wait – is there an exit wound, or just the entry?'

He gave her a desperate look, and felt cautiously round the back of her arm. It was sticky, the flesh cold, but it seemed to be unscathed. He found her cotton umpire's hat and did as she suggested, tightening the bandage until she told him to stop. Her dark red fleece was invisibly saturated with blood – it was impossible to tell how much she might have lost – but he tucked it back round her, remembering distantly that casualties should be kept warm.

'We have to get you to hospital,' he said at last. 'What's the next stop?'

'Linlithgow, I think,' she said, sinking lower in the seat, trying to find a comfortable position. Tom pushed himself back quickly out of her way, then thought to take off his own padded shirt and spread it over her as an extra layer. 'I don't know if there's a hospital there.'

'There's one at Falkirk,' said Tom, brightening. 'I used to know a research guy there.'

'Someone in A&E might be more useful at the moment,' Catriona remarked with a small smile. 'Might be an idea to see if the train actually stops at Falkirk. Otherwise it could be tricky to get off.'

Tom stood up and looked about, and spotted a girl with spiked black hair pushing a refreshment trolley. He felt in his pockets, suddenly remembering that they would have to buy tickets. The girl was not interested in that, and not much interested in Tom at all after he said he did not want to buy tea or coffee. She was able to tell him, though, that the next stop after Linlithgow would indeed be Falkirk Grahameston. Following her came the ticket inspector, who was pleased enough to sell Tom two singles to Falkirk and tactfully averted his eyes from the slumped form of Catriona on the opposite seat.

'So that was your chums the protestors,' she said, after the inspector had gone.

'Aye, that was them. And that's them away, I hope.'

'Will they follow the train?'

'I think they just want to keep me away from the lab. They're taking this jail fever thing very seriously.'

'The thing is,' said Catriona, struggling a little to face him, 'I'm sure I know one of them. It's just – when you see people out of context …'

'You mean the last time you saw him he wasn't chasing you through the dark streets of Edinburgh with a gun?' asked Tom with a grin. She grimaced back.

'I should hold my arm up and put my feet up on the seat,' she murmured. 'I'm sure that's what they taught us in our Guide First Aid badge.'

'Probably right,' agreed Tom. He leaned over and tried to rearrange his padded shirt to hold her arm at an angle, then pulled her feet up beside him on to the seat. She looked tired. Outside, the lights of the by-pass signalled the edge of Edinburgh. They had a long way to go.

They passed Linlithgow as Catriona slept. Tom glanced out at the floodlit castle and spiky church tower, then back at his travelling companion. Her colour was a little healthier, and sleep was lifting the dark circles there had been under her eyes. Her lips were softer, the hostile frown he was used to had gone, and at her temples her hair, as blonde as corn silk, swept smoothly back to that ridiculous plait, which lay like some kind of guardian serpent across her shoulders.

'Och, get real,' he muttered to himself, and turned to scowl at his reflection in the dark window.

The train did not stop at Polmont, but slid on through an increasingly urban landscape again. He watched industrial buildings going by, then sixties housing estates and older housing, dense and strewn with parks and fine kirks, punctuated with warm lit windows. It must be Falkirk. He tapped Catriona's boots gently, and to his relief she opened her eyes at once.

'I think we're nearly here,' he said. She pushed herself up and looked out of the window.

They took a taxi to Falkirk General, asking to be dropped at the Accident & Emergency Department, which the taxi driver seemed to know well. Inside, Saturday night was happening with a vengeance. A man with a face dripping from the ragged curved scar from a broken bottle sat alone staring into oblivion; two competing babies screamed at their anxious parents; a couple of drunks embraced and wept in the corner, and through the mêlée white coats and nurses' uniforms flashed, sometimes with stretchers, sometimes with wheelchairs, usually with the walking wounded. They reported to the receptionist, and Catriona said that the wound was a graze. They were directed to sit down.

'A graze?' Tom queried.

'I hope it is,' said Catriona, a bit tight-lipped.

'It's a bloody great hole,' said Tom hotly.

'Aye, well. If we have to sit around here explaining bloody great holes to the doctors, and then to the police, we'll never find Rob.'

Tom sat back in his seat, a hollow feeling inside. The adrenalin had gone. He had forgotten about Rob.

The receptionist must have considered the graze serious enough, because it was only twenty minutes before Catriona was called by a nurse with nicotined fingers to disappear down some shiny hospital corridor. Tom raised a hand to wave her goodbye, and bent forwards again to rest his elbows on his knees and wonder what to do next.

The obvious thing, he supposed, would be to go back to Edinburgh and try to get to Fife. He had a vague recollection that Crook of Devon was somewhere near Kinross, and the quickest way to get there was by the Forth Road Bridge and straight up the M90. What they would find when they got there was anyone's guess. It was a tiny place, blink and you'd miss it, and he could not understand why anyone setting up a countrywide protest would base it there. Unless of course they lived there, or something. And in these days of the Internet, he supposed, you could organise even a worldwide protest from somewhere like Crook of Devon. There had been big anti-capitalist riots in Seattle and Washington

D.C. and London, and those had been arranged on the web.

He became aware of a pair of flat white shoes on the floor in front of him, and looked up. A nurse smiled professionally down at him.

'Mr. Lindsay?'

'What? No, no.

She frowned.

'Oh. I thought you were sitting with her.'

'With whom?'

'Mrs. Lindsay.'

Something clicked belatedly in Tom's head.

'You mean Dr. Lindsay? That's her name, not mine.'

'Ah, she kept her own name! Sorry,' the nurse laughed. 'She's asking for you.'

Blinking, Tom rose and followed the nurse down the grey corridor and round the corner, where she showed him into the first of eight or nine cubicles curtained in green and white gingham. The nurse then hurried off.

Catriona was sitting on the high bed, legs dangling, with a fresh new bandage on her bare arm. Shocking in this context, her blood red fleece lay like a pool beside her on the white paper sheet. She looked up as he came in, severe and serious.

'How's it going?' he asked awkwardly.

'Ssh,' she whispered. 'I saw them.'

'Who?' But his heart was already flickering.

'The men who were chasing us. The doctor came into the cubicle, moving the curtain, and I saw them go past.'

'And did they see you?'

'No, I don't think so.'

'It's only a matter of time, though, if they're looking. Can we leave now?'

'I think so.'

He turned to pull back the curtain.

'Wait!' she snapped. He turned back. 'I know now where I've seen the thin one. It was when I saw him in a white corridor, I think.'

'Well? Don't keep me in suspense!'

'I've seen him at the dig. He works for Elysian Fields.'

Tom raised his eyebrows, thinking.

'Do you think it means anything?'

'He's a protestor against SAIDS cures in his spare time?'

Tom scowled at the floor.

'I don't see … But we'd better go.'

'Where?'

'I thought back to Edinburgh and over the Bridge to Fife.'

'Taxi back to the station, then.' She slid off the bed and picked up her jacket, pulling it on carefully over the bandage.

Tom slid the curtain back and instantly closed it again. He gestured frantically. The men in suits were outside, heads together in conversation.

Tom and Catriona looked at each other. Neither of them breathed. Then Catriona beckoned him to follow her.

The cubicles were divided from each other by the same gingham curtains. Moving quickly, she managed to slide into the next cubicle, fortunately empty, and across it into the third one, where a man lay unconscious on the narrow bed. Then they were flummoxed: the curtains curved out from the wall and around the front of the cubicle, so here there was no gap. They took a deep breath and stepped out into the corridor, not looking back but walking swiftly away from where they had seen the men. Ahead two corridors crossed: without speaking they both turned right. At the end of the corridor was a plastic door with darkness beyond. They ran for it.

Outside and round the corner they found themselves in a vast car park. They had no sooner ducked behind the nearest car than they heard the familiar heavy footsteps and peeped over the bonnet to see the two men in suits standing, dark and dramatic against the security lights, scanning the car park. Then they began to move slowly forward.

Tom and Catriona, bent more than double, edged away. A patch of shadow where one of the tall lights was broken let them scuttle to the next row back and hide again. The men in suits glanced at each other and then began to move apart, one strolling away from them, sideways, towards the front of the hospital and the main gate, and the other one still coming steadily forward, not rushing, looking carefully from side to side as he came.

Virtually on their hands and knees, Tom and Catriona moved back another row, then another, gradually at the same time heading away from the main gate behind on their left, where their first pursuer was now venturing into the car park again.

'Damn,' said Catriona under her breath. Tom looked at her, questioning. 'See what they're doing? They're shepherding us into that corner.

'Shit.' The car park was surrounded by three metre high wire fencing, and the only gate Tom could see was the main one. From here, they stood no chance of hailing a taxi. Catriona leaned towards his ear again.

'Can you hotwire a car?'

He looked at her. She seemed to be perfectly serious. He paused, and then nodded. He reached up and gently tried the door of the car beside them.

'No, not that one!' Catriona gasped, a bit too loud. They both froze, waiting to hear running feet. Nothing happened. She pointed at a sticker on the windscreen, 'Doctor on Call'.

'Aw, shit, Catriona, we're stealing a car. Why bring ethics into it?' He tried the car behind them. It was locked. He made a face at her, and, watching the approaching hunters, they quietly moved back another row.

The next car opened. Tom leaned in and eased the plastic panel off the steering column, feeling in the darkness for the ignition wires. Catriona crouched behind him, looking out for danger.

They both jumped when the engine sprang into life.

'There!' said Tom proudly, feeling he had justified his position as the male half of this team.

'Get in!' said Catriona. 'I'll get in the back.'

'Catriona ....' Said Tom suddenly, watching their hunters trying to locate the engine noise in the vast car par.

'What?' she snapped.

'I can't drive.'

'What?' She stared at him. He shrugged.

'Oh, for – ' She shoved him bodily into the passenger seat and flung herself into the driver's seat, getting the car moving almost before she had sat down. It was parked nose out, by good luck. Catriona slammed the door and they were off.

'Oh, two *very* annoyed heavies!' cried Tom in delight, looking back. The men in suits tried a run, but it was clearly pointless. 'Ahm, shouldn't you be changing up a gear about now?'

There was silence above the engine noise. He looked at Catriona. She was biting her lips so hard they were pale in the orange car park lights.

'What?'

'Gears,' she said, through gritted teeth. 'Arm. Handbrake was enough.'

He glanced down. Her left arm, the wounded one, was flopped weakly in her lap. The car continued in a pointed but stately progress in first gear.

'Can you change gear?' she asked, a hint of desperation in her voice.

'Ah ... think so.'

'Can you find second when I say so?' He nodded, trying to see the little map on the top of the gearstick. They were at the main gate. She slowed down, waited for a passing car, then pulled out, accelerating again. 'Ready? Three, two, one – now!'

He slipped the lever back into neutral, gulped, and pulled it back a stage further. The cogs bit, and the car gained speed smoothly. He laughed in relief.

'Wey hey!'

'How the hell,' said Catriona bitterly, 'did I land myself in a mess like this with the only man in the western world above the age of fourteen who can't drive?'

'I hotwired the car, didn't I?'

'I think that was just to get my hopes up. Are you ready for third, or have we exhausted your technical potential?'

He found third more easily.

'Next time I'll hotwire an automatic for you.'

'I'd be grateful.'

'Any particular colour?'

'Don't be petty.' There was a long silence as she tried to maintain a speed through traffic that would allow her to stay in third. Tom kept his hand on the gear stick, sweating slightly, ready for instructions.

'Second!' He shoved it with an awful shriek and Catriona looked like thunder. Tom was faintly surprised that the car in front did not spontaneously combust. 'Where are we going, anyway?' she asked, as they waited for the junction lights to change.

'I thought it would be best if we went back to the Forth Road Bridge. You wanted to go to Fife, you said, and so do I. I think I know where the protestors are based.'

'And it's in Fife? That's funny. First,' she added, and waited for him to fumble the stick into place before she moved off smoothly. 'Second. You're improving. You know I said I had spent the afternoon looking through a postcode book? I went back to take a closer look at Rob's whiteboard, and as far as I could see there was a KY at the beginning of where you might expect a postcode to be if it ended in that 5PM we saw.'

'KY is certainly Fife,' agreed Tom.

'I couldn't work out what came in between, though,' she went on. 'And third. And fourth. But there were only a few places that ended in 5PM. There was –'

'Was Crook of Devon one of them?' asked Tom suddenly. She turned to stare at him.

'Actually, it was. How did you know? I've never even heard of it.'

'I think we might be looking for the same place. This is too confusing.' He explained about the missing scrap of paper as they manoeuvred themselves on to the motorway.

'Does that gearbox have fifth?' Catriona asked, and Tom struggled to see in the dim light.

'I think so.'

'Then fifth. So you think the protests have something to do with Crook of Devon, and there is a possibility that that was where Rob was going to after the dig. And you say those men were chasing you, yet I recognised one of them as being from Elysian Fields. What's the link? And which of us are they after? And why? And what,' she added, her voice shaking slightly, 'what have they done with Rob?'

'The link could be Roslin,' said Tom after a moment's thought. 'The Establishment, the dig and Elysian Fields are all there.'

'The traffic's very heavy for this time of night,' Catriona said absently. 'Is there a radio? Switch it on and see if you can get any travel news.'

Tom could manage radios. He fiddled with the controls and ended up with something that sounded like Radio Forth, just about news time.

'... died today. He was the forty-eighth victim of the mysterious SAIDS infection since the Millenium. The youngest person to contract the so-called jail fever, a child in Edinburgh Royal Infirmary, said to be stable but still very seriously ill.'

'You can't get away from it, can you?' Tom sighed. 'But at least the girl's still hanging on.'

'On a related topic,' continued the newsreader, 'the pathologist who has carried out the post mortems on all the Scottish victims of jail fever, Dr. Joanne Eastleigh, was killed in a hit and run accident today near her home in the Marchmont area of Edinburgh. Dr. Eastleigh, who ...'

'What?' said Tom and Catriona at once. They stared at each other.

'Her poor wee daughter,' said Catriona. 'Dr. Eastleigh's husband - I think he left her about two years ago, ran off with his practice nurse to the States. The child's only about three.'

'You don't think,' said Tom slowly, not wishing to appear completely paranoid, 'that this might be – connected?'

'Connected? Dr. Eastleigh doesn't work in Roslin.'

'No, but think about it.' Tom was getting quite excited. 'We four were all there yesterday – not in Roslin, I mean just all together, at the Infirmary and then at that weird museum store place at Granton, when Rob realised that Alf had gone missing. And then you and Dr. Eastleigh and I were together at your department. And now Rob is missing, and we're on the run, and Dr. Eastleigh is dead.'

Catriona was silent, biting her lip. Into the pause the radio carried on speaking.

'And AA Roadwatch has told us that there are huge tailbacks on the Forth Road Bridge this evening. Police are attending the scene, trying to clear the blockage.'

'Oh, shit,' she said, and began to look around. 'Where's the next turn off? I can't believe we're in a stolen car.'

Tom switched off the radio and rooted around in the glove compartment.

'There's a map here. Where are we?'

'Your guess is as good as mine. Somewhere between Falkirk and the Edinburgh bypass. Oh, look: there's the sign for Linlithgow. Let's turn around here.'

'But turn around and do what?'

'We want to get to Fife, don't we? If they've killed Dr. Eastleigh, what will they do to Rob?'

'So how do you intend to cross the Forth? Swim it?' asked Tom.

'There are other bridges, you know. How do you think people managed before they built the bridge?'

'Wasn't there a ferry?' asked Tom. Catriona sighed.

'There was a ferry. There is also a bridge at Kincardine: I suggest we go for that. We could be a long time waiting for the ferry: it closed in about 1964.' She saw the countdown signs for the Linlithgow slip road ahead, and reached through the steering wheel with her good hand to flick the indicator switch. 'Stand by for the gears,' she added.

They had not tackled a roundabout before. The gearbox groaned its protest, and Catriona scowled as Tom wrestled with the gearstick. Her injured arm twitched as if longing to do the job properly. They sailed round the roundabout majestically in first gear and finally found second on the slip road back towards Falkirk. Catriona glanced into the rear view mirror as they filtered on to the motorway again.

'That's funny,' she said, half to herself.

'What?'

'That car was behind us before. It must have turned at that roundabout, too.'

Tom resisted the urge to turn in his seat and looked instead in the wing mirror on his side. The car behind them was large, dark and discreet. It was difficult to see, but it looked as though the men in the front seats were wearing suits.

'Could be our friends,' he said, trying to sound casual. 'Could be plain clothes police. Could be a couple of confused businessmen out for a drive, trying to find a different way over the Forth.'

'Could be time for evasive manoeuvres,' said Catriona. Tom waited.

'Well, what are you going to do?' he asked at last.

'I was hoping you might have an idea. I have to say the ones you've come up with so far have been pretty good,' he admitted, and was rewarded with a surprisingly bashful smile.

'Ah. Well, the only tactics I know are the ones where you stick to brightly lit streets and drive to the nearest police station. I don't think I really want to do that in a stolen car.'

'We could try to explain …'

'We should have gone back and tried to explain to Inspector McAlester. But we still need to get to Fife.'

They drove in silence for a while, both lost in thought. Tom could feel on the back of his neck the eyes from the car behind, and he could not resist checking every now and again to see if it was still there. It always was. Not immediately behind, not all the time, but always in the range of the wing mirror, as if attached there by a rubber band.

VI

It was a day or two's hard walking in the drizzling rain before Eliot finally arrived where he had intended, on the hill above the harbour of North Queensferry. The great expanse of the grey Forth lay before him, the silvery sea to his left, and ahead in the distance the hills of Midlothian blue-green and undulating.

Unpractised at this kind of thing, Eliot tucked himself uncomfortably amidst some gorse, and settled down to watch what was happening. Below him, the little village, full of its own importance simply because it was the way to somewhere else, bustled about the ferry. The boat was almost the same size as the one in which he had travelled from Norway, though it looked more sound. Eliot knew that looks could be deceptive with boats.

He sneezed, and wiped his nose on his sleeve, smelling the brine in his coat and the brine from the sea below. He still had a slight ague from his night in the hedge, though the hot broth and bannocks had driven off anything worse. The last couple of nights he had found first a barn, then an outhouse, to sleep in, and had fared much better, living lightly off the remains of the food that the monks had given him. He planned to have a hot pie before boarding the ferry, for he could remember a good pieman in the village whose meat rarely caused problems. But before he could think of that, he needed to see that the village was safe for him.

From his vantage point, he could actually see the pieman, plying his very successful trade to the travellers boarding the ferry from a neat little stall with an awning over it. One or two pedlars hung around, hoping that some passenger would suddenly recall a need for thread or buttons, or a present for the wife or the mistress, or the latest rude song ill-penned on a scrap of paper. Eliot had done a bit of that himself in his time, building things up, when days had been bad. It was a young man's trade, though, standing out in the rain, walking miles from place to place to sell a scrap of ribbon or a spool of thread.

Around the traders were local women, benefitting from the interest in the ferry. They had bright shawls over their heads against the rain, and did not linger to chat, darting out to the quay from their little houses. It was hard to follow their movement, like birds in the trees in spring, flitting around each other in incomprehensible patterns. Eliot scowled at himself for this frivolous thought, then laughed. He was growing soft.

Then he caught sight of something that froze the smile on his face. The awning on the pie stall flapping damply, and showed the edge of someone who was standing behind it. He was tall and wore a dark cloak, and Eliot knew, without having to be told, that this was the Sheriff's man. He would never be allowed to reach the ferry.

Suddenly he realised how his acquaintance in Boulogne must have felt. Unable to leave, unable to communicate, with the power to help if only he could have reached the person who needed help, he had instead sunk into the inns and alehouses of Boulogne, desperate to find someone to tell. And Eliot had not believed him, had refused to help. He sat in his gorse bush and shuddered at the thought of what had happened to the spy that night, and of what might in the end happen to him. And at last, helpless, he turned and crawled away, back up the hill and out of sight.

He slumped against a rock over the brow of the hill and thought. His only real option now was to go to Stirling. It was a long way, but there was no other reliable crossing of the Forth from here to Stirling Bridge. And also, if he started now, while the sheriff's man was still expecting him to take the ferry, he might make good progress and reach Stirling long before they thought he was thinking about it. Filled with a new energy, he slithered down the rest of the hill on the wet grass and back to the path he had been following, turning west again to follow the line of the Forth. No pie, then, he thought sadly, and set himself to remember all the things he knew about Stirling.

VII

'Kincardine Bridge,' said Tom, pointing to the motorway signboard.

'That's the one,' said Catriona.

'Toll bridge?' asked Tom, feeling in his pockets for change.

'No, not as far as I remember. They're still there, aren't they?' She jerked her head back towards the sleek black shadow behind them. 'Why aren't they doing anything?'

'Not much they can do out here, I suppose. They'll wait till we go somewhere where we'll have to stop.'

'Like Kincardine, you mean?'

'I don't know the place. Doesn't the road just go through, like the Forth Road Bridge?'

Catriona laughed shortly.

'No, it's a tiny place. We might well have to stop: parked cars by the side of the road, and so on. And the police training college on the other side of the river,' she added, suddenly nervous again.

'Is that so?' asked Tom, casually interested. Then, struck by an idea, he said, 'What does it look like?'

'I don't know,' said Catriona. 'There's woodland or shrubbery or something round it, as far as I remember. There's a gateway and a big blue and white sign saying 'Tullieallan Police College, or something like that.'

Tom stared ahead, thinking hard.

'And is there a gate in the gateway?'

Catriona frowned.

'Can't remember. I can't picture one, no.' She glanced at Tom, then with automatic caution up at the rear view mirror. The dark car was still there. 'Why the sudden interest?'

'I think we should pay a call to the police college,' he said, with a smile. He felt happier than he had for nearly an hour.

Kincardine was asleep in the dark, the street lamps making the houses and shops golden orange in their pools of light. The bridge was well signposted, and they drove through steadily, with only the occasional oath from Catriona at Tom's gear changes. The dark car followed them at a discreet distance, and was only one car behind them as they slid on to the flat bridge. Tom watched in the mirror as the shadows of the bridge's upperworks flickered across the windscreens behind them, and in a moment they were over and away. The dark car followed.

Just around the corner, Catriona snapped,

'Second!' and Tom, ready for it, flicked the lever across and in. In that moment Catriona turned hard right. Headlights flashed past the blue and white sign, and their car bumped and surged up the dark driveway of the Scottish Police training college. They followed the drive around the corner, allowing their tail lights to vanish from sight, then Catriona braked. With a certain amount of churning they turned the car between them, and it slipped quietly back down again to the main road. They took a good look in each direction. There was no sign of the sleek black car. The road was empty. Catriona let in the clutch and they darted back across Kincardine Bridge, laughing like idiots.

'Where, now?' asked Tom, when he had got his breath back.

'Yes, what exactly has that achieved?' asked Catriona, 'apart from making them angry?' She had sobered up so fast she seemed embarrassed by her lapse into laughter.

'Well, with any luck they'll think we've gone to report them, hand ourselves over to a hundred police cadets.'

'Hm. Well, presumably we still can't go back to the Forth Road Bridge. So the next one upstream is Stirling.'

'Upstream ... it's like going back in time, to when the geography mattered.'

'It still does,' she said shortly. 'Why do you think we're looking for a bridge in the first place?' Tom heard her tone of voice, and bit back what he had been about to say. Could she not allow herself any relaxation? He wondered how often she laughed. Instead, he said casually,

'So what do we know about Stirling, then?'

VIII

Eliot permitted himself a long, yellow-fanged grin. He felt pleased with his progress. From the hill above the ferry he had moved with speed and decision towards Dunfermline, an abbey town where one more stranger would not be much remarked. He kept his head down but ate and drank well, staying unobtrusively at the abbey guest hall for the night, and making his way out with the crowd the next day, an innocent traveller seeing the sights. All the same, he kept his wits about him, and saw no sign of any in pursuit of him.

There had been royalty once at Dunfermline, when Scotland had her own king: Eliot approved of kings. They tended to spend money. A country without a king was an uncertain place, where even the rich kept their gold in their coffers and the poor kept their heads down: not the place for a merchant.

From Dunfermline it was about twenty miles to Stirling. He broke it in two. On the first day, starting well on a hearty breakfast he reached

Alloa by nightfall. Here the Forth was curling, but flowed fast: he supposed he could have hired a boat to take him across, but he had no wish to draw attention to himself.

He stayed the night in the only inn, a dubious place run by a slatternly woman not much used to guests. Eliot saw the fleas in the bed before ever he was bitten and made himself a nest of his coat on the bare floor instead, glad that the woman had not exerted herself to put down rushes which would probably have been infested, too. He slept well after his exertions, and rose only slightly stiffly for breakfast.

But there was no breakfast to be had there that day. One of the other guests, a tall man in a dark coat, had been knifed in his bed. The landlady had taken it as a personal affront, and was running about the kitchen screaming, while the maids, none of them over twelve years of age, wept hysterically by the cold fireplace. The other guests tried to prevail upon Eliot to stay with them and together call the sheriff – not the Fife sheriff now, but equally alarming to Eliot – but he saw too much of the dead man's appearance in himself to want to linger. The whole nasty business delayed his departure, and when he was at last on the road he found himself to be so hungry that he had to stop for a substantial dinner in a tiny place called Tullibody, with Stirling still a few miles off. Further, as it turned out, on foot, for he had to skirt the flailing loops of the Forth on its broad flat river plain, and find a way between it and the woody headlands above it. He could see Stirling for a good while before he reached it, but at last the crossing was in view, and he paused by the side of the road, cautious now, to see if this bridge, like the ferry, was being watched.

IX

'I'm starving,' Tom announced, as they reached the outskirts of Stirling. For once, Catriona agreed with him.

'I've had no dinner,' she said.

'Nor me.'

'You were just finishing chips when I saw you at the Tron – what was that, just a snack?' Tom had forgotten that: it seemed like days ago. 'Anyway, the car's starving, too – we need some petrol. Any sign of that black car?'

Tom squirmed round and peered behind them.

'No. It's not very original, is it? A black car. If I were a bad guy I'd drive a nice quiet blue or red car, much less obvious.'

'If you could drive, of course,' Catriona added. Tom looked

sideways at her.

'How's the arm, then?'

'I wish I'd hung around for the painkillers they promised.'

'They might have paracetamol at the petrol station.'

'I'd rather have aspirin.'

'It's bad for you: you'd be better off with paracetamol.'

'Don't tell me what's good and bad for me!' Catriona shouted.

There was a shocked silence. Tom could hear the echo of her cry resounding in the little car. What the hell was wrong with the woman? True, she was stunning to look at, but at this rate she was looking much too much like hard work.

With only a muttered series of gear changes, they pulled into a petrol station and Tom got out stiffly to fill the tank. At least he could manage that level of car technology, he thought grimly. Catriona sat in silence behind the wheel, staring at nothing in particular. Tom went to pay, and returned with a packet of soluble aspirin, a bottle of mineral water and a bar of chocolate, all of which he wordlessly handed over to Catriona. She took them and gazed at the little aspirin packet as if she hadn't seen one before.

'I'm sorry,' she said at last, and sounded it. Tom nodded, not trusting herself to speak. 'Didn't you get yourself anything to eat?'

'I didn't fancy yesterday's BLTs. Can we park and go and find a chippy, or something?'

'Sure. I could do with stretching my legs, too.'

They were back to the strained politeness they had found themselves with yesterday, but started the car off smoothly enough and, after a few minutes of hesitant driving, parked near the station. Catriona took two aspirin and carefully broke the chocolate bar in two. She offered half of it to Tom, who accepted it, and smiled. Catriona smiled back, rather stiffly, and they left the car and headed up into town.

It was completely dark now, and the streets, frequented by late takeaway collectors and pub leavers, were patterned gold and brown in the street lamps. Most of the food shops were closing up for the night, and they had to walk some distance up the hill before they eventually found a Spartan, formica-fitted Chinese prepared to provide them with a couple of reasonable meals. They took what they could get, and found a seat in a little triangular park on which to eat them. There was a road high behind them and another below them in front, but they were quiet, lined with venerable stone buildings. Beyond the lower ones, they could just see the flat, curling valley of the Forth, the shadowy wooded hill with the mock ruined Wallace Monument spiking the top, and the dim outlines of low mountains beyond.

'All this just to get to the other side of that little river,' Catriona mused. Tom grunted, his mouth full of beef and black bean sauce. 'I wonder if I'm right: if Rob is really there?'

Tom swallowed.

'Is – ah – is there something between you two?' he asked, trying to sound concerned and sympathetic. Catriona looked down at her dinner.

'Not sure,' she said at last. 'I mean, I like him –' (you're on your own there, thought Tom) ' – but I – well, I thought recently maybe it was going to be more than that.' She looked sideways at him, but there was none of her usual hostility. She seemed still contrite after her outburst over the painkillers. Tom felt encouraged.

'Do you want there to be?' he asked. She looked away again.

'Not sure,' she said again. She sighed. 'You see, there was someone – someone very important – for years … and I'm still not sure …'

'Oh, right,' said Tom, understanding at least in part. 'How long ago did you split up?'

'We didn't. He died.'

Tom's throat was seized with embarrassment. He could not think of a reply.

'He was an archaeologist too,' she went on, still staring down at the curling Forth. 'We met as undergraduates. He worked in Africa, in the north – not Egyptian sites, other stuff further west. The last time he came back, he wasn't well: nothing serious, we thought at first. You always get something, particularly on a dig: they're not usually near a five-star hotel. But he went to the doctor, and the doctor was worried enough to take samples and send them to the London School of Hygiene and Tropical Medicine. They said he was fine, but he wasn't. He was getting worse. Vomiting, diarrhoea, sweating: it was as if the more fluid left him, the faster it became. He drank gallons of water, took salt tablets, all the stuff, and the epidemiologists' she said the word with a careful lack of emphasis, 'kept saying they could find nothing, there was nothing they could do. He grew weaker and weaker, and they took him into the Infirmary. He weighed six stone, and he was a tall man. And he just went on getting worse: they put him on drips, they gave him blood transfusions. He was three stone when he died. You wouldn't believe in this day and age that a man in a Western country could die like that. The bloody flux, that's what they called it centuries ago.'

She broke off, and silence fell between them again. It was the longest speech he had ever heard her make. And perhaps she told everyone about this after only a couple of days' acquaintance (a couple of days? It seemed like years), but he had the definite impression that she did not, that this outburst was as uncharacteristic as it seemed. As if to confirm his thoughts, she added,

'I don't usually go on like this. But I felt I owed you an explanation, at least. I have a low opinion of epidemiologists – there were one or two in particular that were very casual about the whole thing – but that doesn't mean that I can scream at you for offering me a paracetamol.' She gave a little half-grin, her face still rueful, not quite meeting his eyes.

'Ah, don't worry about it,' Tom said, struggling to find neutral words. 'We've had a stressful couple of days between us. And you were in a lot of pain.' He finished his takeaway and looked round at her. 'You not eating?' he added hopefully.

'Slowly.' She was having difficulty holding the foil dish in her left hand. Tom lifted it away from her grasp and held it out at a better level, watching her as she spooned up the rest of her food, eating it neatly and gratefully. Funny woman, he thought, but maybe she has reason to be.

X

Eliot watched the bridge for over an hour, until it began to grow dark. The bridge lay, a little arched, just where the river narrowed before a bend: he had not seen it since before the great battle of which the monks had told him, when Wallace had split the English forces at the bridge and his soldiers had picked them off in batches as they crossed, like blackberries off a bramble. You had to admire the man: and anyone who could bring some kind of pride to this woebegotten country had to be of some use.

He saw no sign of anyone showing much interest in the bridge or the people crossing it, busy now to go home before nightfall. Up above the river, the rounded castle sat on its long crag, with little lights beginning to pierce the heavy walls. Below it, and spreading back the way he had come, downstream, was the town itself. Behind it all lay forests, the banked and ditched hunting demesne that belonged to the castle. It would have made a good place to hide for a while for anyone with more country sense than Eliot, as long as you were not had up for poaching. It would be a leafy and less frequented place at this time of year. But he would find no information there. He had to go on to the town, where he would start to ask one or two discreet questions, and find himself some dinner.

He crossed the bridge without incident, and began to make his way up the long road from the bridge into the town. The castle surged slowly by on his right, and then he was amongst tall buildings – not as tall as the mountainside that faced you on an Edinburgh street, oh, no! – but three or four storeys, some of them, for where royalty went a court followed, and there had been royalty, English and Scots, in Stirling Castle. And courts had money, and money brought merchants, as well he knew.

At length he came to a place where two streets ran parallel but one a little above the other, the upper one leading back to the gates of the castle itself. The inn he chose was not the first he came to, nor the quietest. He picked a busy, cheery looking place, where he felt that stabbings in the middle of the night would be least likely. The landlady was large and red and looked as though she could deal comfortably with any threat to her business or her guests. It was probably a bit more expensive than some of the places he had passed and rejected, but he had plenty of gold left and anyway, it was worth it.

A pig was roasting on the spit and he dined well off it, jammed on a four-man bench with five other men, each of them twisted sideways to reach the table, hungry fingers clutching at greasy pork and fresh, crumbly bread. There were chickens, too, who had lived well off corn and laid down their contented lives to let others live well off them. A couple of fine-looking girls bounced, smiling and joking, among the diners, filling tankards from tall ale jugs, bringing more bread and more pork to the tables, kicking stray bones over towards the walls out of the way.

There was a man across the table from him who had the tanned skin and distant eyes that Eliot had once known to be his own – a traveller, used to strange sights and foreign skies. It was not like him to strike up conversations with strangers, but the man, catching his eye, held it, and stared at him in uncertainty.

'Forgive me, sir, but have you lately been abroad – in France, perhaps?'

Eliot was wary, but saw no benefit in denying the man's guess.

'I have, sir. If I met you there I do not remember.'

Not put off by Eliot's shortness, the man gave a brief laugh.

'No, sir, I do not doubt it. We met only for a moment, and I was beardless then. You, too, if I may venture, have changed your appearance.'

Eliot took a mouthful of chicken, and did not comment. No one around them in the noisy room was paying them any attention at all.

'We met,' said the man, nothing daunted, 'in the company of a loyal Scot.'

Eliot was incautious enough to give the man a hard stare. His acquaintance, the spy in Boulogne on whose posthumous behalf he was here at all, had always, to Eliot's thorough disgust, described himself as a loyal Scot. The other man nodded a little.

'Damned hot in here, eh? Maybe a breath of air?'

Eliot sat back, and pondered. Friend or foe? How could he tell? The ale was strong and he was tired, and though everyone else seemed to be enjoying themselves tremendously, the noise and heat and rich food gradually built up until his head ached as if it was going to burst. Dinner was over, anyway, and he took up his ale mug and, with some difficulty, extracted himself from the crowd on the bench and squeezed his way through the room to the door, ducking to avoid the low beams.

Outside, the air was clear and the noise following them from the inn seemed to echo in his ears, throbbing. They found a bench against the wall and sat, the man wrapping about him a thick, dark cloak.

'How was our friend when you left him?' he asked.

'Dead,' said Eliot. The other man twitched, but otherwise remained expressionless.

'Are you here on his behalf?'

'Look,' said Eliot, turning to face him, angry at his own uncertainty, 'you were there, you met him and you were coming back here. Why didn't he give the damned job to you? Didn't he trust you?'

The other man blinked, and said,

'Not so loud! He did trust me, yes. And he trusted you, and told me of his hopes that you would be able to help him. But I left France just as you arrived in Boulogne, and it was by no means certain that I would return to Scotland. I have been in London, you see – not an ideal route for such dispatches as you carry.'

'Oh,' said Eliot, and turned back again to stare at the street.

'But,' said the other man, quietly, 'as it happens I am now in a position to be able to help you. You are seeking, I think –' and here he glanced about carefully, 'a certain leader who is in hiding?' Eliot did no more than nod. No one had trusted him before, and he had to be careful. 'Then you must make for the Lothians,' said the man. 'There is a river there, the North Esk – do you know it?'

'I have some idea of where it is,' Eliot replied, dourly. He had hoped to be heading for a town.

'Somewhere on that,' said the other man, shrugging.

'Is that the best you can do?' asked Eliot in disbelief. The man's care and secrecy had made him hope for more.

'Ah. Well, yes, really. I think it's north east of Penicuik, maybe south of Eskbank? Or thereabouts. That's where I would start, anyway.

'Where you would start? Holy Virgin, I'm wondering why I started at all!'

'Well,' said the man, 'I suppose you could hand the papers over to me …'

'Oh, aye,' said Eliot, surveying him coldly, 'and what makes you think I trust you further than I could spit?'

The man, a head shorter than Eliot, looked slightly nervous.

'I think I'd better go now, then,' he said. 'I'll be staying here if you need me ...' and he rose, clutching his cloak, and returned to the inn.

Eliot sat on for a bit, setting his mug beside him, polishing his spoon thoughtfully with a piece of bread. Could he trust the man? For all he tried, he could think of no reason why not. If he had wanted to kill him and steal the papers, why go to the trouble of a long conversation? Knives were more expressive than words. He thought the man was probably genuine. When he had put the spoon away in his satchel, and washed the bread down with the last of his ale, he rose and decided to walk to the end of the street and back again, to stretch his legs.

XI

'Come on, then, we'd better be going,' said Catriona, as Tom tipped the empty takeaway dishes into a bin. 'We've only to get down there and cross the Forth and then there'll be no further obstacles.'

'Apart from whatever we find at Crook of Devon,' he said. She looked at him sideways, worried. 'I mean, if they have kidnapped Rob, or if he's there to give them what for for nicking your old body, they – whoever they may be – might not want to give him up that easily.'

'I know,' she agreed. 'Let's go.' She stood up and turned around, then gasped. Tom twisted to look. On the road above them, the one that led up to the castle, a dark car had just parked, and two men in suits got out.

'Holy shit, here we go again!' muttered Tom. The men were looking straight at them. There was no one else about. There was nothing else to do. They ran.

XII

When the men broke out of the shadows, he was ready for them. He ran.

He had not thought that he was really paying attention to anything beyond his aching head, but something as he passed the lane end caught his attention, some minuscule movement, and his hackles rose like a hunting dog's. All that remained was to decide whether to stay and fight or to flee, and the appearance of the fourth man swung that decision. He ran.

He ran back towards the inn, but one of them was too fast for him at that side. He had to swerve sharply to avoid a snatching hand, and clutched his coat about him to stop them catching it. The length of his legs was giving him an advantage for now, but he did not knew where he was going. He slipped, staggered and grabbed at the wall to hold him up, found he was at the end of another lane and plunged down it, bouncing from one wall to the other, staggering into the darkness.

XIII

'How well do you know Stirling?' Tom panted. The little lanes and narrow streets had kept them safe so far, tripping and stumbling in the confusing glow of the street lights. The men behind them were either making no better progress or, more worryingly, were simply waiting to tire them out, up and down Baker Street and King Street, round by the Dumbarton Road and up by the Corn Exchange again. Tom peered for the street names to try to keep some track of where they were, how they could get back to the car.

They could not go much longer. Catriona was clearly fitter than he was, but she was sweating with pain. His legs felt like jelly. And still their pursuers came, almost silently, through the alleys of the old town.

XIV

The blundering series of alleys, lit by the occasional pool of light from a window, led Eliot up and down from street to street, sometimes drawing away from his pursuers, sometimes feeling them almost on his heels. He ran breathlessly, but they were silent in pursuit, even their footsteps light on earth and stone.

He dodged around yet another corner, completely lost now, and immediately tripped and fell. He landed hard in the gutter, winded. Wild-eyed, he stared into the darkness, trying to see them before they fell upon him, but miraculously the blows never came. Soft footsteps paused, moved back, went past the head of the alley again. He pictured them like dark hounds, sniffing to catch an evasive scent.

He looked about him, breath back now, still lying in the gutter. Just a little further down the alley in which he had fallen was a howff – he had not even noticed the lights or the noise until now, or the stink of bad ale. He might not be safe in there, but at least he could confuse them for a while. He rolled gently, carefully, on to his stomach, retching at the stench of whatever it was he had fallen into. He listened. There was no sound from behind him. He rose slowly on to his knees and, keeping low in the gutter, he crawled like a fox in the shadows of the wall, slinking towards the howff doorway. At the last moment, in the last inch of shadow, he rose quickly and slipped inside.

There was a cry from the street, and with a desperate leap he vanished into the crowd.

XV

They were back in the lanes again, up nearer the castle now, near the old jail. Feeling their pursuers drop back a little on the hill, Tom had surge of confidence: maybe they would make it after all. He ducked into a dark alley, sloping downwards, and Catriona followed – too closely, as it happened. He tripped over a stinking heap of binbags that clung to his legs and she fell on top of him, knocking a precarious stack of empty cooking oil drums. They toppled, held, then crashed resoundingly on the cobbles and began to roll, bouncing, down this alley and one that forked off it.

Tom felt Catriona flatten herself over him, tense and still. Running footsteps approached from the street, paused, then came cautiously into the alley. Tom steeled himself for an attack. He tried to hold his breath, afraid that the least thing might give them away. The darkness was thick and smothering.

And then, miraculously, the footsteps passed, running lightly in pursuit of the distant oil cans. They waited, lying in the binbags for as long as they could bear, then gently detached themselves from the rubbish, if not from the stench.

'You know, I used to be quite fond of this fleece,' Catriona muttered.

'They'll come back when they realise they've lost us. What's that?' asked Tom, half-peering, half-straining to hear, entirely trying to ignore the fact that his legs were sticky. Catriona considered.

'Trad jazz,' she remarked at last. '"Flying Home", I think it's called.'

'This must be the entrance,' said Tom, and then rather stupidly noticed that there was in fact a sign up, saying so. 'The Fat Domino Jazz Club,' it said, with below it, 'Tonight: Donny Jamieson's Hot Jazz Five. Tickets £3 on the door.'

'I think I hear them coming back,' said Catriona, staring down the alley.

'Got six quid?' asked Tom.

XVI

The howff was popular.

The wooden benches were full to bending point, and people stood and lounged around them, tankards in their fists, faces beaming scarlet in the light of the filthy tallow candles and crusie lamps. The fire was a redundant heater but useful for cooking the chickens: the fowl, once cooked, were hurled off the spit on to the tables where the drinkers tore the legs off and ate avidly, spitting bones into the trampled straw on the floor. Beside it on either side stood two fiddlers, each frantically competing with the other and cheered on by the drinkers so loudly that both were inaudible anyway.

Eliot pushed his way through the crowds, finding his way to the darkness at the back of the room. It was only when he felt he had hidden himself, knees bent to disguise his unusual height, that he finally turned to see where his hounds were. Three men, discreetly clad in the unremarkable serving livery of a minor nobleman, could be seen surveying the room, edging through the crowd, though clearly they had not seen him yet. He kept his head down, peering from under the brim of his hat, cheering the fiddlers on with the rest so as to blend in. The hunters came closer. He felt his way backwards, still watching them, and found the cool render of the back wall behind him. He began to grope his way along it, grinning at the drinkers he displaced, his eyes all the time on the hunters, their dark livery linking them across the room like a net, ready to scoop and enmesh him.

XVII

The trumpet howled and spat, the trumpeter tortoise-shouldered in his intensity. The bass player stood with his arm companionably around his instrument, smooching with it while he chatted with the drummer, paying only a nodding courtesy to the trumpeter's solo. The trombonist fingered a few notes thoughtfully, and a scrawny singer took up the trumpeter's last notes with an unexpectedly plump and luscious voice as the audience applauded.

'They're worth three quid,' said Catriona appreciatively. They had worked their way to a table on the extreme left, quite near the band but also in semi-darkness. The club was crowded and there were people standing and occasionally dancing. Tom ordered two huge colas from a waitress.

'You know something about jazz, then?' he asked her.

'I used to.'

The Other Archaeologist, he thought to himself darkly, he must have been a jazz fan.

The drinks arrived and they emptied them almost immediately, dehydrated from the chase. But as Tom put his glass back down he noticed a familiar movement near the door. He nudged Catriona. She looked around as the two hunters came into view, quartering the club with their eyes like hounds.

'Oh, my earring!' exclaimed Catriona, and slid efficiently under the table. Grinning, Tom followed.

They re-emerged behind several layers of people, even nearer the band now but against the matt black painted wall. With their backs to it, they began to edge along. There might be a stage door.

XVIII

Eliot felt the wall stop behind him: lo and behold there was a doorway. He wondered where it might lead – some inner room, perhaps, without any other exit? But the hunters were drawing nearer – he had to try it.

XIX

The wall stopped suddenly behind Tom and he looked round, surprised. They had reached the emergency exit, lit from above in green and with a warning notice above the bar handle – 'The Door is Alarmed.' He grinned: it was nothing to what he was at the moment. He glanced back past Catriona. The hunters were drawing nearer. He saw the green light from the door reflected in her hair, and suddenly had an idea.

XX

The door opened easily when his hands twisted the rope latch. He felt inside with his foot: the floor did not seem to drop away drastically. He stooped, still watching the hunters, and slipped quietly through the door, not sure if even the men next to him had noticed.

XXI

Tom took Catriona's elbow and, as she turned, nodded to her. She frowned. He jerked his head back at the fire door, and she saw his had tighten on the bar handle. She gave a little smile, and nodded back. Tom took a breath, and pushed sharply down on the handle.

The door certainly was alarmed. So was everyone else in the place: the trombonist's slide came off in his hand and the drummer made a hideous noise with the cymbals, but no one cared as the fire alarm and sprinkler system simultaneously exploded into life. People leapt from the little round tables, sending drinks and snacks spilling on the floor as they scrabbled for the door. The hunters, too, had the same panicked, confused look that the alarm imspired. All this Tom and Catriona grasped in a split second, before hurtling out into the night.

XXII

Eliot turned as he left the howff and found himself not in an inner room but outside, under heavy eaves. He was in a yard, but the walls were not impossible, and, look, there was a gate, even easier. He pulled at the rope latch on it and shot out into the street, then slowed, trying to get his bearings. He was further down the hill than his own inn, and he wondered if he should return to it or whether he could even find it again. He could not leave the town at night, however: the gates would be locked. He walked briskly along the street, his heart calming with every step, but still alert to possible pursuit – or even being stopped by the night watch. Only when he had put two or three junctions and turns between himself and the howff without incident did he begin to think he might just have got away with it.

XXIII

It was downhill all the way to the car park near the station, and they ran most of it, nearly falling several times as the momentum was too much for their feet to keep up. They rounded the final corner laughing, and could clearly see the car in the distance. Three steps nearer, and they could just as clearly see the two representatives of the local constabulary with their notebooks and radios out, prowling around it.

'Oh no,' breathed Catriona. 'Did we leave anything in it?'

'Don't think so.' Tom stared at the scene for a moment, then sighed.

'I suppose we'll just have to get another one, then.'

Catriona stared at him.

'Is it something about your upbringing, or something?'

'What?'

'This ease with which you steal cars? Did you joyride a lot as a teenager? Oh no: then you'd at least have known how to drive.'

Tom laughed, refusing at this stage to take her too seriously, and amazingly she laughed too. They turned away from the car park together.

'Oh, come on, let's find another car park. I'm not nicking motors under a pollisman's nose.'

The next car park was not far, but as they entered it they saw that once again they were not alone. They jogged to the nearest car, but as Tom tried the handle, its alarm started to go off. They jumped. The hunters hurried in the direction of the sound.

'I've an idea,' muttered Catriona, and vanished further into the car park. In a moment, Tom heard a car alarm start down there, then another. Clever woman, he thought, crouching by the next car. The hunters at the gate stopped, confused.

The next car was locked, but not alarmed, even when he pushed it. He set off three more alarms. Catriona was evidently darting about, for alarms were sounding all over the place now. The hunters would know the police would arrive soon – and so did Tom. But he could not find an unlocked car, and his skills did not extend to lock-picking. If he could get Catriona's attention, he would signal that they ought to leave this car park, and try somewhere else.

A white van pulled up at the car park entrance, effectively blocking it. The police at last. But no: when the back door opened, plain clothed men leapt out, and the hunters went to talk with them – damn it, they had reinforcements! Now what?

He could only see a little of what was going on: the party of hunters seemed to split, and then came together again – but this time, they had Catriona.

But as Tom watched, he grew very puzzled. Catriona approached the van, without any apparent hesitation. She exchanged a few words with the men there. Then quietly and calmly, she stepped up into the back of the van, using her good arm to pull herself up. The men followed, and when the doors were shut, the van moved off.

When the police arrived, a moment or two later, the alarms in the car park were switching off, one by one. The officers shone their torches around a few cars, saw nothing suspicious, and left. They did not see Tom, sitting on the gravel between two cars, shocked into oblivion.

XXIV

Eliot rounded the last corner on to the broad street where, oddly, the inn he had left looked exactly the same as it had earlier. He had half expected by now that everyone would have gone off to bed, but perhaps the chase had not taken so long after all.

He strolled up the street, smiling to himself with some satisfaction that despite his less than perfect physical fitness he had still managed to shake off three younger men. It occurred to him that in fact, he had shaken off four men: there had been four back here at the inn, but by the time they had reached the howff, there were only three.

He had just begun to wonder if that was significant when the fourth man stepped out of the darkness and hit him hard on the head. As he passed out, he heard the strange sound of wheels on the cobbles, and felt something soft falling over his face.

5 – ELYSIAN FIELDS

I

This time it was the movement that roused him, but his memory came back almost at once and he was as cautious as ever in opening his eyes and feeling what was around him.

His roughened fingers grazed and caught on the smooth, distinctive surface of a very expensive silk.

That was a little unusual. It made him much more uneasy than simple rough wool would have done. The silk was both above and below his hands, and he spread his fingers wide, pressing downwards to feel a thinnish mattress, and upwards to find little weight of bedding over him. He lay flat on his back, and opened his eyes slowly to find himself in almost total darkness. Above him, moving slightly, he saw a chink of dim light, and the draught made him realise that he was in a small, bed-sized chamber, curtained on either side. The movement, he distinguished now, was that of wheels: he was in some kind of well-appointed litter, and outside it was nearly dawn.

He sat up, trying not to rock the litter and show anyone outside that he was awake and moving. He felt around him. His coat, he discovered, was laid across his feet, and the heavy hems seemed to be intact: the motive had not been robbery, then, but no surprise there.

But why had they even bothered to remove his coat? Why not simply throw him straight into the litter? In a sudden panic he felt around in the darkness.

His satchel had gone.

II

By the time Tom moved, he was cold and stiff. It was only the sound of the police van returning for another look that roused him, but though he stumbled off once it had passed, it could not be said that he was entirely conscious.

Catriona had gone off with those men as if she had known them all her life.

Had she? Or rather, had she been on their side all along? She had known where Alf was stored, and how to get him, and she had been the last person really to speak to Rob before he, too, had disappeared. But what would her reasons be for working with these people?

As soon as he tried to work that out, he realised that he was hitting one major stumbling block. When it came down to it, he hardly knew Catriona at all.

Right, well, she was an archaeologist and seemed fairly intelligent. She had the looks of ... well, best not to go there, just now. She had ambiguous morals when it came to nicking cars, and was probably fitter than he was. And she had been working all summer on a dig where they'd excavated a body showing that SAIDS had existed – and been survived – seven centuries ago.

He felt like writing it all down, just to show himself how much – or how little – he knew about her.

Anyway, what was he going to do now? She wanted to go to Fife, presumably to look for Rob: well, she was making her own way somewhere now. Maybe he himself should just go back to Edinburgh and find Inspector McAlester. Mind you, he thought on reflection, he did not fancy explaining this evening's curious events even to as kind a police officer as McAlester. He had the impression that the vague confusion concealed a sharp brain and a hardness he had not yet encountered.

And besides, he had his own reasons for going to Fife. The protestors who were disrupting his work, possibly sabotaging it, and certainly threatening him with bodily harm of some severity, seemed still to be based in Crook of Devon. Nothing Catriona had done or had had the opportunity to do affected that. And whatever she had done, whichever side – if there were sides – that she might be on – that did not detract from the fact that Rob had vanished, Alf the archaeological corpse had vanished, and Joanne Eastleigh, whom he himself had known and at least admired, if not been close to, was dead, in suspiciously coincidental circumstances. If Catriona was implicated, then he himself was the only innocent person left who had all the pieces to the puzzle – or as many as were yet available.

He walked, blindly, for some time. Eventually he came to a wide junction in a modern part of the town, where his bootlace broke. He stooped to fix it, and noticed a transport café a few yards away, whose cold yellow lights made him think of hot tea and comforting, greasy food. He felt cold, tired and unbearably lonely. He fished in his pockets. He still had money, anyway. The tea and the grease beckoned, and he did not resist.

He joined a short queue at the counter. A young lad in a soiled white cap was serving the man in front of him, and Tom could not see much past that – the customer was enormous. From the back, Tom mostly noticed the sheer breadth of the man's shoulders, emphasised by a black vest top stretched taut over a set of muscles that would not have seemed puny on a Russian Olympic weightlifter. The man's arms, three times the width of Tom's own, were so grey with old tattoos that if he had ever contracted SAIDS, the characteristic blotches would have been nearly invisible. His head was mostly covered in glittering grey bristle, but there were traces of scars there, and Tom found that he had no particular wish to know how he had got them.

The man paid, and half-turned to pick up his mug of tea with one hand while he pushed his change into a pocket with the other. He had a face even a mother would have hesitated over, and it was about a foot above Tom's. Tom made a nervous movement, and the man turned fully to face him. He stared at Tom for a moment. Then, in a thick Fife accent, he said,

'You looking for a fight?'

Tom froze.

The lad behind the counter vanished.

So much for the old 'fight or flight' think, he thought numbly. What about just plain 'stand still and shit yourself'?

His mouth was open. The man continued to stare.

Tom shut his mouth, and swallowed. Then in his best, non-confrontational, 'I'm-not-really-here-and-who-are-Rangers-and-Celtic-anyway? kind of voice, he said,

'I beg your pardon?'

'I said,' the man answered patiently, 'you're looking very white. Are you no well?'

Sweat broke out in relief on Tom's forehead. He began to gabble.

'No, no, I'm fine, fine, really, had a long day, tired, not much sleep last night, you know, lots of work on lately, not getting out much …'

'Aye. You'd best get yourself a good cuppa. Ali! Get this guy a mug of your strongest on me.'

The thin lad reappeared with a fresh box of teabags, nodded to the big man and threw a teabag into a clean mug. He handed the brew to Tom, and the big man led him to a table by a darkened window. Outside, an occasional car cruised around the roundabout.

'Name's Billy,' said the big man, settling himself down.

'Tom,' said Tom.

'I forgot the sugar,' said Billy, slapping the table. Tom leapt out of his seat as though it had scorched him. 'You're awful nervy,' Billy added, looking at him in concern. 'When did you last eat anything?'

'Ah …' He had no idea. A vague memory of chips surfaced, but he could find no context for them.

'Just sit yourself down, son,' said Billy, 'and get started on that tea.'

The tea was scalding, and made him shiver as he drank it. By the time Billy had arrived back with two plates of food, he was ready for it, and tucked in with empty-minded enthusiasm. Billy ate his own food contemplatively, and when he had finished, remarked,

'My missus says there's nothing like a good fry-up for the nerves, that and a strong cup of tea.'

'What do I owe you?' asked Tom, reaching into his pocket, but Billy waved a huge hand graciously. Crumbs sprayed from a final slice of fried bread.

'Fellow traveller in need,' he said. 'That's my truck out there, with the red and white cab. I call it Morag, after the wife.'

'That's nice,' said Tom, nodding out of the window at the truck.

'Car out there?'

'No, no, it's –' Tom broke off. His initial panic had gone, but he wondered how wise it would be to involve himself in even casual lying with this man. And ... well, he had an awful desire to tell somebody about what was happening to him. He was no professional spy: he had no oaths of secrecy, and no training in this kind of thing. He badly needed to talk it over, if not with someone, then at least in front of someone. He tested the waters. 'I walked here,' he said.

Billy raised his grey eyebrows – not far, it was not that expressive a face.

'Walked from where? Your car broken down?'

'No. I don't have a car.'

'You on the run?' asked Billy, with only a minor frown.

Tom took a deep breath.

'In a manner of speaking, yes. Um – someone's been trying to kill me.'

He began, encouraged by Billy's interest, to tell the story of his past few days, simply at first, wondering how great Billy's understanding could be of epidemiology and archaeology, then less straightforwardly as Billy's nods and comments and questions prompted him. It turned out that Billy listened a good deal to the radio as he drove his truck, and he wasn't that keen on all this modern music crap. Radio 4 suited him very well.

Tom reached the point of their escape from the pursuers in the middle of Stirling, and paused. Both their mugs were empty now.

'Another?' he asked, and Billy nodded.

'But make it quick, eh? This is better than the afternoon play.'

Tom grimaced, and went to fetch two teas.

'So what happened yon blonde, then?' Billy asked the moment he returned.

'She abandoned me.'

'Aye, women,' agreed Billy, with all the self-satisfaction of the happily married. Tom explained what had happened in the car park. Billy frowned. Tom frowned too at the memory, and they sat for a moment in silence.

He looked up from his tea and stared, first about the bright, grubby café, then at the equally bright reflections in the black windows. There were several other customers now, grey-pale in the late night and the unsympathetic fluorescent glow. Most were sitting individually, but the two nearest to them, though at separate tables, had struck up a conversation across the narrow aisle.

'Ah'm headin' for Perth, me,' said one, a thin lorry driver who must have made the most of power steering. 'Where're you aff till?'

'Bloody Aberdeen,' said the other in a Scouse accent. 'Then bloody Inverness,' he added, with impressive despair.

'Aye. Perth for me, then back Embro,' the thin one replied, satisfied with his lot.

Billy had been listening.

'I could give you a lift up to Kinross way, if you like,' he offered. 'Were you thinking of going up after her?'

'I was thinking of going up on my own account,' said Tom sourly. 'She can go hang, for all I care.'

'Oh aye,' said Billy. 'Aye.'

III

The thin mattress was nonetheless comfortable, and Eliot was exhausted after his long walk and the chase through Stirling's steep streets. He could do nothing as yet about his missing satchel: instead, he slept.

When he finally awoke, properly, he felt, if anything, worse. His head ached, and the various cuts and bruises from the chase, his capture and from that fall in the gutter with its mixed blessings, were enumerating themselves each time he moved. The fall, too, had left a residual but persistent stink about his clothes.

There was a slight difference about his little prison now that he had opened his eyes, and he realised that he must have slept for some time, for the light at the chink between the curtains was now that of full daylight. The litter was moving less certainly now and there was more noise outside: above the thudding of the hooves of the horses accompanying him there were people talking and calling, dogs barking, the heavy surge of an ox cart heading past in the opposite direction, and occasionally the sharp slap of a whip, nearby, as though his captors were forcing their way along a busy street. The whipcrack was always accompanied by an exchange of some pretty insults, from which Eliot deduced that his captors were Scots. It was not much of a surprise: what he had to take to Wallace was as dangerous to Scots as to English, he supposed.

The litter jerked sharply and he flailed his arms out to stop himself being rolled out. They appeared to be trying to turn it into a narrow lane or gate: there was a lot of backing and bumping, and some short-tempered shouting. When at last the litter moved smoothly forwards, Eliot could feel and hear it scrape its length along a wall to his left. There was a cry of alarm at this, followed by some resigned groans and a dull thud as someone kicked one of the wheels in frustration.

They ran over earth now, Eliot thought, and then the daylight was blocked out and he was plunged again into dusk. The angry voices faded away and instead there were the soothing clucks and whispers of men working with the horses, the clink and squeak of harness being removed, and one by one the horses were led away, too. There was the creak of a door being swung and then closed. The last of the light went, and Eliot heard bolts being shot home. There was silence.

Mere silence was not, however, enough to reassure a cautious man like Eliot. He waited. He could still smell the filth of the gutter on his hose and his coat, and behind that there was a faint smell of horses and a stronger smell of hay, sweet, making his nose tingle. Somewhere beyond that, he thought he could detect the distant scent of roasting meat. He remember that he must be hungry, and was instantly starving.

He went on waiting. Nothing changed. The only sounds he could hear were those of people and horses crossing the earth yard outside, and the occasional scuffle in the building he was in, which – after a moment's alarm – he identified as a cat chasing rats.

At last, he sat up carefully, touched the curtains with a surprisingly delicate hand, and pulled them apart by half an inch. He looked out.

He was, as he had thought, in a dark barn, large enough to hold a thin heap of hay (for it was not long till harvest time) and the large and splendid litter in which he had been travelling. The cat was sneaking along by the door, under which there was a gap allowing in some light. Eliot was surprised at its dimness – it was clearly already evening again, and they had travelled all day. He wondered where they were, and who had been in such a hurry to bring him here. Whatever it was, he did not intend to give them the satisfaction of staying. Thanks for the ride, gentlemen, he thought to himself, but here's where I go my own way.

He pushed the curtains back further, and swung his large feet over the side to slide, as lightly as he could, down to the floor. He reached back into the litter for his coat, and paused to admire the scratch, clearly visible even in this light, right along the side of the litter. Someone's fine lady wife would be having a few words with her treacherous husband, for it was obviously a lady's litter and its livery was the same as that he had seen on his pursuers. He had a sudden desire to do it some more damage, and felt in his boot to find that the knife he had slipped there had gone. He sighed, continuing to walk around the litter, noting the fine paintwork and neat leather tooling, and noticed a bundle hanging from one of the luggage hooks at the back. He peered more closely in the dim light, hardly believing his eyes. It was his satchel.

He glanced around again, half-suspecting a trick, but there was no one there but the cat. He reached out, and plucked the satchel from the hook.

It was dustier than it had been, from hanging outside during their rapid journey. It was fastened, and he unfastened it quickly, and crouched on the floor by the barn doors to use the best of the available light. He pulled the satchel open, and peered inside. The dispatches were still there.

He sat back on his heels, half-relieved, half-bewildered. Had they simply been in too much of a hurry to look at them? and then too flustered about the litter and the scratch and all the rest of it to remember to take them away with them when they left him in the barn? It was possible.

There was a dull clunk and he glanced back down at the satchel. His knife fell out.

So they had at least opened the satchel, then. Perhaps they had not seen the dispatches? Or realised what they were? His gaze fell on the half-loaf of bread he had been carrying, and the pie he had bought at the inn for the next day – today. He gave them both a rudimentary examination for signs of tampering, and then fell on the pie ravenously, not pausing until it had vanished into his long jaws. He sat back again, and noticed how the evening light was continuing to fade. His captors would also be dining, he supposed – and then what would they do?

This was difficult. He was not much of a man for tactics and strategy, he knew, beyond trying to make someone buy something. That and a healthy scepticism had usually seen him well on his way – sometimes a little faster than he had planned, true. If it would have made any difference, he would have found every man to whom he owed money, and paid them now, with interest, if he could change places with them. He was scared.

They might just be waiting until they had eaten to bring him out and torture him. They might be too tired to bother this evening, and think him well-secured in here.

And where was 'here'? He had been assuming that it was an inn, but what if it was in fact home for them, the laird's house that went with this fine litter? No, that was unlikely: they would surely then have taken him indoors, then, probably to a cellar or a lockable tower room. Here, he felt sure, his presence was being kept secret.

That might mean that this barn was not as secure as his captors thought.

He rose, stiff-legged, and looked about. He would have to move quite quickly now, or he would be able to see nothing. The barn was one storey high, but with a kind of shallow loft above where the litter stood, probably for storing ropes and such. He went back to the litter and looked around at the wooden wall behind it. It was sturdy and whole, no doors or windows there. The hay pile was low enough for him to see that it was the same all around: the only door was the main one, and he had heard it being locked. Besides, he did not think that emerging straight into the stableyard would be a good move. He eyed the loft.

The first thing that struck him was that there was no ladder. Then he realised that there was nothing to stop him – apart, perhaps, from general physical weakness – from climbing up on to the top of the litter and pulling himself up into the loft: it had not rail or wall, he thought, to get in the way. He slung his satchel, now fastened, around his neck, slid his knife back into his belt, and pulled on his heavy coat. The prospect seemed immediately more difficult. He sighed, and began by placing one foot on the high shaft of the litter, and gradually worked his way on to its roof. He tried to stay at the edges of it, where the wooden supports would bear his weight better, and reached up to get a good grip on the edge of the loft above. He was just about to heave himself up, when it all went wrong. A rat ran over his fingers. He jumped. His foot slipped, and with a thick ripping noise went straight through the fine leather roof of the litter.

Stuck half-in and half-out, Eliot could hardly pull himself up for the silent laughter that shook his thin body. How were they going to explain that to the fine lady, then, eh?

He had to wait some time for the laughter to ease before he finally heaved himself free and then up and into the loft. It was much as he had expected. Coils of rope of different thicknesses lay neatly about, and there were piles of dusty sacking. No one had been up here for a while, he judged, sniffing the dust, and then belatedly realised that the reason he could see all this so well was the presence of an open window, about two feet square, facing west and tucked into the gable wall before him. He nearly began to laugh again.

Instead, he edged over to it. The window did not look out upon the stableyard, but over a lane which seemed to form the back of a row of rigs, the long strips of land with their tightly joined houses at the far end. He was not sure quite where he was: it did not look like a big place, so not Edinburgh or Linlithgow. Maybe they had taken him back north – that would be a blow. Now that he knew he had to make for the Lothians he wanted no further delays.

Just below him was a grassy bank, not too steep, but possibly concealing a ditch. He had no wish to jump and risk a broken ankle. There was no one about, no one even in sight, though windows of the rig houses were lit in the growing darkness. He glanced back inside the loft at the ropes. His next step was obvious.

He tied the end of stout-looking coil to a roof beam, knotting it as best he could. Where were sailors when you needed them? he thought. The knot looked thoroughly unreliable. However, he tugged and pulled at it, giving it all his weight to bear as he leaned across the loft, and it only tightened. He grinned to himself.

Then he returned to the window. Once again he looked hard to left and right, and examined the rigs one by one to see if anyone was taking an undue interest in the barn. Then, cautiously, he fed the other end of the rope out of the window till it hit the ground, and carried on until it led straight up to the roof beam. He looked down. It formed a long, pale line to the ground, showing him the way to safety. He checked the knot once more, wrapped his coat about him over his satchel, and took a deep breath. Then, feet first, he scrambled through the window, banging elbows and knees and scraping one ear as he went.

This is good, he thought, his hands now on the rope and his legs wrapped round it. This is fine. Now, how do I move?

And in that instant, the problem was resolved. The rope snapped, and he fell into the darkness.

IV

The rain, promised for weeks, began to fall as Billy swung the vast truck out on to the road and followed the signs for Fife. The cab of Billy's truck was cosily domestic, with a huge tartan tea flask, a box of homemade biscuits and photos of his wife Morag. By the time they had reached Kinross Services – a bijou little service station with a craft shop – the water was pouring on to the windscreen as fast as the wipers could push it off, not in drops but in waves.

'I canna put you down here,' shouted Billy over the riot of rain on the roof. 'I couldna do it to a rat. Come on, I'll take you as far as you need to go.'

'Aren't your bosses pretty strict?'

'I'm self-employed, me,' said Billy proudly. 'It's no problem.'

Tom looked out at the rain. Crook of Devon was not much further, but he would never find another lift there in this downpour. He paused enough for decency, then agreed.

'Crook of Devon, then,' said Billy with satisfaction. 'Do you ken the address? Not that there's much to it, mind.'

'I have only a postcode. You'd better just put me down in the middle and leave me to wander.'

Billy snorted, squinting horribly through the washed windscreen, and started up again.

He was right, there was nothing much of Crook of Devon. Tom peered out of the window on his side of the cab, struggling to make out anything beyond a few isolated bungalows. Then a tall, dark barrier appeared, smooth and black, and he gave a yelp. Billy stopped the truck with a snort of hydraulic brakes.

'What did you see?' asked Billy, straining to find something outside that looked remotely distinctive.

'See the sign?' Tom pointed excitedly. 'It was the hedge I saw first – looks as if it has been bought by the yard. But the sign swings it – look.'

Billy scowled into the semi-darkness, and read with difficulty, aloud:

'"Elysian Fields, Food Science Research". What's that?'

'It's the link,' said Tom happily. 'I don't know how yet, but I'm dead sure it's the link. Damn, I can't see in.'

The gate, a large double one, more than the width of Billy's truck, glinted in the headlights. It was wire, and perfectly transparent, but beyond it the hedge doubled back and anything beyond it was invisible.

'Climb up on the outside of the cab,' said Billy reasonably. 'There's a wee ladder at the back of you there. Watch your footing, though: it'll be slippery in this.'

Tom made a rueful face at him, and opened the cab door. Instantly his left arm and leg were soaked, slapped with cold water. He shuddered, and stood on the step, glancing back at Billy. The huge man nodded encouragingly, a curiously comforting presence. He felt for the ladder, found it, and pulled himself around and on to it.

Once up at the roof of the cab, he had to push his dripping hair off his face and wipe his eyes before he could see anything at all. Beyond the tall, thick hedges was an enclosed area, partly grassed and partly tarmac, shiny under a number of bright security lights – not many, Tom noticed. There were about half a dozen cars parked by one of the nearer buildings, and beside them a white Transit van. It might have been the one that Catriona had left Stirling in.

That building looked like offices, or perhaps – Tom could see one window lit, from an internal corridor, to show one or two details that looked familiar – perhaps laboratories. Beyond it, only two-storey, was a taller building with only one row of very high windows, perhaps some kind of factory, or production plant. Across to the left, close to but not quite adjoining the second building, was another one, small, one storey, with a heavy chimney. All three buildings were squared, smart, functional and modern: the whole place could have been planted there, complete, surrounded by its hedges, or it could have been anywhere else. It gave off an air of complete self-containment.

Tom scrambled back down the ladder and slid clumsily back into the cab, dripping.

'This is where we part company, then. Thanks for everything, Billy.'

'Aye, well. You take care, now.'

'I will.' He held out a hand, and it disappeared completely in one of Billy's own. He pushed the cab door open, and was about to slip down to the road when there came a clank from behind him. He looked round quickly.

'I dinna ken how you think you're getting in,' said Billy calmly, 'but you might be needing the lend of these.'

He tossed over something heavy, and Tom caught it awkwardly. It was a pair of wire cutters.

When the truck moved off, roaring, it left behind a broad wake of diesel fumes and loneliness. Tom was already drenched, the water running down his cold bare legs into his sock tops, and he watched the lights of the truck disappear up the road and at last out of sight. He felt a strong urge to go running after it, yelling. Then he turned to look at the wire gate.

The gate was at a corner of the hedged-in compound. Tom walked to the corner and looked round it, but found nothing but a field. Tom did not know much about fields, and in the saturated darkness he had little wish to push back the boundaries of his knowledge. It looked like crops, he decided, mostly on the basis that he could see no cows. Catriona would know – and would probably dig it up, too. He sighed, and turned back to the gate, hefting the wire cutters. If there were security cameras he could not see them, and was so wet he barely cared. He began at about his own head height and worked his way methodically downwards, clipping the wire at the edge of the gate, hoping it would be less noticeable there.

The wire cutters were sharp, but his hand still ached by the time he had opened a slit long enough for him to step through, pulling his knapsack after him. As he had seen from his vantage point on top of the truck cabin, he now found himself inside a short, high tunnel of hedges, tarmac-surfaced and empty. He paced forward, neither fast nor slow, looking about him, smelling the wet leaves, and stopped when he reached the end of the inner hedge. Cutting through the gate had been easy: to turn this corner seemed to require much more courage.

At last he took a deep breath, and edged his head round the clipped twigs, his fingers twined in them for support. There was no sign of life in the car park. Some distance to his right was the laboratory-like building he had seen over the hedge. Straight ahead was the one with the tall chimney. He decided to stick to what he knew best, and head for the laboratory.

He breathed in again, counted to ten, and darted across to the cover of the parked cars outside the building. He stopped there. Apart from the rain, all was silence: no dogs, no shouts, no running footsteps. He squeezed between the cars – he seemed to have spent all this endless night in car parks, knees bent, head down. He reached the wall of the building and crouched down. Still no sound. The windows were only six feet off the ground. One wide casement was open, must have been opened in the muggy heat of the day and forgotten when the downpour started. The rain splattered from a drainpipe next to him and flooded over his feet, but he paid it little attention. Instead, he rose slowly and carefully, touching the concrete walls for balance, and stretched up to look in through the open window.

V

Eliot lay winded in the ditch, the rope in pale coils over him and its frayed, rotten, stinking end telling its own story of betrayal. When he had his breath back, the first thing he did was to swear thoroughly. Then he tried and found that all his bones seemed to be whole, though there would be a few sharp bruises if he did not move soon.

Moving soon did not prove to be the problem he had thought it might be. He heard footsteps in the barn beside him – footsteps too heavy to be those of a cat or a rat – and then there came a shout. He was off down the path and away from the barn before he had considered how to get up, and the frayed rope was over and into the end of someone's rig where it would attract less attention. As soon as he could do it without making too much noise, he jogged for a few yards, but found it was too dark to see his path safely. Behind him, distantly but not distantly enough, were the jerking patterns of lanterns quartering the area outside the barn. He hurried on.

Where in the name of all things good and holy was he? Which direction should he be heading? Anywhere away from that damned barn just the now, he reckoned, tripping and catching his balance again. At least he was rested and fed – he could go all night now if he had to – if he really had to.

As it turned out, he had to. It was summer, it never really grew dark, which was good and bad as he staggered along rutted roads and sometimes through hedges and over pasture, through woodland, past darkened cottages or occasionally, at a crossroads, the ghost of a gallows creaking in the dusk. The pursuit seemed to follow him all night, never near enough to make him desperate, never far enough away to let him relax. They had dogs, joyous, energetic dogs, happy in their work. Eliot hated dogs. For the sake of the dogs, he flung himself in pools and stumbled up and down streams, trying to shake off the scent, but he could always hear them, faint and bewildered, until he no longer knew if the voices of the hounds were in the field behind him or in his dreams. At last, muddy to the thighs, he waded one last stream, pulled himself sodden and weary up into a tree, and lodged in its branches he fell sound asleep.

He woke to a heavy grey morning. He was alone. It was already warm, and his clothes had partly dried on him, but his coat was about him, his satchel was tucked into his lap, and he was alone. As far as he was concerned, the day was fine.

He poked around in his satchel and pulled out the half-loaf of bread, now on the stale side. It made for hard chewing, but he got some of it down his craw before taking the time to think about where he might be. He knew he had crossed the stream, mumbling below him, to reach this tree, and from the vague brightness in the sky behind him he realised that for the last part of his stravaigings last night, he had been heading east. If he was south of the Forth, that would be fine. If his captors had taken him back over Stirling bridge, though, he would have a good part of his journey to make again.

He slid down out of the tree and stretched. Around him was pasture land and he could see traces of sheep that even he could recognise. There was no point in heading south or north at this stage. If he went west, he might be doubling back, or he might even be heading for the west coast. No, he would go east. If he found himself at the Fife coast again, he would take the boat from the Queen's ferry, for they would surely not be watching it now. If he found himself west of Stirling he would have to keep heading east anyway, and if he was south of the Forth, he was just about on his intended route. He took a draught of water from the stream, and turned his face to the dim sunlight.

He found himself back on a road quite soon, a track baked dry underfoot in cart ruts and boot tracks. It was tiring walking, but it was going the way he intended and surely was heading somewhere of some use to him. He found a few berries in a hedge and ate them, feeling the sweet juice as a luxury on his tongue, delighted with its flavour. He passed a few people as he went, a beggar eyeing him with suspicion, a man with two cows and a wall eye, a lone pilgrim muttering to himself. None of them looked approachable, and Eliot walked on.

At dinner time he came to a house more worthy than some of the hovels he had seen, and from its proximity to a small wooden church too it to be the priest's house. He was not wrong, for a cleric answered the door to his knock, and as Eliot had hoped invited him to share his dinner. It was black bread, broth and fish, a combination that suited Eliot well and made him think that it might be Friday.

'And has your parish a name?' asked Eliot, after grace had been said.

'Aye,' said the priest, setting to with his broth. He was a young man, but clearly not much used to the conversation of outsiders. Eventually Eliot's encouraging (or threatening) look penetrated the priest's concentration on his food.

'Balerno,' he said, as if no one else could be expected to know.'

'And where's that from Edinburgh?' asked Eliot, not to let the matter drop.

'Och, it's eight miles,' said the priest. The implication was that this was a distance no one would consider worth travelling.

'In which direction?' Eliot persisted.

'Yonder,' the priest waved. Eliot thought quickly – north-east. If he kept going due east from here, he would meet the Esk not far from Eskbank. It was not the most direct path, but if he headed upstream, south west from there, he should be able eventually to find what he was looking for – if he could cross the Pentlands safely, or if he could find the Esk, or if the man at the inn at Stirling was telling him anything remotely true.

VI

The room was empty. It was a laboratory, in fact: the principal things in this one that did not appear in Tom's own workplace were a rank of filing cabinets and a central bench with one or two trays of seedlings on it, looking forgotten. The room light was off, but the corridor beyond was lit and illuminated the lab through frosted glass internal windows. The door to the corridor was ajar.

Tom glanced back, then, with a leg-up on one of the drainpipe supports, he pulled himself up and through the window. It was easy to slip across the plastic-topped bench and drop down on to the floor – no slight sound he made could have been heard over the rain, anyway. He tiptoed over to the inner door, then froze as two blurry figures came into view in the corridor, their outlines wavering through the frosted glass.

'So it's all contained, then, is it?' asked a soft, transatlantic voice, then before the other could reply, added, 'Oh, wait a minute – I've to check something in here.'

The central workbench had cupboards beneath it. Under normal circumstances, Tom would never have considered jamming himself into such a small space – but then, he did not actually consider it this time. He just did it. As he pulled the cupboard door gently to, he could hear rubber-soled shoes, two pairs, squeaking on the tiled floor. He prayed they did not notice his wet footprints.

'There, damn it, I knew he'd leave the window open,' continued the American. 'He's been whining about the heat in here all day. This rain means the security men don't even want to leave their office – it could have been open all night.'

There was the clunk of the window being closed, and the noise of the rain diminished.

'So what happened?' the man continued. A Scottish accent replied.

'Okay, we've got all the material back, now, all that hadn't been used. It's being destroyed over at the incinerator. That includes the old body.'

'Excellent. That thing gives me the shivers.'

'And the two archaeologists. Funny, the way that turned out.'

'Well, we'll just have to watch what we sponsor in future.' He must have leaned back, for Tom heard the bench creak above him. 'We'll be switching operations here, soon, anyway. Did the second archaeologist, the girl – did she know anything?'

'She had some link between the body they dug up and her colleague and Fife – don't know if it went any further than that. Of course, she'd been shot, which might have led to questions. And then she was with the epidemiologist we've been working on – but she didn't seem to think much of him. Pure coincidence she was there when we tried to bust him.'

Didn't think much of him, eh? thought Tom in his cupboard. He'd soon show her – but wait – what had the man said about the incinerator?

'... dealing with him?' the American was asking.

'By what the girl said, he knows zip,' said the Scot. 'I think it might draw too much attention if we took him out just now. Leave it to go the way we originally planned, eh?'

'If you're sure it's safe ...'

'We still have the other things to wrap up in Edinburgh. We can get our own guy there to do the lot – tidier, and then he's expendable, too.'

'He always was going to be expensive. So where's our man Buchan now?'

'The lads left him in Stirling, with the police on his tail and no wheels.'

'I guess he'll go back to Edinburgh, then. Find him, and keep a track of him.'

'Yes, sir.'

'Now, I've got to go and kick the butts of those security guards. Like what do they want – umbrellas?'

The Scot laughed, and their rubber shoes squeaked back out of the lab. Tom did not hear the door close.

Catriona was innocent. There, she was.

But was she still alive?

VII

Vicky seemed barely alive.

Shona would have given anything now for Vicky to cheek her, to break something or shout at her or run around flailing her teddy, or anything she would normally tell her off for. But Vicky still lay on the bed, and Shona still sat on one side, and Andy still sat on the other, and the nurse with the kind eyes and his colleagues glided in and out, unrealistic behind their masks, and the machines kept the air alive with humming.

Andy had had the tests, too, now. The warden had gone with him, wearing the mask with which he, too, had been issued and looking nervous, but Shona had stayed with Vicky, holding her hand or endlessly smoothing her pretty hair. They kept telling Shona that they had no idea how Vicky was living for so long, but the longer she held on the better chance she had. Shona didn't care why. They talked of antibodies, of the possible effects of a full blood transfusion, of possible contaminants at the prison, of someone wanting to come and see Vicky from some local research establishment, and Andy seemed to be answering them articulately. Shona just went on talking to Vicky, and when her voice ran out, silently praying.

VIII

Eliot limped wearily into the village of Dalkeith two days later.

Since he had left the laconic priest, he had pushed himself hard, and though he had never felt under threat – well, no more than anyone walking through the Pentlands in the dawn and the dusk – the sense of urgency he had felt to some extent since he had woken on the May Isle had intensified since his escape from the nameless barn. He felt driven, and had hardly slept, unable to rest until he had walked just a few more paces, reached just that next corner ...

Dalkeith was tucked between two rivers, the north and the south Esk. There was not much to it: if it had not been for Dalkeith Castle to the north, a practical building where one of the Douglases oversaw his estate, there would have been nothing to mark it out at all. Eliot felt less danger here: the Douglases were a loyal Scottish family. The good Sir James' father had died in London's Tower four years ago. Sir James himself, as far as Eliot knew, was still in Paris.

He bought several pies in Dalkeith, and began walking again while eating the first one still hot. He was at a point where he knew that if he once sat down, he would not rise again for hours: feet always hurt more if they are allowed to rest a little. It was not very long before he reached the North Esk, and, fearful either of losing his way or of missing completely what he was looking for, he resolved to follow the river faithfully from there to Penicuik, if necessary, and not to cut any of its meandering corners. Ahead of him, the river emerged from thick deciduous woodland under a leaden sky. Eliot stuffed the remains of his pie into his mouth, and wiped across with the back of one hand. Then he stooped to take a draught of water and stood again, stretching his back and kicking up his heels to ease his knees and thighs. The scars on his neck and elsewhere felt stiff again, and he wondered if they would ever disappear.

It was late dinner time when he set off, the only vague sunlight high in the sky, and he walked slowly despite himself. The river did indeed wind, between woods and fields, and past the occasional tower house, but he made himself stick rigorously to its wandering banks, and ploughed on.

IX

Tom crossed the car park again, feet splashing in the rain, every sense alert for a team of security guards with freshly kicked butts. An incinerator presumably needed a chimney, he had thought quickly, and there was definitely a chimney on this site. He had slipped out of the cupboard and back through the window, leaving it closed but not fastened, and was now making for the building at the far corner of the site.

Catriona was innocent, but for some reason Elysian Fields, the food science research company that had sponsored the Roslin dig, wanted to destroy her, her colleague Rob, and the seven hundred year old corpse they had dug up. They also wanted to destroy him, though (a bit of an insult) that was less urgent. Was all that the 'material' that the Scot had talked of destroying? Or was there something else – something that needed to be hidden?

The building had a metal door with a bolt. He suddenly realised that if he found Catriona there, dead, he was going to find it very hard to live with himself.

His hand trembled as he reached to draw back the bolt. The door swung out towards him with the ease of use, and a steady churn of machinery hit his ears. He moved inside.

The room was not large, but was dark and warm. To one side of him, taking up most of the space in the room, was a conveyor belt, three or four feet wide, intended to feed waste material from a chute above and behind him. Tom imagined it must lead from the factory-like building nearby. Around it, perhaps thrown there for disposal later, were large paper sacks filled with something heavy, to judge by the way they sat. The conveyor belt was moving, with unremitting sloth, towards the fiery mouth that was lighting the whole room with a dull, infernal glow: the incinerator. Sweating, Tom shivered.

But things did not seem to be going according to plan. On the conveyor belt at the moment were four long white cardboard boxes, of the kind that importers of flowers or plants sometimes use. They were labelled only 'Elysian Fields. Plant Material' in that soft green writing Tom now knew well. All four were clearly destined for destruction, but though the conveyor belt beneath them was moving, they were not. The foremost of the boxes had somehow managed to screw itself round at an angle, and had caught on stacks of the solidly packed paper refuse sacks, and the other three had jammed up behind it like telescoped carriages in a train crash.

He could try to switch the conveyor belt off, but he was afraid that that might attract attention somewhere. If the waste chute from the factory was backing up, people would notice soon enough anyway. He moved forward slowly and lifted the lid on the box nearest the door, farthest from the incinerator.

Inside there were packed plants, lying on their sides and slightly withered-looking. He had no idea what they were – long and leafy, but beyond that he could say they were not cabbage or grass, and from the lack of thorns he thought they probably were not roses, either. On impulse, he pulled one out, folded it as best he could and pushed it into his rucksack. Then he replaced the lid tidily and moved on to the next box.

He let out a yell before he could stop himself. No plants here: instead, a wrinkled, wizened corpse stared at him with eyes from hell. Shaking violently, he made himself stop and listen. No sound of any pursuit: he looked again at the corpse. It was not Catriona, anyway, nor even Rob. This must be the archaeological find that had started all this trouble. He cleared his throat, and even managed a grin.

'Hiya, Alf,' he whispered.

The movement from the fourth box was sudden. He jumped, and stared at it. The long box, caught between paper sacks, twitched again, and the lid shifted slightly. Holding his breath, he tiptoed over to it, and pulled off the lid.

There was a wild tipping movement and a wave of gold seemed to envelope him. He staggered back, clutching whatever it was, and in a second found it was Catriona, her mouth obscured by packing tape. Her hair had escaped from the plait and seemed to be everywhere.

Tom pulled off the packing tape as she winced, and then, because he knew he would never have the nerve again, he kissed her hard on the lips.

'Ow,' said Catriona after a moment, but without hostility, then added, 'What about untying me?'

Abashed, Tom tackled the knots on the baler twine around her wrists. They were unimaginative, and she was quickly freed.

'What is this place?' she asked, crouching to untie her own ankles. Tom was still a little shaken by his own boldness as he watched her.

'It's an incinerator plant,' he said, 'at the Elysian Fields site in Crook of Devon.'

'So it was Elysian Fields,' she breathed. 'What the hell are they up to?'

'Damned if I know,' said Tom. 'By the way, I take it this is Alf?'

He pointed to the conveyor belt. The boxes had moved a little, but sice the one behind Catriona's had been shoved out of line, it too had caught on the paper sacks.

'Yes,' said Catriona, 'that's Alf. He looks just the same as he did after the post mortem … What's he doing here?'

'Heading for the incinerator. Along with you, some plants, and whatever's in this box – more plants, I expect.'

He showed Catriona the contents of the plant box, and then between them they pulled the lid off the last box.

For a long moment, there was silence. Then Catriona said,

'Rob.'

Rob looked, apart from the singed hole in his chest, as if he were asleep. His fingernails were still rimmed with earth, and there was some grass stuck to his boots. Tom put out an uncertain hand and touched Rob's forehead.

'He's quite cold.'

'Yes.' She said nothing for a moment, then, still staring at Rob, she asked,

'Do you think we could lift him, between us?'

'We can't take him with us, Catriona.'

'I don't mean that,' she snapped back. 'I mean we should try to get him – and Alf – off this conveyor belt. I mean – he's evidence, isn't he?'

She was as white as a sheet, but Tom was impressed. Between them, they managed to lift the plant box, then Alf, then finally Rob, down on to the floor and to slide them under the conveyor belt. Then they replaced all the lids, and stacked Catriona's empty box on top. Tom hauled a paper refuse sack across in front of them for luck.

'We'd better go,' he said. 'I cut through the gate to get in – it won't be long until they notice the hole.'

'I take it you didn't drive here,' Catriona said suddenly.

'Of course not. I hitched.'

'Oh,' said Catriona. 'Good. But how do we get back to Edinburgh?'

'First things first,' said Tom. 'How do we get out of here?'

He opened the big metal door to the car park – and the first thing he saw was a guard dog.

X

Eliot had a feeling that this was the right place.

That was it, no evidence, no proof. The river had dug itself a deep gorge, winding between grey cliffs darkened by spray at the bottom and capped with leafy green. He had walked about six miles from Dalkeith, he reckoned: it was mid-afternoon, and already the water was in shadow. To justify his instincts, he decided that from certain points on the cliff-sides you could see anyone entering the gorge from downstream, which was the way most likely travelled. If that was the case, then he himself had already been seen – if the man he sought was being as careful as he ought to be.

He slowed his pace, finding his way up the river stone by stone, content just now to take his time. Ahead of him, a little spit of land jutted out shallow from a taller corner, making a small beach on which stood a few saplings. He decided to take a rest there.

He settled himself down against the sturdiest sapling, stretching his back and his legs, turning his ankles in his boots to ease them. The river ran busily past him, its noise like the breeze echoing up the cliffs till it met the birdsong in the trees far above. There was no sign that human life existed. He waited for a moment, trying to stay alert, but his head rolled back against the sapling's smooth trunk and he stared at the grey sky above him until his eyes closed.

Having a knife at your throat was as bad a way to wake up as any, he thought, what seemed like seconds later. He held himself very still, eyes fixed on the grey sky, and after waiting an eternity said,

'All right, then, who are you this time?'

The knife twitched. Then a deep voice, with a sigh in it, said,

'I was going to ask you the same thing, man.' He waited, then added, 'Thing is, see, I've got the knife.'

'True,' admitted Eliot. It did not sound like one of his captors from Stirling. Though some of them, too, had sounded educated, they at least knew who he was, he supposed.

The knife twitched again.

'I'm waiting ...'

'My name is Nicholas Eliot. I'm a merchant.'

'A Scot?'

'From the borders. But I havena been home for years.'

'What does that prove, one way or the other?'

Eliot scowled.

'Nothing, to my mind. But it might interest you to know that I am a loyal Scot, and I come from a loyal Scot in Boulogne.'

The words were out: he might well have condemned himself out of hand, or the words might mean nothing. He held his breath, and felt his pulse beating his skin against the knife blade. He tried to resist the urge to swallow.

The knife blade moved slowly away, and as his captor moved round to stand between him and the river, he found himself looking at a big man, with sandy hair and blue eyes. His face was lined and he had the inescapably grimy look of one living rough. The knife he held was a good one, well-maintained, and clasped in a competent grasp.

'Would – ' Eliot broke off, annoyed at himself for being in awe of anybody. He was his own man. 'You wouldna be Wallace, would you?'

'If you're from a loyal Scot in Boulogne,' said the big man quietly,

'I'd be Wallace.'

'Good,' said Eliot, 'I'll be damned pleased to get rid of these dispatches: they've caused me enough trouble now.' He felt, with a cautious eye still on Wallace's ready knife, for his satchel. He undid it and pulled out two cold pies, the straw wrapping that came with them (which always got loose and ended up everywhere), and finally the wad of papers that he had carried so carefully all the way from Boulogne. Wrinkled with seawater, rumpled by the journey and scattering crumbs, the papers were solemnly handed over to their rightful recipient. Eliot breathed a sigh of relief.

Wallace glanced down at them, flicking through the three or four closely-written sheets.

'This will take a while. Where are you for now?'

'I had not thought,' said Eliot in surprise. 'I had no idea how soon I might find you.'

'Come and break bread with me, at least,' said Wallace. 'Though it is no great castle, and no great reward for your services, still I should be pleased to hear your story, if you will tell it to me.'

'But where do you bide?' asked Eliot, looking about him.

'Just here. You were on my doorstep.' And he showed Eliot the entrance to a cave, worn discreetly into the rock just behind where Eliot had been resting. Eliot shivered at his own prescience, and when Wallace's back was turned, surreptitiously crossed himself.

They fed off Eliot's cold pies and some fish Wallace had caught in the river, roasted on a little fire that Wallace smothered with green leaves as soon as the fish was cooked. Nevertheless the meal was a good one: Wallace turned out to be a grand talker and gave some accounts of battles that the monks on the May Isle would have relished. Eliot on his side told of the death of the Scot in Boulogne and of his own travels since, of May and of Stirling. When he told of his escape from his captors, though, Wallace seemed worried.

'You escaped so easily,' he explained, 'with all your belongings and the dispatches intact. Are you sure they did not let you go?'

'For what purpose?'

'Well, to follow you. Maybe they looked at the dispatches, saw they were for me, and put them back so that you would continue with your task.'

'You mean they let me go just to use me to find you?' Eliot was not pleased. 'Look, son, it wasna that easy to escape from yon barn. Do you think you're Rome, that all roads point to you?'

Wallace was affronted.

'There have been plenty threats, you know. That's what these papers are about – did you not read them?'

'Read them?' asked Eliot, even more cross. 'What makes you think anyone ever took the trouble to teach me how to read? Numbers I can manage,' he added, with pride.

'Oh, aye,' said Wallace, calmer. 'Well, according to the dispatches, there are certain Scots lordlings who would be happy enough to see Edward of England find and capture me.'

'Aye, your man said that much. They want to take you out of the race for the Crown, and they want to win favour with Edward so that he'll maybe support them when they race for it themselves.'

'Neat, is it not?' agreed Wallace. Eliot could not now see his face clearly, for outside it was dusk. 'These papers explain the plot and name some likely plotters. The chief of them is, I believe, the most likely: Nicolson of Rosehill. He's a keen supporter of Robert Bruce's claims to kingship. Whether Bruce know of this plot or not, it will win him favour with Edward – Nicolson will make sure of it.'

'If it works,' added Eliot, grimly.

XI

The nurse came in with the consultant that evening. It was not unusual. The consultant always looked exhausted, and the nurse always looked kind. Andy had asked her their names, but she had shrugged, shaking her head, and turned back to Vicky.

But this evening, after the consultant had made his usual examination of Vicky, nodding and frowning, he did not go. He leaned heavily on the end of the bed, and coughed softly, to attract their attention. They both turned to look at him.

'We have had the blood tests back from the labs now for the blood we took from both of you. You, Mrs. Larssen, are completely clear, though of course we'll test again. However you, Mr. Larssen ...' Andy sat upright and straightened his shoulders, waiting for the blow it was clear was coming. 'Your results have been a bit of a puzzle to us. We're talking to the scientists out at the Establishment at Roslin now – they've developed a test for SAIDS, seeing traces of it in the blood – but it looks very much from your blood sample that you have traces of SAIDS cells in your blood.'

'Andy?' said Shona, staring at him. Andy, too, was looking confused.

'Does that mean I'm coming down with it? That I'm going to die?'

'But I thought it was quick ...' whispered Shona. She eyed her husband, almost distrustfully.

'Come on, doctor,' said Andy, the calm beginning to crack, 'tell me – do I have SAIDS?'

'No,' said the consultant, 'you don't. But it looks very much as if you *have* had it.'

XII

The guard dog was alone: the security man must have baulked again at actually leaving the building. The rain was still coming down in torrents and the German shepherd looked cold and miserable. Tom dropped to his knees.

'Here, boy!' he called softly. The dog looked round, unsure. 'Come on, boy, here!' He could sense Catriona staring at him as he willed the dog over to them. The dog, with a why-not air, eventually trotted across. Tom reached into his bag and found an old piece of chocolate, which the dog swallowed before he could possibly have tasted it.

'You all alone, boy? Eh?' Tom asked, rubbing the dog's sodden ears. 'Come in here, nice and warm and dry. There's a good boy.' He ushered the dog into the incinerator room, nudged Catriona out into the rain, and followed her, giving the dog a farewell pat before closing the door on it. The room seemed well ventilated. Catriona was still staring at him, her loose hair instantly darkened in the downpour.

'Impressive,' she admitted at last.

'Oh, watch it, Catriona, you'll be all over me in a moment!' Tom replied, unable to keep a thoroughly smug smile off his face. She grinned back, but he thought it was probably best to resist kissing her again then and there, and turned his face towards the laboratory building.

'We need to find out what they're doing here,' he said. 'Those are offices and laboratories over there – if we can find some records or something to take back to Inspector McAlester ...'

'It might make up for the stolen car and the breaking and entering, you mean?' She looked at the building, squinting through the rain. 'How do we get in?'

'There's a window open round the front. I've been in already – it's no big deal – oh. Unless your arm's still giving you jip?'

'Well ... let's just see how we go, will we?'

There was still no one in sight. The guard dog evidently appreciated the warmth of the incinerator room: he barely made a token scratch on the door, and Tom left it unbolted anyway, unable to bear the thought of locking an animal in unnecessarily. Then, with as much caution as before, they crossed the car park again back towards the laboratory and the main gate. They turned the corner, finding the few cars parked as

Tom had left them, and he led the way to the drainpipe and the window by which he had entered before. It was fastened.

'Damn,' whispered Tom, peering up at it. 'The security guards must have done their rounds after all. We'll just have to go, then.'

'Not necessarily,' said Catriona. She was apparently feeling in her pockets. 'Can you give me a leg up?'

Tom bent and made a step for her, and he saw something metallic flash in her right hand as she reached up, fiddled for a moment, then swung the window open again. Then, with a push that nearly floored Tom, she swung herself in through the window and disappeared. A step on the drainpipe and Tom followed.

'How did you do that?' he whispered, when they were both safely in the lab. She opened her hand.

'Trowel,' she said simply. 'An archaeologist is never without one.'

Tom had a fleeting vision of what life would be like if he were never without an electron microscope, and dismissed it as hysteria.

'Those filing cabinets seem most promising,' he said, looking about him. The first one needed the skilled application of Catriona's trowel again, but once inside, the field was Tom's.

'Records of experiments ... research plans ... research papers ... too much to take all of it,' he muttered. 'Wait, wait, wait ... what's this? Turbot?'

'Turbot?' repeated Catriona. Her teeth were chattering. 'It's cold in here,' she explained. Tom was sweating: he had not noticed. 'Actually, that's misleading,' she added. 'I've no idea whether it's cold in here or not: this is just blind terror.'

Tom nodded absently. Adrenalin was quietly filtering into the part of his brain that he usually used for work: drop by drop, the excitement was rising.

'I've got it,' he whispered, almost inaudibly. 'I've got it.'

'What?'

'Jail fever. SAIDS. I know what causes it. It's all here ...' He skim read the file he was holding, the papers rattling in his shaking hands. 'Listen,' he said, 'in case one of us doesn't make it: the disease is caused by the oil from oilseed rape.'

'How?' asked Catriona quickly.

'It's genetically modified. In order to make it more frost resistant, so they can get more crops in in a year, they've used genes from a deep sea fish – a turbot from the North Sea. Somehow the modification has jumped species and the antifreeze – that's basically what it is – kills humans.'

'Oh, my,' breathed Catriona, wide-eyed. 'And Elysian Fields did the modification?'

'In this very plant,' Tom nodded, stuffing the papers into his knapsack. 'Come on: we've got to see if we can get something on their staff, names or something.'

He led the way out into the corridor. All was quiet. The building was small: stairs ahead led to the upper floor and to one side of them was what seemed to be the main door, the orthodox method of coming in. To the other side was an office, lit from within, but apparently empty and with the door shut. Through the corridor window, clear this time, they could see a large desk, neatly kept, two armchairs, a sofa, a side table with several files laid flat on it, and two elegant wooden filing cabinets.

'That looks as if it might have the important stuff in it,' remarked Catriona.

'Not if it's like our director's place,' said Tom. 'He only keeps papers that mention him and a copy of Who's Who, and one of his filing cabinets actually holds his drinks cabinet.'

'Shall we try it? I could do with a whisky.'

'Why not?'

She put her hand on the door, turned the handle, and opened it. At once an alarm screamed.

Catriona belted into the room and grabbed the files from the side table. By the time she emerged, Tom had already tried the front door.

'Locked!' he shouted. 'Back to the lab!'

They ran down the corridor. They could hear footsteps above them, doors slamming, and they flung themselves into and across the lab to the open window. While Catriona scrambled out, Tom took a moment to shove the files she had collected into his knapsack, then followed her out of the window. She stood there, looking baffled, until he pointed to the end of the hedge that concealed the gate. At that moment, two men in uniforms appeared around the corner, between them and the hedge. They ran for it.

The men, taken by surprise at their turn of speed, followed. Catriona and Tom made it to the corner with seconds to spare, but the men were gaining on them, and suddenly Tom felt a tug from behind nearly lift him off his feet. The man had grabbed his knapsack, then in a high tackle knocked him to the ground. They rolled on the wet tarmac. Tom scrambled to his feet and grabbed the ankles of the second man as he passed. He fell, but the first guard was up again, racing after Catriona. Tom could see she had reached the gate but was scrabbling to find the hole he had cut. He ran towards them, but was felled in his turn by the second guard. He could taste grit and blood, mouth full of pain. The man rolled on him and sat on his chest, pinning his arms down to leave his face open to attack. Tom was stretched across his stuffed knapsack: there was a roaring in his ears, and even the first fist on his jaw did not diminish it. He could not breathe. The rain poured into his open mouth, choking him. Just as he was about to black out, the roaring noise rose to a terrible crescendo and a crash echoed through the wet air.

XIII

Eliot left the cave at dusk. It was not the most sensible time, perhaps, to set out on a journey, but Wallace had given him directions to Roslin, the next village, and he would be able to find an inn there, not sleep on the floor of a cave. Besides, he was not anxious to have anything more to do with this matter, now that he had discharged his duty. A night in Roslin, a couple of days' walk back north to Leith, and the next boat for the Baltic – that was him. As long as it was no relation to that ill-begotten barrel that had brought him over here in the first place.

He was happy enough wandering along in the dusk. He felt in danger no longer – no one could want anything from him, his duty was done and the loyal Scot in Boulogne could sleep in peace at last. He wondered inconsequentially about the link boy, the torch bearer who had been killed with him on that dark French street. Could the peaceless souls of those killed because they were in the wrong place at the wrong time ever be laid to rest? Who could atone for their death, except their killers?

This train of thought was interesting, but morbid in the summer dusk, and Eliot was not entirely sure that his acquaintances on the May Isle would approve of it. He bared his teeth in a grin: he supposed he ought to get word somehow to Brother Fillan that his prayers for Eliot's soul were no longer required.

The walking was rough, but nothing to what he had been doing over the Pentlands lately, and as he strolled on the moon rose, green-white, showing him his path.

The valley broadened and he thought he had reached the point where Wallace had told him he could take a short cut across some pasture land and reach the village itself, which was a little distance from the glen. He left the dappled woodland and struck out unconcernedly. To his right was scrub, straight ahead was a low hill with some kind of shepherd's hut tucked into its lea, and the smooth field before him was cut across by a shadow in the silver light which, from its shape, showed the meanders of a little burn.

He had just forded the stream, no great trial, when a movement ahead caught his eye. Four men were emerging from the shepherd's hut – and from what the moonlight showed of their clothes, they were not shepherds.

He stood still where he was. Short of lying in the stream, there was no cover to be had for some distance in any direction. He stood quite motionless, hoping that in the strange moonlight only a movement would attract their attention.

But they seemed to be heading straight for him.

He waited for an instant when they did not seem to be looking, and slid back down quickly into the stream. But it was too late: the two nearer men had seen him, ran forward and grabbed him by an arm each. He was brought up, dripping and foolish, before a short middle-aged man in a fine velvet cloak. A younger man, almost as finely dressed but with very prominent front teeth stood by him, and they regarded Eliot, the older man with disdain, the younger with some surprise.

'Who is this?' asked the older man. His accent was English, Eliot was sure. One of the henchmen holding him nudged him with a persuasive knee.

'My name is Eliot,' he managed to say, with as much pride as he could muster after his initial yelp. 'Who is this?' He jerked his head at the older man, and was kneed again for his insolence.

'He's the one, my lord,' said the younger man, almost reluctantly. Eliot looked at him sharply: even without the colourful oaths, he could recognise the voice of the man who had seemed to lead his captors. So this was probably the owner of that fancy litter.

'You'd be Nicholson of Rosehill, then?' he asked, with a deliberate sneer. He could feel the blood racing in his veins. The young man breathed in sharply, and looked quickly to his older companion.

'You keep your secrets well, then,' said the older man cuttingly, and even in the moonlight Eliot could see young Nicolson blush. 'He'll have to go. He has served his purpose.' He started to turn away, but Eliot was not going to let that go.

'My purpose? What purpose?'

The older man looked back at him and laughed shortly.

'You led us to Wallace, of course. Oh, your friend in Boulogne was genuine enough, and so were the dispatches, but we've been following you for days. Edward of England will thank you for the service you have done him this night – posthumously, of course.'

He stopped and looked about him.

'You'll want to hide him well: we have no wish for other rebel agents to discover his fate and have their suspicions aroused.'

'There was that coffin back in the hut, my lord,' Nicholson offered, trying to regain some credit.

'Some ancient remains. Yes, we could use that. These two will have some digging to do, then. Let us leave them: I have a flask of good wine in my saddlebag, if you will join me.'

'Aye, my lord.' Nicholson and the Englishman washed their hands of Eliot and walked away, talking softly and easily, back past the hut and out of sight.

'You hold him, I'll dig?' suggested one of the henchmen to the other.

'Aye. You'll have to go and get the spade,' the other added, as if he were talking of nothing more than digging a cesspit. Eliot suddenly felt terribly tired. He had been ship-wrecked, ill almost to death, had walked for weeks, been pursued, captured, had escaped, had found his goal, and now at the last minute he was captured again and told it was all for nothing. But this was probably his best chance of escape. Using his fatigue as his inspiration, he waited until this first henchman had gone enough paces to put him out of the way, then sagged convincingly in the arms of his guard. He straightened almost at once, though the man let out a shout and his companion came running back. But by now, from the top of his boot, Eliot had his knife in his hand.

Ah, the old reflexes! He turned and stabbed at his guard, and despite the hard leather cuirass he wounded him, he thought. But the other henchman was back now, and before Eliot had a chance to withdraw his blade the second man chopped down hard on his wrist. Eliot's fingers sprang open, the second man wrenched the blade from his companion and, as Eliot spun in shock, stabbed him full in the chest.

The old reflexes ... Weariness overwhelmed him, and he felt himself fall on to the soft river earth like a mattress, like straw on an inn floor, like a bracken bed in a mud hut. Even with his eyes closed he could see those blasted monks fluttering about him. That pretty brown-eyed girl was there, too, he thought, but all he could see were the brothers, Brother Peter, officious and fidgety, Brother Mungo, excitable, and Brother Fillan, still praying for his soul. Had nobody told them that he had made it? Their kind brown wings swooped around him until the fire went out, and there was darkness.

XIV

The rain was still falling into Tom's mouth as a huge hand clamped around his arm and pulled him to his feet.

'Billy!'

The truck driver nodded briefly and made a swift movement. The security guard who had been about to attack Tom again lay suddenly some distance away, his nose broken. Tom swallowed hard.

'Come on, then, lad – this your lady friend?'

'That's the one,' Tom grinned at Catriona's stunned expression. 'This is Billy, Catriona: he gave me a lift here from Stirling.'

'In this?' Catriona asked shakily. Tom looked where she was pointing, and gasped. Where the wire gate had been, and the first ten metres of hedge, there was instead the slightly scraped, shiny, wet, red and white bulk of Morag, Billy's truck.

'Ye get all ye come for?' Billy asked, winking at Catriona.

'Ah – yes,' said Tom, still staring at the truck.

'Then hop in – Edinburgh, is it?'

'Quick,' said Catriona, 'before they send reinforcements.'

'She has her head screwed on,' Billy agreed, giving Catriona a leg up so that she could scramble, one-handed, into the cab and across to the passenger seat. Tom followed, and Billy leapt up behind him as the first of Catriona's reinforcements appeared around the corner of the inner hedge. With expert nonchalance Billy revved the engine and reversed the huge truck a few delicate metres, then, tossing hedge and gates aside under the mighty wheels, the truck set off down the road up which Tom had travelled what seemed like hours ago. He looked out at the rain, now easing, and sideways at Catriona, white with exhaustion, her hair drying about her like a dark veil, bruises starting to show on her face and hands. She caught his eye and gave a little smile which almost brought tears to his exhausted eyes. He grinned back quickly and turned to look at Billy, vast and competent behind the barrel-sized wheel.

'What made you come back?' he asked, finding new pains in his jaw.

'Ye didna look like the kind that could make it on your own – not your kind of thing. Don't get me wrong, eh? You've got the brains, all right, but some of us have different talents.' He grinned contentedly, into the darkness. Tom felt he ought to be offended, but he was too tired.

'But why me? Why this? It wasn't your fight, not that I'm not grateful!'

Billy's face fell. It was like watching a mountainside shift.

'See all that stuff you talked about before? All they mystery illnesses and maybe food contamination and what-have-ye?'

'That's what it seems to be, yeah.'

'Well, you ken my Morag?' He pointed at one of the cheery photographs of his wife with which the cab was adorned. 'New variant CJD, last summer. Dead in weeks, okay? If people like you can stop it, I'm here to help.'

They rode in silence for a long time after that. A sickly dawn was starting to appear when it occurred to Tom that he ought to check and see that the papers he and Catriona had snatched were safe in his knapsack. He shrugged it off and pulled it on to his lap to feel inside it.

The three bundles of papers were damp, but otherwise unharmed. The first one, the one reporting on the experiments with turbot, made interesting reading, particularly the last few paragraphs on the random toxicity of the resulting rapeseed oil. He read it through, then turned to the two files Catriona had snatched from the office with the alarm. Each had 'For Destruction' written in black marker pen across the front. Catriona looked over his shoulder.

'Oh, what's in those?'

'I hope it's something good. I couldn't believe it when you ran into the room instead of out when the alarm went off.'

'Ha! I wasn't going to let them away with all they've done just because of a feeble alarm!'

Billy said,

'That's my girl!' quite cheerily, and Tom told him quickly about the contents of the first file again, before opening the top of the two in front of him.

'Receipts,' he said after a moment. 'How boring.'

'Recent ones,' added Catriona, looking at the dates on the top few. 'I would have thought they would need to keep these for tax purposes.' She examined them more closely. 'You say they were making rapeseed oil back there.'

'That's right.'

'Then I suppose, in the current climate, they might want to destroy evidence that says they've been delivering gallons of the stuff to SecureGuard at Her Majesty's Prison Sinclair House, Old Dalkeith Road, Edinburgh?'

'Oh, aye,' agreed Billy in a voice heavy with irony, 'I'm sure they'd like us all to know that. You reckon that's what's done it, then? Caused SAIDS, like?'

'I reckon,' Tom nodded. 'I mean, they tested all the foodstuffs, but they had no idea what they were looking for. I doubt they would ever have seen it.'

'I thought they weren't allowed to grow GM crops here,' said Billy.

'They are, under licence, but they're not supposed to sell them. They can get Part C consent for trials just now, but it's all supposed to be open and regulated. I doubt that is.' He waved at the papers.

'It still doesn't explain Alf, though,' said Catriona.

'Maybe we'll never be able to explain Alf.'

'Forth Road Bridge,' remarked Billy, sweeping the truck round and down towards the huge suspension bridge. 'Where is it you're wanting to go in Edinburgh?'

'St. Leonard's Police Station,' said Catriona firmly.

'You go there,' said Tom suddenly, handing her the files, 'and take these. I want to go to the Infirmary.'

'The Infirmary? Why?' asked Catriona.

'That wee girl is still alive,' said Tom. 'Maybe this information will help to keep her that way.'

XV

He seemed to watch them as they dug his grave. They did not like it.

'Close his damned eyes,' insisted the shorter henchman, whose name was Davie.

'You close them. I'm no going near him again.'

They had only one spade between them, so it was slow work. They had debated whether to carry Eliot to the coffin, which the lairds had said was over by the wee hill, or to carry to coffin to Eliot. The ground swung it in the end, because it was softer here, by the river. Davie dug for a bit, then stood guard while Al, the bigger one, poked around at the bottom of the hole.

'I dinna think it's long enough for yon long box.'

'Aye, it is.'

'I dinna think so. Should we go and fetch it?'

'Good idea. I've had enough of his company for a bit.'

They both felt his gaze on them as they walked away, but neither said anything to the other.

The coffin was a long grey lead box, with some plainish decoration. Davie said he had heard the lairds say it was ancient, dug up here by the farmer and abandoned as an unchancy thing. It weighed a lot. In the end they found some thickish sticks and half-heaved, half-rolled it over to the bank of the burn where they discovered that Al was quite right: the hole was a few inches short. He scraped away again for a bit, while Davie tried to force the coffin lid off with Eliot's knife. Eventually it seemed to be loose and he called Al up to help him. Between them they slid the lid off.

'Holy Virgin,' Al muttered, and they both crossed themselves. The skeleton lay in the bottom of the coffin, quite bare. Davie looked reluctantly over at Eliot.

'He's a big lad – he'll no fit in unless we take all this fellow out.'

They picked out the bones one by one, with their finger tips, and laid them on the grass near the grave. Then they lifted the coffin, not noticeably lighter, and lowered it into the grave, now just big enough for the purpose.

'Now him,' said Davie, with revulsion. 'Close his eyes.'

Al tried, but Eliot's eyes would not close.

'I wish I hadna tried,' he grumbled. 'That's worse now.'

They dragged the body the short distance to the grave, over the soft grass, the head lolling lazily between them. They rolled him down into the coffin.

'He's too big for it – look, his feet are out the end,' said Davie, implying that Al was going to be the one to do something about it. But Al said,

'I'm going to throw –' and staggered towards the burn. Davie sighed, and stepped down into the grave. He pulled Eliot's knees up with a jerk and kicked the long feet down into the coffin. Eliot's head rolled to one side, the horrid gaze seeming to pass over Davie's face in the cold light of dawn. He shivered.

He clambered out of the grave and his feet met something hard on the grass – Eliot's knife. He tossed it down into the coffin and called Al back to help him with the lid.

'Praise Heaven for that,' Davie concluded when they had the lid firmly down. 'Now kick in these other bones – there, that'll do. Now put the earth back, then the turves. Get moving, the sun's near up.'

They finished as the sun rose, tramping down the last turf, and turned wearily to where their horses were tethered beyond the little hill. Even when they had passed it, however, neither could shake off the impression that they were not alone.

XVI

Edinburgh was coming to life for the day. Shopkeepers sluiced the night's debris off their pavements and besuited briefcase carriers queued, grey-faced, at bus stops. They stared blankly as the big red and white lorry surged past, and Catriona, waking again from a web of golden hair, confessed to an urge to wave at them. Billy grinned.

'I can take your young lady to the pollis,' he announced, but I'm no sure I can get Morag round by the Infirmary.'

'It's no distance,' said Tom. 'I'll walk.'

Billy dropped him at the corner of Melville Drive, and Tom turned to wave before hurrying across the Meadows to cut round the back of Simpsons Maternity Pavilion to the Infirmary.

He was halfway to the laboratory building holding the electron microscope he had been using when he remembered he had no idea where the little girl suffering from SAIDS had been taken. He returned to reception.

'Hallo,' he said to the grey-haired lady in the twinset. 'I'd like to speak to the consultant who's dealing with the SAIDS cases.'

'The what, dear?'

'The SAIDS cases. There's a little girl here, suffering from SAIDS.'

'Are you family?'

'No, I'm –'

'Then I'm afraid I can't tell you anything, dear. Patient confidentiality, you see?' She smiled kindly, but from her position of secure responsibility was eyeing his unshaven chin, his bruised jaw and bloody lip, his torn shirt and, if she could see over the counter, his bare legs, bruised, scraped and muddy.

'My name,' said Tom, knowing it sounded unlikely, 'is Dr. Thomas Buchan. I work as an epidemiologist at the Establishment at Roslin. I am working on the SAIDS outbreak and I think I might just have come up with something that might help that little girl. Will you let me talk to the consultant, please?'

He doubted if she had heard much past his first sentence – the magic word 'Doctor' had done it again.

'Dr. Buchan,' said the lady, writing it down. 'I'll try and page Mr. Lewis for you now. He gets in early these days.' She vanished for a moment to do whatever this mysterious process required. Soon she returned.

'He'll be round in a minute,' she said, 'if you'd like to take a seat.' She waved towards a group of fake-leather benches by the door, and Tom had barely settled himself when a weary-looking man, in a white lab coat with the folds still showing, emerged through a swing door and spoke his name. Tom stood up and shook hands.

'I must apologise for my appearance, Mr. Lewis,' Tom started, shamed by the lab coat, 'I've been working on this all night, and I haven't been home.'

'No problem,' said Lewis. 'We had three more cases last night – I've barely slept myself. Any contributions to a solution gratefully received.'

'Any survivors?' asked Tom.

'None.' He glanced at Tom out of the corner of his eye. 'You say you're from the Establishment?'

'That's right.'

'Hmm. Then one of your colleagues is here already.'

Can't be Uncle George, Tom thought, not at this premature hour of the day.

'Gavin Price?' he asked.

'That's right. He's here to see the girl – says you've been working on some blood samples.'

It seemed like an age ago.

'I haven't seen Gavin for a few days,' Tom admitted. 'We were working on her blood, yes, but we went our separate ways for a bit. I've been looking at cause, and I think Gavin's been looking at cure. He'll be stunned when he hears what I've got!' He grinned, imagining Gavin's face. Gavin always liked to get there first.

'It's an infection control area, I'm afraid,' Lewis explained, handing Tom overalls and a mask. 'The parents are in there, too: I suppose you've heard she's clear, but he appears to have had it and recovered?'

Tom's shocked expression was lost behind his mask, and Mr. Lewis did not see it as he led the way into the SAIDS unit.

Ahead of them, a figure recognisable as Gavin chiefly by the number of freckles visible around the mask was talking to another man in the corridor.

'I just think they should take a break some time,' he was saying. 'That woman's going to have the shape of the chair permanently etched on her behind at this rate.'

'I know, I know,' the other man agreed, 'but she in particular won't shift. Oh, hi, Mr. Lewis.'

'Staff Nurse Johnston, Dr. Buchan.' The man shook Tom's hand.

'Tom!' Gavin looked very surprised to see him.

'Ah, sorry I stood you up at the Ceilidh House, Gav. I was, er, called away urgently.'

'No harm done,' said Gavin cheerfully. 'Willie and I got out of our heads and he crashed on my floor.'

'Not that out of your head, by the look of you. Is that why you're up here this early? Wife kick you out for bringing Willie home?'

Gavin gave a short laugh.

'You've heard about the father having immunity?'

'Yes, Mr. Lewis just told me. What's the story?'

'No idea. I'm here to get more samples of his and his daughter's. And to try to talk them into taking a breath of air or something. That woman's glued to her seat.'

'Well,' said Tom, gathering the nurse and the consultant back into the conversation, 'I think I know what's causing this.'

'Well, go on,' said Mr. Lewis anxiously.

'I think that it is piscine antifreeze from North Sea turbot, the genes of which have been bred into oil seed rape, from which oil has been supplied to the Prison Service.'

There was a long silence. Then the nurse ventured,

'North Sea turbot? Do you think there's any connexion with the fact that Mr. Larssen – that's the child's father,' he explained to Tom, 'is Norwegian?'

'Have you evidence for this?' asked Mr. Lewis, frowning as if he was testing the theory against all the facts.

'I believe so,' said Tom. 'I have paperwork, and I think I might have plant samples.'

'Bloody hell,' said Gavin with reverence. 'So what are we looking at here is really a kind of food poisoning?'

'That's about the height of it.'

Suddenly a man appeared further down the corridor. He was blond almost to the point of being white, and his skin was pale.

'Nurse!' he called, and Staff Nurse Johnston jogged down the corridor towards him. Mr. Lewis followed. Gavin looked after them, then took Tom by the arm and led him a few paces in the opposite direction.

'So where's this evidence?' he asked. 'Where did it come from?'

'From Fife,' said Tom, eager to tell his exciting story. 'You remember I asked you if you'd heard of any institute in Crook of Devon? Well, there is one: a branch of Elysian Fields.'

'What, that food research place in Roslin? They're a GM bunch?'

'That's right. I went there last night, and you won't believe all I found.'

'You went there alone? That was a bit risky, wasn't it?'

'Well, as it turned out, it wasn't too bad. Gav, they've killed people to keep this secret, and I think they're linked with those protestors that were threatening us. Think about it: who really had an interest in keeping the truth about SAIDS a secret? The people who caused it, of course. They must have someone on the inside, someone working in the Institute. That way they could sabotage our experiments, delay the whole process. Who do you think it could be?'

'I don't know. Look, I really want to see this evidence for myself – show me? Where is it – is it that mouldy old daysack of yours outside?'

He was already leading Tom back through the doors to the bare little room where they had donned their protective overalls, hurrying him out of his mask, pulling his own off with a practised movement.

'Come on, Tom, you've got me all excited now – where is it?'

'Gav ...' Tom was belatedly on his guard. 'Gavin, did you tell your friends I'd be at the Ceilidh House at eight last night? Is that how they knew where I'd be?'

'Just show me the evidence, Tom, there's a good lad.'

Gavin and the electron microscope. An insider doing the break-in. Gavin so keen to blame the protestors.

'You did all of that, didn't you?' he asked, hearing his voice like somebody else's. 'What about your family? Your wife?'

'My wife's left me,' said Gavin bitterly. 'She said I didn't make enough money to be out working all day and half the night. She took the children. But this way I make more money, and my contract keeps being extended. I'm hoping she'll come back soon.'

The voice was Gavin's, but it too sounded as if it had been loaned to someone else. Tom felt a shiver down his spine. He was too tired for this.

'I'm not giving you the evidence,' he said flatly. 'What'll you do about that?'

'I'll have to kill you,' Gavin said. He was fiddling with something in his hand. 'They've told me anyway I'll have to kill you. I'll just shout out that protestors have rushed in and attacked us – there have been enough of them about. I'll maybe have to cut myself or something, too, make it look more realistic.' He had half turned away.

'Tell them the big guy with the hood did it,' Tom suggested. This was completely unrealistic. Gavin wouldn't kill him, would he? 'That'll add a touch of artistic verisimilitude.'

'What big guy with the hood?' asked Gavin, and swung suddenly round. In his hand flashed a scalpel.

All hell broke loose. The swing doors crashed in, Tom dived for the floor and Gavin, seemingly propelled from behind, landed flat beside him. Tom heard running feet and cries of alarm, though it had to be said that his eyes were firmly closed and he had his hands over his head. There were sounds of a struggle, and he thought he heard Gavin grunt, then at last there was peace. He opened his eyes.

In front of him were the toes of a large pair of yellow wellingtons. He looked up, past baggy trousers and a regrettable waistcoat, to see the ramshackle, kindly face of Inspector McAlester beaming down upon him. He groaned, and sat up. P.C. Williams was calmly bagging Gavin's scalpel, discarded on the floor. Gavin was nowhere to be seen.

'Have you quite finished, Dr. Buchan?' asked McAlester. 'I think you'll find little remains to be done.'

'Did Catriona give you the papers?' he asked anxiously.

'The papers, and the plants, and the address in Crook of Devon. That's how we knew you might be in difficulties here,' said McAlester with kindly satisfaction. 'The third file – the one Dr. Lindsay says you didn't read? – was a kind of payroll. Dr. Gavin Price was on it and we traced him here. The Fife police are on to Crook of Devon now. We're busy here with matching Dr. Price's car with the one that killed Joanne

Eastleigh – and a spot of taking and driving away in Falkirk …'

'Ah. And the breaking and entering in Fife, of course,' said Tom sorrowfully.

'I gather all evidence of that has been obliterated by Mr. Scobie's – Billy's – reckless driving. You looked so respectable, Dr. Buchan: what has become of you?'

But the smile on McAlester's face made light of his words, and Tom found himself relaxing – into the bruised, battered, exhausted, starving wreck that he was.

Suddenly the swing doors to the SAIDS unit burst open, and Staff Nurse Johnston appeared. He ripped off his mask, revealing himself as a very young man with a round, angelic face.

'It's Vicky Larssen!' he cried, entirely oblivious to the police presence. 'She's regained consciousness!'

XVII

The day was cool and cloudy, more natural weather for Edinburgh. Tom was back in jeans, though they rubbed his knees where he had scraped them across the tarmac drive in Crook of Devon. There was no security guard by the gate there at Roslin, though the sign, 'Elysian Fields – Food Science Research' still shone clean and reassuring on the other side of the drive. He ducked under the gate and walked on.

The grass was growing green in the damp soil where the dig had disturbed the earth – you could hardly tell where the trenches had been. The university's tent was still standing where it had been when he had last seen it, though the car beside it was no longer Rob's.

He strolled across to the tent, peered inside, then walked on around it. Catriona was standing on the other side. The wind was catching her loose hair, bundling it around her and flinging it free again. She turned at the sound of his approach.

'Hi,' he said.

'Hi.'

'Doing all right?'

She jerked her left arm, which rested in a sling. He glanced back at the car, raising his eyebrows.

'Had to hire an automatic,' she said. 'Couldn't find anyone willing to change gear for me. Something to do with how much I shout at them.'

'I'm sorry about Rob.'

She made a face at him, indicating that she doubted it but saw it was kindly meant.

'What are you here for?

'I walked over from the Establishment to see – if anything had changed.' He nodded over at the smooth green hedges.

'No sign of anyone. Fortunately they paid upfront for the dig.'

They smiled at each other.

'I came to empty and strike the tent.'

'Want a hand?'

'Okay. As long as you do it properly.'

'I can follow orders!'

They turned, and disappeared inside the tent.

On the little hill, a tall figure, cloaked, stood and watched until they had vanished from view. Then it, too, left.

Looking at the field, you would have said that nothing had ever happened there.

About the Author:

Lexie Conyngham is a historian living in the shadow of the Highlands. Her Murray of Letho and Hippolyta Napier novels are born of a life amidst Scotland's old cities, ancient universities and hidden-away aristocratic estates, but she has written since the day she found out that people were allowed to do such a thing. Beyond teaching and research, her days are spent with wool, wild allotments and a wee bit of whisky.

Reviews are important to authors: it would be lovely if you could leave a review where you bought this book, particularly if you liked it!

If you'd like the chance to follow Lexie Conyngham's meandering thoughts on writing, gardening and knitting, take a look at www.murrayofletho.blogspot.co.uk, or on Facebook or Pinterest (Lexie Conyngham).

Finally! If you'd like to be kept up to date with Murray, Hippolyta and Lexie, please join our mailing list at: contact@kellascatpress.co.uk. No details are passed to third parties, not even for ready money!

The Hippolyta Napier series:
A Knife in Darkness
Death of a False Physician
A Murderous Game

The Murray of Letho series:
Death in a Scarlet Gown
Knowledge of Sins Past
Service of the Heir: An Edinburgh Murder
An Abandoned Woman
Fellowship with Demons
The Tender Herb: A Murder in Mughal India
Death of an Officer's Lady
Out of a Dark Reflection
Slow Death by Quicksilver
Thicker than Water

Also by Lexie Conyngham:
Windhorse Burning
The War, The Bones and Dr. Cowie
Thrawn Thoughts and Blithe Bits (short stories)

www.ingramcontent.com/pod-product-compliance
Lightning Source LLC
Chambersburg PA
CBHW020126180626
46810CB00004B/1421